The Trial of
Jonathan Haughton

James Sane

For Christina, Faith and Deanna.

1

He awoke in a bed – tired, alone and confused. He squinted his eyes until his blurred vision gradually came back into focus but at the same time, they ached from the bright lights that shone down from the ceiling. He slowly looked around the plain and featureless room. His initial guess was that he was in a hospital ward. It certainly smelled like one but lacked the generic bedside-friendly look one would normally associate with a public hospital, and seemed more like a high-tech research laboratory. He then looked down at himself as he lay on the bed. His body was covered with various tubes and wires which led out to strange drip-bags that dangled on a frame and to machines that whirred and beeped repeatedly. Soon, he was fully conscious but lay there, motionless and growing increasingly distressed. He dared not move too much for fear inadvertently causing himself further injury – and yet he had no idea how he ended up there in the first place – no memory of why. In fact, to begin with, he had no memory of anything at all aside from who he was, but then gradually, like a shallow stream, they began to trickle back. It was a painless sensation but strange all the same. It was like computer files in his mind being opened one after another. He soon started to recall what he was – a soldier, covert operations, and driver specialist. He remembered a mission he and his team had been building up to, but no recollection of the mission itself. He lay back down and concentrated hard but recalled nothing more after.

A few minutes more passed by for what seemed like forever, until the door to the room opened, and in walked two mysterious men dressed in long white laboratory jackets. The man naturally assumed they were doctors. Both men seemed pleased to see the patient was awake and had pulled through whatever surgery he had undergone. As they carefully sat him up on the bed to examine him, the patient slowly opened his mouth to try and speak but struggled to get even one word out. The only noise he could make was reduced to stuttered whispers as if he had never spoken before in his life.

"Now rest easy, sir," one of the doctors reassured him. "You have been through quite an experience and there is much for you to take in."

The doctor took the man's wrist and checked his pulse, while the other doctor examined his tired eyes. The man was weak and exhausted but continued his efforts to speak and force out at least a syllable. The doctors stepped back slightly and observed him as the sounds became more frequent. They watched and waited for him to say something coherent.

"Can we help you, sir?" one of the doctors asked slowly. "Is there anything we can do for you just now? Can we get you anything? Anything at all?"

They waited patiently as the man continued to force out sounds. The stammered whispers gradually became mumbling murmurs, which became louder with each passing second until he eventually began to speak clearly.

"I..." he began slowly and delicately. He looked directly into the eyes of who he presumed to be the senior doctor. "I'm hungry. I want something to eat."

"I'm not surprised," the doctor replied with a smile. "My assistant here has a tray of food ready for you. A strong appetite is very common for somebody in your condition."

The doctor signalled his assistant forward, who then wheeled across a tray of food into view and positioned it in front of the man. The patient looked down at the dish with a raised eyebrow in surprise at what he saw – not disappointed or dissatisfied, but rather pleasantly surprised. Instead of the stereotypical 'hospital food' he had been expecting, or even a mundane pack of sandwiches from the nearest vending machine, the man found himself being treated to what, for him, would be the 'perfect feast'. It was a large dish of chicken wings, accompanied by a variety of spicy dipping sauces. In addition to that was a twelve-inch chicken and red onion pizza, a side plate of French fries and a large bottle of cola – chilled. This was hardly the kind of meal he expected somebody in the medical profession to recommend but there he was, being beckoned by so-called medical experts to just 'dig in' – and that he did. Wasting no time, the man dived in and began to stuff his face with the heavenly meal. He gorged primitively as if he hadn't eaten in years and relished every second of the experience. The doctors watched with a smile, with one of them taking notes and nodding in approval at what they were observing. As he ate, the man kept watchful eyes on the two men in white. After all, there was a reason why he was there and why he was being treated like a celebrity.

"Hungry?" the lead doctor commented. The man nodded and forced a tight smile as he attempted to show appreciation despite a mouthful of chicken.

"Thought you might be," the doctor continued with a satisfied smile. "According to the details we collected, this is meant to be your favourite food."

The man nodded in agreement as he continued to eat.

"Normally we would have had something healthier ready, like a salad or a pasta meal," the doctor went on, "but the research and current guidelines recommend encouraging you to familiarise yourself with your surroundings based on what you would see as normal. This can include favourite foods, familiar smells, even music if you like."

"And after some time," the other doctor added, "we'll expose you to familiar faces, such as friends, relatives, work colleagues, etc."

The man paused and looked slightly confused. What did the doctor mean by 'familiarise'? His thoughts then brought him back to the bigger issue of why he was in hospital in the first place, and he was immediately aware that somebody he hoped would have been there when he woke up, was not.

"Cassy?" he inquired. At the same time, he began to look around. "Where is Cassy? Is she here? Is she okay?"

"Cassy is fine, I believe," the lead doctor reassured him, "and you will get to see her once we've helped you get back into the swing of things. And on that note, allow me to introduce myself. I am Dr Wint and my quiet assistant taking notes over there is Dr Morecambe."

"Doctor..." the man inquired again, still frantically looking around the room. "Why am I here?"

"First things first," replied Dr Wint as he leaned closer towards the man. "We need you to confirm to us who you are."

"What?" the man remarked in confusion.

"Your name, please?" Dr Morcambe asked. "Your full name, please?"

"My name..." the man began as he answered slowly. "My name is Haughton… Jonathan Kenzie Haughton."

"Correct!" Dr Morcambe replied, making a gesture with his pen as if he were ticking a box on his notepad.

"Your birthday is May 12th..." Dr Wint then said suggestively.

"August!" Jonathan corrected him. "11th August."

"And your favourite colour..." Dr Wint then suggested, "...Green?"

"Red!" he answered.

The doctors looked at each other with nods of approval, but Jonathan was unimpressed. He pushed the rest of his meal away and sat further back on his bed.

"Would you tell me what this is all about?" he asked impatiently. "What happened to me? Why I'm here?"

"Do you remember much before waking up here?" Dr Morcambe asked him. Jonathan paused for a minute to think about the question.

"I don't know," he replied. "I guess it rather depends how long I have been lying here. Have I got amnesia or something, Doc?"

"We don't believe so, Mr Haughton," replied Dr Wint. "In fact, we are hoping that your long-term memories are all intact. Otherwise, we wouldn't have done our job properly."

"But I'm still not sure why I'm here," Jonathan replied. "I've no idea how I've ended up in a hospital, being pumped full of chemicals and hungry as hell. I just..."

Jonathan paused momentarily as a sudden realisation hit him.

"The mission!" he guessed. "I'm guessing our target was a little less welcoming than we were led to believe. Did anyone else make it out okay?"

Dr Wint sighed and moved closer to Jonathan.

"Now look, Mr Haughton," he said. "Right now, you probably have many questions, and we will do our best to answer them as best we can. However, the process is a delicate one and it is important that you trust us for the time being. I assure you we all have your best interests at heart."

Jonathan's expression became more impatient. He wasn't used to being in the dark with what was going on around him and he certainly didn't appreciate being spoken to in riddles. He responded with a more aggressive tone in his voice.

Dr Wint was unfazed and remained calm.

"Mr Haughton, do you remember anything about your mission?" he asked. "Anything at all?"

Jonathan calmed slightly and began to reflect on what he could remember.

"To be honest, Doc? No!" he answered.

"No matter, Mr Haughton," replied Dr Wint. "With the permission of your former superiors, I am at liberty to disclose to you that there were...complications regarding the mission of which you speak. From what was released publicly, several things went wrong, for everybody involved. For unknown reasons, the armoured vehicle used to transport the team spun out of control and crashed, killing all on board."

Dr Wint's careful choice of words hadn't gone unnoticed by Jonathan.

"*Former* superiors?" he inquired, still confused.

"One step at a time, Mr Haughton," Dr Wint replied patiently. "Firstly, we need to know what the last thing you remember was."

"Literally the last thing before waking up here," Dr Morcambe added, "no matter how trivial."

Jonathan paused again and took a deep breath as he attempted to recall everything that had happened to him. His memory was still cloudy, but he was not yet sure whether it was down to his exhaustion or his injuries.

"If I'm honest, Doc, I'm not really sure what I remember. I've been drifting in and out of consciousness and have been having vivid dreams..."

"Concentrate if you can, Mr Haughton," Dr Wint advised. "It's important."

Jonathan obliged and began to clear his mind, but after a few moments, he shook his head in disappointment.

"No," he answered. "The last thing I recall was the day before we were due to set out."

"Go on," Dr Wint encouraged him.

"I said my goodbyes to Cassy that morning and drove away," Jonathan continued. "I remember stopping off at the *Forever Together* clinic en-route to update their memory banks and..."

"And what?" Dr Morcambe asked,

"And... now wait a minute!" Jonathan suddenly realized. "Did you say that the crash killed *everyone* on board?"

"According to official reports, that's right," Dr Wint replied with a nod.

"But how can that be?" said Jonathan. His facial expression twisted slightly in confusion. "I was supposed to be the one driving!"

"Well, not exactly," Dr Morcambe commented.

"What's that supposed to mean?" demanded Jonathan. "Did I go on the mission or not?"

"Well, technically..." Dr Wint remarked without finishing. Jonathan turned his head back up towards Dr Wint and looked him in the eyes again.

"Doctor...My mind's a total blank. Do you know what happened to me out there? Why can't I remember anything?"

Dr Wint placed a comforting hand on Jonathan's shoulder.

"It is probably for the best that you are sitting down, Mr Haughton," he said. "This isn't going to be easy to take in. It never is."

"Take in what?" Jonathan inquired as his heartbeat began to rise in anticipation. His body was still connected to the machines, which began to register his increased anxiety and signalled their results to the two doctors through a series of rapid beeps.

"As far as you are concerned, you are Jonathan Kenzie Haughton," Dr Wint began to explain. "You were born in Nottingham, England and moved to Chicago, United States, when you were five. You enrolled in the military at the age of 20, in which you have maintained an outstanding record; being repeatedly selected for covert missions around the world and decorated for your efforts on several occasions. You have been with your girlfriend, Cassandra Summers, whom you refer to as 'Cassy', for 6 years in an ever-growing relationship that included some mutual enrolment in the *Forever Together* scheme as part of a joint life-insurance policy – hence your regular six-month memory uploads."

The doctor stopped there to allow Jonathan to process his report. He nodded slowly and silently.

"As you know," Dr Morcambe added, "the *Forever Together* institute is a highly sophisticated and expensive scientific endeavour to preserve the memories of deceased relatives upon their passing...to help relieve the sense of loss of the bereaved."

"In a nutshell," Dr Wint remarked, "a clone replacement of the deceased."

"I know," Jonathan replied. "Cassy and I both signed up to it. We paid extra for the memory uploads."

"But why so frequent?" Dr Morcambe asked. "Every six months, when most people on the scheme pay to go just once every two years?"

"I want my replacement to be as close to being 'me' as possible, if that makes any sense," Jonathan explained. "Due to the nature of my work, I reckon there is more chance of me dying than most folk out there. More frequent uploads mean that my replacement will have all my most recent memories, should that fateful day ever come. Nothing but the best for my Cassy. Nothing but..."

Jonathan stopped again as another realisation suddenly hit him. Up to now, he had been reasonably concerned about the mission, how bad it was, and what had happened to him and his comrades; but now he had another thought – one he hoped would not be true, but one that would logically explain the lack of memory since his previous upload at the clinic.

"Doctor..." he stammered nervously as his heart began to race again. "Where am I?"

Both Wint and Morcambe gave Jonathan a look of both concern and anticipation as they prepared to deliver what he expected to be difficult news.

"To put it bluntly, Mr Haughton," Dr Wint delicately explained, "following the most recent upload at the clinic, Jonathan Haughton set off for a final briefing in preparation for the mission; after which the team was mobilised the following day...but the vehicle they were travelling in crashed and they, including Jonathan, never made it home."

"Including Jonathan???" Jonathan exclaimed. His eyes widened in surprise.

"Never made it home," Dr Wint repeated. "He was declared missing in action and later dead. His body was never found but there wasn't much left of the wreckage. The mission, whatever it entailed, was abandoned."

"After which Cassandra Summers, following an understandable period of mourning, eventually filed for the activation of the replacement clone," Dr Morcambe added. "That was three months ago."

Jonathan's breathing intensified as he began to take in the news of who he *used* to be...and what he was now.

"It will take some time to adapt to the world as a clone replacement, Mr Haughton," Dr Wint continued, "but we are confident that with the rapid progress we have made so far in getting you ready, you should be released very soon."

Jonathan grew increasingly agitated as the machines continued to beep and buzz wildly. Like a caged animal seeking freedom, he threw the food table to the floor and began to frantically rip out the wires that were attached to him. The two doctors rushed forward to try and restrain him and calm him down, but he managed to push them away, and after ripping away the final tube, he bolted from the room. Wint crawled to his feet again and frantically hit an emergency button on the wall, which activated an alarm. Out in the corridor, the confused and panicked Jonathan staggered about and covered his ears as the deafening alarm echoed around him. He tried to find his bearings but within minutes, several more scientists had converged on his position and attempted to restrain him. He tried to fight them away but was eventually subdued. Another scientist moved in with a syringe and jabbed the needle straight into Jonathan's thigh. The tranquilising chemical took a minute or so to take effect, giving time for the scientists to carefully move him onto a nearby clinical bed, where he finally succumbed. As the group of scientists attached the restraints, Wint and Morcambe appeared, none the worse for wear, to examine their patient again.

"I don't think he took it too well," Dr Wint commented.

"You think so?" Dr Morcambe sarcastically concurred. "Do you think there's something wrong with the protein? You'd have thought it would have kicked in by now."

"I don't know," Dr Wint replied, "but either way we cannot let him out of here in his present condition. He's going to need more time."

"And what of the client?" Dr Morcambe then asked. "Do we let her know?"

"She doesn't need to know about any of this just yet," replied Wint. "Just tell her...he's not quite ready...which wouldn't be too far from the truth."

Wint then leaned over the sedated Jonathan and looked down at his face, as if he was still conscious and listening.

"In the meantime, Mr Haughton," he silently said to him, "welcome to the world."

2

Cassandra Summers ('Cassy' to her friends) had always prepared herself for the possibility of losing Jonathan. She was well aware of the hazards of his occupation and had made peace with the possibility that she might never see him again. Whenever he set off for deployment, she treated each kiss goodbye as if it was their last, but it never made it any easier. When she was notified of Jonathan's death she was devastated. They all were – all the wives and girlfriends of the men who perished in the accident. The funeral that followed brought little closure for them. Nobody knew exactly why the mission had gone wrong and what little they found in the wreckage was barely salvageable, and the remains of the soldiers so unrecognisable that Cassy was lucky if any of what she had cremated was her beloved Jonathan.

For several months Cassy was melancholic and inconsolable. She sank into a depression and isolated herself in her home. With so much on her mind at the time, the thought of activating Jonathan's clone, in which they had invested much, never occurred to her. That was until she was contacted directly by the *Forever Together* clinic. They told her they had received notification of Jonathan's passing and required her official consent for activation. They also reminded her that should her consent be denied or withdrawn; the 'product' (the clone) would be subject to compulsory 'disposal'. Although they did not divulge the method to her, Cassy was well aware of what 'disposal' meant. At first, she was sceptical. She didn't realise how far gone the cloning process had come until they told her that it was nearly ready for activation. As such, she felt uncomfortable about disposing of it. She also felt it a duty to look after the clone and preserve Jonathan's memories. After all, both she and Jonathan had invested so much to ensure his memories were properly uploaded onto the system. Furthermore, Jonathan's regular visits to the clinic prior to his death ensured that any clone replacement would be up to date in terms of thought and behaviour. This presented Cassy with the extraordinary possibility of resurrecting the life she had shared with Jonathan and continue as if nothing had happened...in theory anyway. That phone call was two weeks ago.

She arrived at the clinic with excitement and anticipation. They told her that she was to come as quickly as possible because he, the clone, had now been activated. When she arrived, she was greeted by one of the clinic's representatives and directed to a separate waiting area and offered refreshments. Within a few minutes, she was greeted by Dr Wint – a man she had seen several times before on previous visits.

"Miss Summers!" said Dr Wint in a welcoming tone. "Welcome back to the clinic on what I would say is a..."

"Is it ready?" Cassy asked abruptly. Dr Wint's eager expression sank quickly, along with his smile.

"Well...no, not exactly," he replied. "Although the product has been successfully activated, there have been a few teething troubles."

"I don't understand," Cassy remarked in slight confusion. "Why bring me out here if it isn't ready yet? Has something happened?"

"Please sit down, Miss Summers and I'll explain as best I can," said Dr Wint. Cassy complied and sat attentively.

"How much do you know about how the cloning process works?" he then asked her.

"Very little," Cassy answered. "I left much of the know-how to Jonathan. The decision to prepare a replacement clone was originally his idea after all. Aren't they grown in tubes or something and have no belly buttons?"

"I'm afraid that's one of the many myths surrounding cloning, Miss Summers," said Dr Wint with a light tone of amusement in his voice. He went on, "The process of human cloning is a rather delicate one. The clone still needs time to grow and develop and as such, still requires a means of delivering the necessary nutrients. The umbilical cord is as natural to our clones as it is to people born the conventional way. Many people don't realise that it takes a lot of attempts to successfully create a stable embryo – hence the monetary costs for trying. Now, if left to grow naturally, that embryo would develop into a human being – a replica of the original and would start off much like the original – a foetus and then a baby."

"A baby?" Cassy commented. "But that would take..."

"Years, I know!" Dr Wint nodded back. "Years for the clone to reach the age that the original individual was at the time of their death. Naturally, this wouldn't be of much use to many of our clients out there, such as yourself, who seek to continue on from where they had left off."

"So, my clone isn't..."

"No," Dr Wint said reassuringly. "Your clone is not a baby, but a fully-grown adult."

"How?"

"In order to satisfy customer demand, we include a couple of alterations to our clones' designs. These of course are completely legal. The first inclusion is a manufactured growth hormone, which causes the clone to age and grow quickly. However, unlike the rare uncontrollable conditions, such as Progeria, these hormones are specifically designed to cease at a certain point. Through this method, we aim to speed up the growth of the clone to adulthood, or whatever age is required. This isn't an overnight process mind you and may take several months, or even years to complete. The second alteration is the inclusion of a special protein, which is placed into the clone with each memory upload. Upon activation the clone, depending on the memories uploaded, will naturally believe themselves to be the original individual because they will perceive those memories as their own experiences. The protein we give them helps to calm them down and come to terms with what has happened until they accept that they are in fact, a clone replacement. This psychological process sometimes takes time and occasionally comes with its own difficulties...and that is why we have asked you to come in today, Miss Summers."

Cassy looked at Dr Wint inquisitively as he explained why he had brought her to the clinic.

"We have been having difficulty getting your clone to come round," he began. "Ever since its activation, the clone has been insistent that it is the real Jonathan Haughton, even though it is not."

"What happened? Did it not get that calming gene you spoke of?"

"The protein? Of course, it did, same as all our specimens," Dr Wint replied. "But for some reason, unknown to us at the time, the protein failed to kick in when the clone was activated. It has done so *now* but all it has done is calm him down and leave him open to suggestion. However, it is still finding it difficult to fully come to terms with its existence. We reckoned the best way to convince the clone could be hearing it from a trusted friend or relative — someone like you."

"I see," Cassy said thoughtfully. "So, you need me to help you bring him round?"

"Any help you can provide will be essential," Dr Wint answered. "Legally speaking we cannot release him to your custody until he fully understands what he really is. The problem here is that your former partner insisted on regular memory uploads when he was alive. We think that with such a high concentration of memories embedded into the clone, he may as well be Jonathan Haughton reincarnated. It might be difficult to get through to him unless we have your help doing so."

"I understand!" Cassy acknowledged.

"So, you will help us, Miss Summers? And help him?"

"Yes," Cassy answered after a brief hesitation. "Take me to him."

"Okay then, if you would like to step this way," said Wint as he rose from his seat and began to guide Cassy towards the doors. As he led her down the corridor he continued to converse and advise.

"By the way, Miss Summers," he pointed out, "if we are to get the clone to accept who, or rather 'what' he is, it is important that we maintain consistency in how we refer to him."

"Oh?" Cassy remarked as she waited for Dr Wint to elaborate further.

"What I mean is," Dr Wint continued, "I couldn't help noticing earlier that you occasionally referred to the clone as 'he' and 'him'. I believe it might be rather early for that, Miss Summers. You may need to work on that when you take him away."

Upon hearing Dr Wint's advice, Cassy reflected for a few seconds and then released a grin of irony.

"You know, it's funny you should say that Doctor," she then said, "because I noticed you doing it as well."

"Yes, I suppose it is a hard habit to break, Miss Summers," Dr Wint conceded with a proud grin, "but once you see the product for yourself, you will also understand why."

3

Cassy had to contain herself when she first cast her eyes on the clone. She couldn't believe it at first. Even though she knew deep down that the man she was presented to wasn't her own Jonathan Haughton, he nevertheless looked and sounded so much like him, albeit a little more fresh-faced than the original. She moved towards him slowly, and as he stood before her, she gently stroked his face and looked into his eyes. She so much wanted him to be Jonathan, and in many ways, he was. There was no reason she could not continue to have that same life through the clone, but first, she needed him to accept who (or rather 'what') he was.

Dr Wint was right about the slow performance of the protein, which, although successful in calming Jonathan down and rendering him susceptible to some suggestion, he still took some convincing of who, or what, he really was. That was where Cassy came in. For hours she sat with the clone, whom she still referred to as 'Jonathan' and worked with the doctors to bring him round. She spoke to him about the mission, and the accident, of which the clone had no recollection. She then drew his attention to the absence of scars on his body and other injuries that the original Jonathan had, but the clone did not (for these were not aspects of a person that could be cloned). The doctors also pointed out the fact that he still had all his wisdom teeth, whereas the original was missing three by the time he had died. They also drew attention to the most visual indicator of a clone – a tattoo-like barcode on the back of his hand, just above the lunate bone. All clones had those. It was a way of registering the clinic's 'products' upon activation and prevent multiple copies from being created.

Gradually, bit by bit, the clone's resolve was broken down until he finally accepted the truth, and once the doctors were satisfied with his mental well-being, Cassy led him away from the clinic and took him home.

Life with the clone took some getting used to for Cassy. It wasn't exactly like she had let a new boyfriend move in with her. In that scenario, she would have needed to show him around the house and explain to him what was where, but in this case, she didn't need to. Jonathan the clone's memories were everything Jonathan (the man) knew and when he entered the house, he took to things like a duck to water. There was no need for him to look around because everything was where he knew it would be. Cassy watched with loving eyes as life appeared to resume business as usual.

"It really is you, Jonathan," she said. "It's as if my Jonathan has come back to me."

"That's funny," said Jonathan as he smiled back at her. "To me, it's as if I never left."

And with that, he moved over to her, gently held her in his arms and kissed her. The initial weirdness Cassy felt went away with each passing second in which they shared their kiss. She knew he wasn't really Jonathan Haughton, but at the same time, he was. He held her as he used to, and he kissed her like he used to. Nothing was different. She was falling in love with him all over again.

"That would have been my final mission, you know," he remarked before he corrected himself, "I mean...*his* final mission."

"I know," said Cassy, "and don't worry about it. I know what you meant."

"Well, I certainly can't go back now!" Jonathan pointed out. "Clone's aren't allowed in the forces. I'm free no matter what when you think about it."

"Yes!" Cassy agreed. "Free to do anything."

"Free to do what I... sorry...what *he* always wanted to do when he left."

He paused briefly as he thought again about his choice of words. "Free to do what *I...me...*have always wanted to do since my activation."

"What's that?"

"Marry me?" Jonathan then proposed before adding nervously, "If it's not too sudden?"

Cassy was taken aback. Was it so sudden? After all, the man asking her now, she had only known for a few hours; and yet, through the genius science of cloning and memory implants, she has also known him long enough. How can this be so confusing and at the same time make so much sense?

But the question itself...she knew that deep down she wanted it too, and without saying anything, she smiled at him, leaned forward and tenderly kissed him again. She then took hold of his hand and slowly led him upstairs to bed.

4

The relationship Cassy and Jonathan wanted was always going to be a complicated one. Although the commercialised cloning of human replacements had become big business, there was nothing in the rules to say that said clones had to be treated in the same way as their deceased predecessors. In fact, most people cloned their relatives for peace of mind – for somebody familiar to have around the house so they did not have to endure the painful grieving process (in theory anyway). It was quite common for replacement clones to be treated very differently by their 'owners' (which, as tasteless as it sounds, was unfortunately what they were). Cassy knew that in the legal sense, Jonathan the clone was effectively her property, but she wasn't shallow enough to see things that way. She wanted to feel that she was waking up to a person in the morning, not 'a thing'. That said, marriage, in the literal sense was easier said than done, as were other limitations bestowed on human clones at the time.

When the development of cloned humans was first commercialised, critics of the practice became increasingly vocal about the potential risks associated with it. Conspiracy theorists and fictional writers of the day promoted stories of unscrupulous people who murdered their spouses and replaced them with more compliant counterparts; while others went further with tales of clone armies taking over the world, or global dictators cloning themselves so they could rule indefinitely. Although presently consigned to science-fiction, the advancements made in cloning technology by this point in time had made such ideas seem more likely and made many people feel uneasy.

To appease the paranoid public (as well as the numerous rich and powerful that had invested much into the programme already), successive governments provided a means to continue the process but with various strict and legal limitations:

'One Body – One identity'
 This law ensures that only one human clone is permitted for release per client, subject to the death of the original individual. To that effect, there can be no more than one person assuming the same identity at the same time. The production, provision, and ownership of multiple copies of a single person is a felony that carries serious penalties.

'On the Rights of Clones'
 The civil rights of clones extend to the right to exist, along with basic rights of decency permitted by the constitution. Clones cannot be forcibly enslaved or mistreated by cruel and unusual measures. Scientific experimentation on clones, without the express permission of the clone, is strictly forbidden.

 Clones are prohibited from joining the armed forces in any capacity, or take up any official, political, or other influential roles. Any prior association that the original individual had with the aforementioned institutions automatically and permanently expires upon their death.

Over time, as the public adapted to the existence of replacement clones, interpretations of these laws were later relaxed where the subject of a clone's formal identity was concerned. Following a hard-fought campaign, The *National Insurance and Identity Redistribution Act* of 2105, (nicknamed the 'New Tamworth Manifesto' after one of its architects), allowed a clone to legally assume the identity of their original counterpart, but only with prior agreement from the original person being cloned. Theoretically, albeit coldly, life could continue for all involved as if nothing had ever happened:

From the *National Insurance and Identity Redistribution Act* of 2105, (AKA the 'New Tamworth Manifesto')

Upon the registered death of the client/original, and the subsequent activation of the cloned replacement, a clone may legally assume the identity of the original copy, including name, title, access to bank accounts and insurance arrangements, etc.

This is subject to recorded permission from the original prior to his or her death and ratified by their next of kin following the completion of confirmatory documentation and a waiting period of no less than three months. This does not extend to the former occupation of the deceased, which will be left to the discretion of the employer — except for those concerning military, political and influential positions, which automatically expire.

'Till death do us part'

Until the rights of marriage have been extended to human clones, the vows of married couples regarding the natural termination of the contract, such as a death, will be upheld. Replacement clones of the deceased will not be recognised as spouses.

Marriage between two clones is strictly prohibited and will not be recognised under rule of law.

Marriage between clone and non-clone is strictly prohibited and will not be recognised under rule of law.

It was the last clause ('Till death do us part') that caused much contention for Cassy and her clone. Although they didn't know it at the time when he proposed to her, legally speaking, they were not allowed to be formally married. However, these restrictions did not necessarily stop them from 'acting' as though they *were* married. Unable to hire an official, Jonathan and Cassy performed a makeshift ceremony at their home and from that day on, they referred to one another as 'husband' and 'wife'. To solidify their vows, not only did Cassy enact the 'New Tamworth Manifesto', which granted Jonathan the rights to his predecessor's name, she also took the Haughton name herself and changed her own name by deed poll. As far as the world should be concerned, Jonathan and Cassy were now 'Mr and Mrs Haughton' – at least in name, if not legally binding.

Over the next year or so, much changed for Jonathan the clone, at least compared to the life his predecessor had had. Firstly, he had to find another job on account of the laws which prohibited clones from joining the army. This didn't bother him too much as his predecessor's tenure had come to an end anyway. Jonathan managed to find a minimum-wage, 9-5 job in a warehouse, where his tasks limited to fetch and carry. The income he contributed became more important months later when Cassy completed their family unit by giving birth to their child – a healthy boy, which they named Jack. Fortunately for them, there were no restrictions on clones with regards to intimate relationships, and as such, the rights that Jack was entitled to were the same as those of Cassy – for it was accepted by most, including opponents of the cloning process, that he was conceived and born the 'natural way' regardless of who the father was.

Over the next year or so, Jonathan Haughton continued to work his hours and help Cassy raise little Jack. They were a family – healthy, complete, and content.

5

There was a vicious storm that evening when Jonathan phoned Cassy from work. He let her know he would be delayed at work on account of overtime for the company to meet its quota. He also asked her to wait up for him as he had forgotten to take his house key with him. Cassy acknowledged and prepared for his eventual return. She placed the meal that she had been preparing on slow-cook and then settled baby Jack down to sleep. Afterwards, Cassy sat curled up on the sofa, watched television and waited.

It was late, around 10 pm when she finally heard a knock at the door. She opened it and beheld a pathetic-looking Jonathan, standing out in the freezing weather and shivering. It was dark and she could not completely see his face properly, but she could tell that he was completely drenched. She guided him in and began to help him with his jacket but before she could get the jacket off, he threw his arms around her and pulled her tightly towards him in a loving embrace.

"Careful!" she exclaimed with a surprised look in her eyes. "You're soaking me...and choking me, come to think of it!"

"Oh, Cassy!" Jonathan exclaimed in a passionate tone. "Oh, Cassy I've missed you so much!"

When Cassy heard those words, she began to take note of a strangeness in his behaviour towards her. As much as she was pleased that Jonathan was home, he was acting as if he hadn't seen her for years. Cassy looked at him in slight bewilderment. She looked down and noticed his wet clothes. They weren't the clothes he had left the house in that day. They looked dirty and tattered. She also noticed a peculiar bandage on Jonathan's hand.

"What happened to your hand, dear?" she inquired. Jonathan paused for a few seconds and then broke off his eye contact with her.

"I don't wish to talk about it right now," he replied. "What's important is that I'm home now. I can only imagine the kind of hurt you must have gone through in my absence. It wouldn't surprise me if you thought that I was dead."

"Dead?" Cassy exclaimed, now more baffled. "I don't understand..."

She began to step back slowly as a horrible realisation began to set in – one that shook her to her very bones. Jonathan, meanwhile, sat down on the sofa to rest his feet. He took a quick sniff of the air and smiled.

"Is that Mexican food?" he asked. "Good timing! Another reason to have come back here before I report back to the barracks."

"Jonathan!" Cassy exclaimed in astonishment. "Is that...is it really you?"

"Yes, my love!" Jonathan responded. "It really is! And I'm home again! I've yet to report back to base but I wanted so much to see you first."

He then took Cassy by the hand and gently guided her over to accompany him on the sofa. Cassy obliged and cautiously sat down next to him. She was still shaking.

"Jonathan," she delicately began to ask. "What happened to you?"

"I... I don't quite remember," Jonathan began to recall. "We were good to go when we set off on our mission. The weather was good, and visibility was fair, at least for jungle terrain – but then..."

"And then what?" Cassy asked.

"And then...nothing!" said Jonathan, still struggling to recall. The events surrounding the mission were a blur and the crash itself a complete blank.

"The next thing I remember was waking up face down in the middle of the jungle and with burning wreckage not too far away from me. I don't remember what happened or why...but it looked like it was just me who had survived."

Cassy's eyes widened further as his response confirmed her fears – that the Jonathan Haughton sitting down in front of her was not the Jonathan Haughton she had waved off to work earlier in the day.

"And I must have hit my head something fierce because when I first woke up, I didn't even know who I was," Jonathan continued. "It took months surviving by myself in the jungle before my memories started to come back – not all at once, but slowly. After a while, I gradually remembered more and more about who I was, what I was doing there...and where I belong. I spend the rest of the time trying to find my way home. Took some fierce walking for much of it...and I managed the rest of the way hitchhiking if you could believe that."

Cassy slowly edged her face closer to his and he looked back at her longingly. She lifted a trembling hand and brushed it delicately against his face. It was rougher than the other Jonathan's face. It was scarred and exhausted.

"Jonathan," she then gasped loudly. "Oh no! No!"

She immediately tore herself away from him and backed away from the sofa. Jonathan looked at her with equal confusion.

"Cassy?" he said. "Are you alright? It's me...Jonathan!" Cassy desperately tried to fight back tears as Jonathan rose from his seat and delicately placed his arms around her.

"It cannot be!" she said, teary-eyed. "You died! They told me you died!"

"I know," Jonathan replied, "and I nearly did. I was lucky. Getting away from that horrible place and back to the States wasn't easy for me, but I'm home now."

Jonathan tightened his arms around Cassy as she tenderly rubbed them with her still-shaking hands.

"It's alright now, my love," he whispered gently as he slowly kissed the top of her head. "I'm home now. I'm home and I'm never going away. I'll report back to the barracks, get that discharge and we can finally be a proper fam..."

Cassy opened her eyes when she noticed that Jonathan had suddenly stopped talking. This time, *he* began to have a realisation of his own.

"Of course!" he said. "It's been that long I almost forgot...did you activate it?"

"I did," Cassy said with a nod, aware of whom he was referring to, "about three months after you..."

"Is it here?" asked Jonathan. "I want to have a look at it. I want to see if it truly is like me."

"*He's* not here just now," Cassy replied, slightly annoyed at Jonathan's insensitive description of the clone. "*He's* out at work."

"Okay...*he!*" Jonathan conceded for the sake of argument. "*HE* truly has looked after you. I never expected *him* to do that. And all my memories, too. All his thoughts and feelings...my feelings...towards you!"

Cassy frantically shook her head in disbelief. "Jonathan," she pleaded. "There's something that I need to tell you..."

Jonathan paused for a minute as his attention was drawn to something in the room which was unfamiliar to him – something not part of the house as he remembered it. There, on the living room floor, was a plastic child's toy. He then tilted his head and glanced through the narrow gap in the doorway that led into the kitchen and beheld little Jack's highchair positioned by the dining table. He then lifted his arms and slowly and began to step backwards.

"Whose toy is that?" he asked curiously. Cassy began to panic and moved towards Jonathan again.

"Jonathan, please..."

"I said," Jonathan repeated in a more demanding tone, "whose toy is THAT?"

"Shh!" Cassy pleaded again. "You will wake..."

"Oh, I see!" Jonathan said solemnly as he looked up towards the ceiling, in sudden disbelief. "I understand. I died, didn't I? And my clone stepped in. Well, I must admit he's been pretty thorough. I bet he told you I was going to ask you to marry me once I got that discharge through from the forces?"

"He did," Cassy panicked. "I'm so sorry Jonathan. I thought you were dead! We all thought you were..."

"Well, no matter," Jonathan said. His tone started to become calmer. "What's important is that I'm home now. I can take it from here and we can be together again. You, me...and the little one...the little one we have both always wanted!"

After she heard those words, Cassy buried her heads into her hands and sank towards the ground.

"I bet his name is Jack!" Jonathan guessed, referring to the child. He clicked his fingers and pointed towards Cassy in a bid to emphasise his point. "I remember we've always talked about having a boy named Jack."

Cassy nodded silently.

The timing could not have been worse for when their discussion was interrupted by the sound of a closing door, followed by the recognisable voice of Jonathan's clone.

"Honey?" spoke the voice. "You've left the front door open! Don't worry I've..."

The clone stopped dead in his tracks at the doorway and stared at the familiar-looking intruder who had entered his home. He looked carefully at him and instantly recognised the features. It was almost like looking in a mirror, but eerier.

"Cassy?" he said in confusion. "What's going on?"

"I could ask you the same thing!" replied the other Jonathan. The clone cautiously walked forwards and began to manoeuvre himself between the other Jonathan and Cassy. Jonathan (the original) then moved forwards to examine his copy. The clone stood there quietly and allowed his counterpart to circle him slowly and look him over.

"My! My!" he commented on the clone. "Those scientists at the clinic *have* been thorough! I certainly got my money's worth, don't you think, Cassy?"

"Jonathan?" the clone remarked. "How can this be? They said that you died! That's why I..."

"That's why you were activated," Jonathan interrupted. "Well, it appears everybody has been misinformed, and now that I'm home again, your services will no longer be needed."

"What?" remarked the clone. He raised his eyebrows at such a challenging statement.

"Look, it's nothing personal, 'other me'," Jonathan explained. "I can see you've looked after my family well while I have been away and for that I am grateful, but now that I'm back, your job is done. It makes no difference to me if you go back to the clinic or if you simply decide to emigrate somewhere."

"I don't think so!" the clone replied defiantly. "This is *my* family! I'm not going anywhere!"

"Well, you can't stay here now that I'm home!" Jonathan growled. "It's not allowed!"

"Jonathan, please!" Cassy pleaded. She moved and stood next to the clone and placed her arms around his. "It's not that simple anymore. I've moved on, and I'm with him now."

Jonathan's mouth dropped as he began to fully make sense of what Cassy was telling him – that she would rather be with his clone instead of him.

"What?!" he exclaimed in disbelief. "Like hell you have! It's really *me* you want to be with. His thoughts and feelings towards you are *mine!* You can't do that!"

"I'm sorry it has to be this way Jonathan," the clone interjected as he began to approach his counterpart. "But you heard her. I love Cassy and she loves me. I'm afraid you're going to have to leave."

No sooner had the clone spoken those words than the other Jonathan viciously launched himself at him and attempted to place his hands around the clone's neck, which was difficult enough with one of his hands all bandaged up.

Nevertheless, he put up a strong enough fight. Tables and chairs tumbled around as they fought and struggled on the floor. As the panicked Cassy tried desperately to force them apart, Jonathan (the original) was momentarily caught off-balance by a lucky shot to the chin. The brief disorientation bought precious time for the clone to shove him towards the front door and, with help from Cassy, they managed to push the original Jonathan out before closing and locking the door once again. Both the clone and Cassy leaned back against the door as Jonathan continued to pound on it from the other side like a madman.

"Cassy!" he yelled. He violently thumped the door again. "CASSY! You're making a big mistake! You can't do this to me!"

Cassy covered her mouth in fear and disbelief while they waited for the pounding to stop. Eventually, it did stop, but Jonathan hadn't gone away. Instead, he crouched down onto the ground and sat back against the door, beside himself in rage, and spent the rest of the evening muttering and cursing aloud.

Neither the clone nor Cassy knew how long the original Jonathan would sit outside. It was several hours later before they looked out through the blinds to see that he had finally gone. Exactly *where* he had gone remained a mystery to them, but the clone knew him all too well...and knew he would be back.

6

Several days had passed since the original Jonathan Haughton had come to their door, and neither the clone nor Cassy had left the house since. Instead, they both phoned in sick to their respective workplaces and, while they remained home, they talked about what had happened and planned their next moves. It was never meant to be this way. Clones had never been activated and released while the original individual was still alive. It had never been allowed. It was one of the fundamental laws that had been woven into the practice of commercial human cloning from the beginning – to appease the most ardent opponents who believed that such advanced technology could be abused to horrifying extremes. Consequently, clones were also forbidden from joining the military or hold important positions of authority. Any deviation from these laws was a serious offence. This worried Cassy, for she was aware of the legal implications of having a clone and the original running around, even if it was accidental. Had the clone not been activated there would not be an issue. But he *had* been activated, and not only that, but he had also fathered her child. It was not an easy position to be in.

"He's right, you know," she said solemnly, referring to Jonathan's aggravated ranting. "If he's still alive then having you around is illegal."

The clone said nothing in response but sat silently at the table. The only signal he gave which showed he was listening was a brief nod of his head as he rested his chin onto his fists in contemplation. Cassy walked over to him and place comforting arms around his shoulders.

"The thing is," she continued, "I'm with you now and that's that. He cannot lay claim to what the two of us have had over the past two years. That wouldn't be right."

"So, what do you propose we do?" asked the clone. "Do we pack up and run? Leave our home?"

"If it comes to it, maybe," Cassy replied, "but *only* if it comes to it. I've made a few phone calls to see if we can get some legal advice on the matter, but unfortunately, most have refused to help and instead cited the various violations of the law we've apparently committed already."

"*WE* didn't do anything," the clone argued. "And neither did the other Jonathan. This has all been a big mistake. If anything, his death had been reported far too soon. Evidently, we need to have some kind of 'Habeas Corpus' clause included in the cloning laws."

"Habeas Corpus?" Cassy asked seriously.

"It's Latin," the clone explained. "It means 'show me the body'...and clearly something the clinic should have demanded before activating me, but it's too late for that now!"

"There is another way," Cassy then revealed. "One of the legal advisers I phoned knows a guy...who knows another guy...who knows a man who *might* be able to help us. Have you heard of a man called Arnold Tamworth?"

"That charlatan from the telly?" the clone replied sternly. "No way! From what I've heard he's a scandal-ridden former politician. An opportunist who refuses to step out of the limelight."

"But Jonathan, dear," Cassy pleaded. "It's Arnold Tamworth! He was one of the architects behind the New Tamworth Manifesto – the very policy that allowed you to claim Jonathan's identity in the first place. Don't you think he'd be best placed to help us on this matter?"

"Hmph! New Tamworth Manifesto indeed!" the clone scoffed. "You know it's not really called that, right? It's just a nickname the media gave it, which he arrogantly encouraged."

"Yes, I know that but…"

"He wouldn't help us unless there was something in it for him!" the clone then argued. "No, Cassy! That's out of the question!"

"But Jonathan, I've..."

"That's final!" the clone snapped, giving Cassy a more serious no-nonsense stare as he spoke.

The two of them continued to discuss ideas on what to do next, particularly if the original Jonathan was to ever come back. This was of course, on the assumption that he had even left. For all they knew, he could still be out there sneaking about the premises. Very soon the mystery of Jonathan's whereabouts was a mystery no more when suddenly, the couple's discussion was interrupted by an angry loud shouting from outside. It was the original Jonathan, who attempted to call the clone out.

"Clone!" Jonathan bellowed. "That's my home and my life. And I want it back!"

The clone got up and peered through the blinds to see his counterpart outside, standing like a gunslinger from an old western, poised for a showdown.

"Is that Jonathan?" Cassy inquired. The clone nodded in response.

"I think he's been drinking!" said the clone. The two of them watched out of the window as the seemingly inebriated Jonathan slowly approached the house again.

"You laboratory freak!" Jonathan shouted again. "Get out here and fight me! To the death! We'll see which one of us truly deserves the name 'Jonathan Haughton'! I'll kill you!"

The clone was not impressed. He clenched his knuckles tightly and gritted his teeth as the rage began to eat away at him. Eventually, he could take no more of Jonathan's aggressive taunts and attempted to make his way to the door.

"That does it!" the clone declared. "If he wants a fight then I'll give him one, and I'll kill him!"

Cassy, however, was having none of it and roughly grabbed the clone back.

"No Jonathan!" she cried as she moved to block his way out. "You've never been a soldier. He'll kill you!"

"Or I could kill *him*," the clone replied. "*That* would certainly be an end to our problems."

"No way!" Cassy pleaded again. "Jonathan, please! You will make it so much worse for us. Don't go out there!"

Soon the clone stopped briefly and began to compose himself once again. Cassy grabbed his shoulders in a bit to try and relax him and calm him down.

"You have so much to live for, my love," Cassy continued. "You have me. You have Jack. Don't throw it all away for him. It's *you* I choose. *You* belong in Jack's life!"

Cassy then stroked the clone's face tenderly as she continued to bring him round again – all while the original

Jonathan continued his provocative tirade from outside. Very soon he was right outside the front door and began to pound on it slowly as he continued to taunt the clone.

"Clone!" he called out again. "You can't stay in there forever, you know! At some point you're gonna have to come out!"

"Go away, Jonathan!" Cassy called back. "Get out of here or I'll call the police!"

"You'll what?" Jonathan remarked. He raised his eyebrows at this peculiar threat, unsure whether or not she meant it.

"Call the police?" he then scoffed. "Go on! Call them! See what happens!"

"I mean it!" shouted Cassy. "I will call them!"

There was a moment's pause as two of them leaned either side against the front door. Cassy leaned back, locked in thought about what to do next, while Jonathan, accompanied by mixed feelings of rage and amusement, placed his forehead against the door from the other side.

"Cassy," he then called with a calm and sinister chuckle. "I think you're bluffing! In case you've forgotten, let me remind you. Having that guy around when I'm still alive is ILLEGAL! You know...against the law! So, if you want to call the cops...do it! Then watch them take your lover away; and when they do, I'll see to it that he's disposed of like the other rejects."

Cassy bit her bottom lip as she listened to Jonathan call her bluff. When push comes to shove, he was right - and both she and her clone were running out of options. "Go away!" were the only words she managed to force out loud.

"Oh, to hell with this!" Jonathan eventually said. "I'm away...at least for now. But tell your 'plaything' in there...that 'laboratory fake'...that it's my home he's taken, and I'm giving him twenty-four hours to leave. Whether I come back with the police or with 'friends' it doesn't matter. Whatever we do will be nice and legal!"

He then stepped away from the front door and began to walk away.

"Think it over, the both of you!" he warned as a parting shot to them. "Twenty-four hours!"

And with that, the original Jonathan Haughton finally walked away and left Cassy and the clone to contemplate his threats. The clone moved towards Cassy and placed his arms around her but there was no comforting her. Her heartbeat raced and her mind filled with anxiety.

"He means it, Jonathan," she said between deep breaths. "We need to get some help!"

"But there is no one to help us," said the clone. "You said yourself that you tried. And once more, he's probably right about the law."

"Is he though?" said Cassy. "There must be another way. Something about the law that we've missed. A loophole of some kind!"

"I don't know," the clone replied as he held Cassy closer to him. "From what I know of them they are pretty watertight."

At that point, the cries of baby Jack from upstairs interrupted their precious moment. Cassy kissed the clone's hand as she slowly unravelled herself from him. She then reminded him it was his turn to check on Jack, which he duly did. He quietly crept upstairs and left Cassy alone to ponder and gather her thoughts.

7

More than twenty-four hours had passed since Jonathan had made his threats to them. The clone stood on guard and readied himself to protect his home from whatever his counterpart had planned – that is if he came back at all. Cassy was feeding baby Jack at the time and seemed calmer and more collected than she had been overnight. Every so often, the clone peeked out through the blinds and carefully scanned the area outside. It was mid-afternoon on the second day when they finally heard a knock at the door. The clone and Cassy looked at each other in anticipation; after which the clone moved cautiously towards the front door.

"Who is it?" he inquired.

A man's voice replied from outside, and to their temporary relief, it was not Jonathan's.

"Ms Cassandra Haughton?" said the voice. "Does Ms Cassandra Haughton live here?"

Cassy moved towards the door and looked out through the window. She saw two suited men outside standing and waiting. She then gave a sigh of relief and began to unlock the door.

"It's okay Jonathan," she said calmly. "I called him over."

"Called *who* over?" the clone inquired.

"I got in touch with someone who said he could help. Please don't be mad at me."

"Mad at you? Why would I be mad...?"

The clone's curiosity was briefly put on hold as Cassy opened the door and greeted the two men.

"Oh, thank heavens you're here," she said to them. "We haven't much time."

"No problem," replied one of the men as he began to address the couple. "I understand you two have been having some domestic issues?"

"In a manner of speaking," said the clone. He looked more carefully at the man who had spoken. His face seemed familiar to him.

"Have I seen you before, somewhere?" he asked the man.

"I don't believe we have met before, sir," the man replied as he extended his hand out in greeting. As he did so, he gave the clone a fixated stare – the same stare that a cobra might give to eye-up a small mammal before making its move.

"And you must be Mr Haughton, right?" he went on. "Mr Jonathan Haughton?"

"Yes, that's me," the clone answered as he took hold of the man's hand. "My wife here tells me you are here to help us?"

The clone didn't have time to process any reply the mysterious man might have given, for what happened next was over so quickly. All he could remember before blacking out was the sensation of being pulled inwards toward the man as he took hold of his hand. The next thing he knew, he was down on the ground and drifting in and out of consciousness. He couldn't see anything properly but could still make out the sounds of different voices around him. He felt limp and helpless as he listened to what the voices were saying.

"What the hell did you do that for?" cried a panicked voice, which the clone recognised to be Cassy's. "You weren't meant to hurt him!"

"I'm sorry, Ms Haughton, but from what you told us over the phone we don't have much time for polite conversation," replied the voice of the mysterious man. "Besides, who puts a table like that in such a narrow hallway anyway?"

The clone then felt his body twist and turn, but not of its own accord. He could feel hands on his arms and legs as the two men began to unceremoniously lift and drag him out of the house.

"Get him into the car, carefully," the man ordered.

"Yes, Boss!" replied the voice of the other man who had been there.

The clone felt his body being bent, crouched, and forced into a sitting position, but he still had no control over the movements. He sat there, presumably in the men's car, still dazed, and confused. He then felt a soft kiss on his forehead, accompanied by the soothing whisper of Cassy's voice.

"I'm sorry, my love," she said to him. "Please don't be mad. These men told me that they will look after you. They want to help you."

The clone wanted to say something back but found he was still motionless. Whatever had happened to him at the door a few minutes earlier, had knocked him for six and rendered him completely helpless. It was the same feeling one would get after waking up from a horrible dream. Like sleep paralysis, unable to move or speak and wondering if any sounds that you make can actually be heard by the outside world.

The clone felt his body jolt suddenly as the vehicle he was in moved off furiously. After which, everything went blank and he passed out completely.

8

Jonathan, the clone, began to regain consciousness. He could feel his head stinging slightly and as his vision returned to normal focus, he quickly realised he was no longer in his house. Almost immediately his final memories came flooding back and he sat up sluggishly on the leather sofa on which he had been placed. He looked around at the unfamiliar room in which he found himself. It was a nicely decorated combination of an office and living room, with all the flair of an ambassadorial guestroom. He concluded that whoever lived or worked in this place was well paid and most likely held authority in an official capacity. Jonathan paused when he caught sight of a mysterious smartly dressed man sat on the sofa opposite from his. The man stared at him from across the coffee table. Although suited, the man wore no tie and sat in a relaxed and casual manner. His whole persona appeared to be of a man on the verge of a midlife crisis – probably in his late-forties or early-fifties but doing his best to look and act as though he was in his thirties. Jonathan immediately recognised him as the same man who had 'greeted' him back at his house.

"Did you sleep okay?" the man asked, with a slight mischievous smirk. Jonathan said nothing. He simply glared at the man as he delicately examined the bump on his head with his finger.

"How about some ice for that?" the man suggested. He pointed towards an ice pack on the table that had been prepared for him. Jonathan looked down at the ice pack thoughtfully. He then picked it up and pressed it gently against his head, all the while he continued to keep a suspicious eye on the mysterious man opposite as he continued to talk.

"Apologies for what happened to your head, by the way," the man continued. "My associates and I were a bit pushed for time and felt it prudent to get you out of there...whether you wanted to go or not."

"My head..." Jonathan began to inquire as the memories of his 'kidnap' became clearer. He then locked eyes with the man with an expression of annoyance. "You...you tasered me!"

"Well, yes," the man replied in a cocky and unsympathetic tone, "but that won't account for that bump on your head. You did that yourself when you fell back against a table."

Jonathan continued to glare at the man in annoyance.

"If it's of any comfort, you needn't worry about me doing it again," the man said. "I left my stun gun with your Mrs before we brought you here. I figured she might need it to discourage the inevitable uninvited guests she'll no doubt receive."

"You...tasered me!" Jonathan repeated with an angrier tone.

"Yes, I think we've established that already, my friend," the man calmly replied.

"I am NOT your 'friend'!" Jonathan barked back. "And I can safely say that you are certainly not *my* fr..."

"Drink?" the man interrupted. He pointed towards the collection of spirit decanters displayed in a cabinet across the room. Jonathan refused, but the man got up out of his seat anyway and moved toward the cabinet.

"Well, do you mind if *I* have a drink, then?" he said. "I work better when I've had a few anyway."

As he walked over to the cabinet to pour himself a whisky, the man continued his farcical dialogue with Jonathan, who was still trying to make sense of what had happened to him.

"I'm surprised you haven't yet asked me who I am, Mr Haughton," the man remarked. "After all, I know all about *you*, so it's only fair that you know a bit about me, don't you think?"

"I think I know who you are," said Jonathan. "You're that politician from the television – that Tamworth guy."

"Arnold James Tamworth," the man declared, taking a half-hearted bow. "Part-time legal advisor and self-proclaimed political upstart at your service!"

"*My* service?" Jonathan exclaimed. "I don't recall asking for your help. And is it standard practice for you to abduct your clients?"

"I prefer the term 'liberated', my friend," Tamworth replied as he began to fill a separate glass. "And whether or not you are my client depends entirely on you."

"And as I said before, you are *not* my friend," Jonathan said angrily.

"Oh, on the contrary, Mr Haughton," Tamworth explained as he offered the other tumbler to Jonathan, "I believe I might be one of the only friends you have right now – and one of the few people you can really rely on."

"You have a funny way of showing it," said Jonathan as he eventually, albeit reluctantly, accepted the drink. "And where's my wife?"

"Your wife?" Tamworth remarked with a raised eyebrow.

"Yes, my wife," Jonathan insisted sternly. "Where's Cassy?"

"Your 'wife' is safe and sound back at the family house; as is your son, Jack," Tamworth explained reassuringly. "And you can thank 'your wife' for having you brought here. It was she who got in contact with me in the first place."

"Yes, I know," said Jonathan, "and I told her I didn't want your help."

"Yes, she told me that," Tamworth admitted. "And as I explained already, we felt our options were rather limited at the time. We had no choice but to get you out of there. Your life might have been in danger had you stayed."

Jonathan looked up towards Tamworth as the man began to explain his predicament to him.

"You," Tamworth began, "are not the 'real' Jonathan Kenzie Haughton. You do understand that, right? You are a clone replica, albeit an extremely advanced one at that. No doubt the memory files downloaded into your mind back at the clinic make you 'feel' as though you *are* Jonathan Haughton, and always have been, but in reality, you are not."

"Get to the point!" Jonathan grumbled.

"You were designed as a replacement for the original Jonathan Haughton following his death," Tamworth continued, "to help ease the loss that Cassy would have naturally suffered. Like other replacement clones out there, you were activated upon notification of Mr Haughton's death, effectively to take his place in a watered-down role and since then you have done a good job. You managed to marry the woman in some 'unofficial' capacity, having lived with Cassandra for a couple of years now, and have also started a family. Compared to other replacement clones out there, you have gone above and beyond your basic remit of simply 'being there'."

"But then the 'real' me came back," Jonathan remarked as he began to graciously sip his drink.

"Yes, now that *is* unusual," Tamworth replied slowly. "In fact, this sort of thing has never happened before. Critics out there, myself included, had often raised the possibility in the past, but as it stands, you are the first such incident – a unique case."

"I must admit," said Jonathan with a thoughtful sigh, "I can understand where he is coming from; my original, that is. After all, I am him in all respects, right down to what his thoughts were before his disappearance. I cannot say in all honesty that I would have reacted differently had it been me."

"Well, to an extent he *is* you," Tamworth agreed, "and Cassy told me all about you...and the 'original' you. Apparently, he was about to call the police that night and have you taken away?"

"Yes, that's right."

"But he thought better of it and left, vowing to be back?"

"Uh-huh."

"So, ask yourself this, Mr Haughton," Tamworth suggested. "When one considers his memories and his characteristics, what would *you* be doing right now in *his* position? Do you think he will return to the house by himself again? Would he come back with the police? Round up a posse? What would *you* do?"

"Maybe all of those things," Jonathan replied. "I'm a soldier, or at least I used to be. I know how to defend myself and my own home."

"From a group of people who vehemently believe that it is *not* your home?" Tamworth argued. "Or that you have no right to even be here?"

Jonathan pondered for a minute as Tamworth continued.

"Whether you like it or not, Mr Haughton, you are a clone. In the current political climate, you have very little in the way of human rights compared to people who are created in the more conventional way. To all extent and purposes, you should not even be alive. With the original Jonathan still out and about, there is no need for you just now – and considering what's happened, do you honestly think he would just casually put you back in your box and keep you on ice for when he really does kick the bucket?"

"So, you're saying he wants to kill me?" Jonathan asked.

"Wouldn't you be tempted if you were in his position?" Tamworth replied. "Assuming he's not the kind of man to kill you himself, he could just as easily have you declared an 'unnecessary asset' and cancel his subscription at the clinic – and you can probably guess what that would entail."

Jonathan thought for a few seconds as he began to make sense of what Tamworth was driving at.

"But surely that's for developing clones back at the clinic," he argued, "not fully-grown ones, like me. It's not like I'm still in my original packaging. I've been out and about. I've l*ived*."

"My point exactly!" said Tamworth. "I'm not sure what people will make of you now. As the original Jonathan Haughton is still alive, it can be argued that you, the replacement, have been activated too early, which itself is against the law. You're only alive today because of some administrative cock-up back at the cloning clinic. Furthermore, the legal requirement for commercial cloning is that when clones are declared 'unnecessary assets' they are required to be 'disposed of" – and there are certain groups of people out there who would happily interpret that ruling to the extremes. So, you see, Mr Haughton, on at least two legal counts, your right to exist in the first place, along with your right to continue existing, is in serious jeopardy."

"Is there nothing in the legal system that can protect me?" Jonathan asked.

"If clones were categorised on the same level as ordinary citizens of our nation then basic convention regarding universal human rights would be your final refuge," Tamworth suggested. "But you and I both know where you stand on that. Although you and your original are identical in almost every aspect, this 'battle' between Jonathan 'the man' and Jonathan 'the clone' is far from an equal one. Legally the cards are stacked very much in his favour and if he wants you out of the way he will push for your 'disposal'."

"Unless I kill him first," Jonathan remarked.

"Oh yeah, let's see how *that* turns out," said Tamworth in a dismissive tone. "If he were to kill you tomorrow then I would wager the world would move on and forget the incident ever took place. He probably wouldn't even go to prison for it and would be, if anything, charged with 'damage to property', namely Cassandra's. But if *you* were to kill *him*? A *clone* actively killing a *human*? And not just any human...but his original? Can you imagine the hornets' nest you'd stir up with that...and the impact it would have on replacement clones everywhere?"

"So, what the hell am I supposed to do?" Jonathan exclaimed in frustration. "I can't just sit around and watch him move back in and push me out! Cassy is *my* wife, not his; and Jack is *my* son! I didn't inherit my child from him and I'm not about to sit by and have my life snatched away from me!"

"But you need to understand that the 'original' Jonathan will see things differently," Tamworth explained. "He will see it as himself taking his life *back* – a life that was originally his, which many would agree he is entitled to. My concerns are more focused on what happens to you if he succeeds, and if it means your 'disposal'..."

"Why not just say 'death'," Jonathan remarked. "Or better yet, 'execution' or even 'murder'!"

"Either way," Tamworth concluded, "I don't see anything right about ending your life in this manner. Not for you, not for your wife and not for your child."

"Is that why you are offering to help me?" Jonathan asked.

"In a manner of speaking," Tamworth replied with a nod. "That said, *how* I will help you rather depends on what our opponents plan to do next. My associates and I brought you here because we believe it is much safer for you than your own home just now – safer from potential baying mobs out for your blood."

"And here?" said Jonathan.

"Rather more fortified, you will find," said Tamworth confidently. "This embassy serves as the headquarters of a well-known and, dare I say, handsome and well-appreciated political figure. The likelihood that this place would be stormed anytime soon without a legal warrant is minimal at best. I believe you are safe here with us for now."

Tamworth then went back over to the cabinet and poured himself another drink.

"Think of it like this, Mr Haughton," he said with a mischievous smile, "You may have just become the first clone in history to be granted political asylum, so make yourself comfortable."

9

Over the next few days, Jonathan, the clone, remained at Arnold Tamworth's place of residence. Concerned for his safety, Tamworth strongly advised him not to leave the premises, at least without a bodyguard, until the legal situation in which he was certain to find himself had been resolved. Tamworth did his best to prepare for each eventuality but was not yet sure who his opponents were and what their next moves would be. He spent much of his time in his office making phone calls to media-friendly colleagues as he attempted to gather key allies within the legal system; the latter he found to be particularly difficult, despite the charismatic persuasive charm he arrogantly boasted. He wanted to make sure that whatever happened could become a public event rather than a single incident that would be quietly swept under the carpet.

Jonathan, meanwhile, grew increasingly bored and agitated. He was desperate to return home to Cassy and Jack but found that bowing to Tamworth's wisdom involved limited contact with them also, at least for the time being. Later that day, a woman entered the room where Jonathan was accommodated. She carried with her a tray of food and placed it down onto the coffee table. She was dressed formally and portrayed a friendly demeanour. Jonathan looked at her as she sat down on the sofa opposite and smiled at him.

"Hello?" he eventually said to her.

"Mina Radcliffe," the woman replied as she keenly stretched out a hand in greeting across the coffee table. "And I assume you are Mr Haughton?"

"Yes," Jonathan answered with a smile, "but you can call me Jonathan if you like."

"I am one of Mr Tamworth's associates," Mina started to explain. "He asked me to bring you something to eat and keep you company during his busy hours at the office. If there is anything I can do for you, or get, don't hesitate to ask."

"Thanks!" Jonathan replied as he began to help himself to the sandwiches on the tray. There was an awkward silence as he ate and said nothing, but he was acutely aware that Mina was still staring at him – perhaps waiting for him to speak, even if the conversation was trivial.

"So, must be hard being in your position, eh?" Mina said, "your original copy coming back and all?"

Jonathan looked back towards her and began to sit up in his seat.

"The hardest part is being made to feel like I have done something wrong," he replied. "I mean, according to Tamworth, there are people out there who think that every breath I take is a criminal offence."

"Sucks to be a copy, doesn't it?" said Mina. "Even if conditions are largely benign, it's never identical to the life the original used to lead."

"What would you know of it?" Jonathan asked. "Do you know many clones?"

"Well, actually...I *am* one," Mina revealed with a shrug and a smile. As she spoke, she stretched out her other hand and showed him the distinctive barcode etched into the back of it. Jonathan was slightly taken aback by this revelation. She looked rather young for a replacement clone. Evidently her original must have died in her prime.

"You?" he remarked. "But you look barely out of your twenties. What happened to your original?"

"She...she passed away," Mina replied hesitantly, "several years ago."

"May I ask how it happened?" Jonathan inquired. "I don't mean to push."

"It was a car accident, apparently," Mina started to explain. "Her name was Collette Steven. After her funeral, I was activated and released from the clinic. Alas, I wasn't the complete package. It turned out that Collette could only afford the most basic memory implants and so I had years of catching up to do."

"So, who were you for?" Jonathan asked curiously. "A husband? Boyfriend?"

"My mother and father," Mina replied. "I mean...Collette's parents. It was she who had filed the documents as a gift for them should anything happen to her. She was aware they had done the same for her and that their clones waiting to be activated back at the clinic."

"So, what happened?" Jonathan asked. "It doesn't sound like they took to you."

"It was mixed, to be honest," Mina replied. "They had a hard time calling me 'Mina' and kept referring to me as 'Collette', even though they despised doing so. They knew I was not really their daughter. They really kept me around because they knew it was what Collette would have wanted, but also because I represented, at the very least, a 'bit' of her.

However, as time went by, things changed. Collette's father wanted to move on properly and felt that having me around prevented him from doing so. After Collette's mother had passed away, he decided not to activate her clone, electing instead to declare both his and her clones 'unnecessary assets' and arranged for both of their disposals."

"So where did that leave you?" Jonathan asked.

"Well, I'm here, aren't I?" Mina laughed. "No, as much as he might have been tempted to dispose of me as well, we had been living together and interacting. Even though I was not his beloved Collette, I had been allowed to grow and develop into my own person. When the new laws were passed, which allowed clones limited and supervised access to their predecessor's identity, he refused to sign over Collette's identification and insisted that his daughter was dead."

"Which she was, to be fair," Jonathan pointed out.

"Still hurts though," Mina replied solemnly. "For him to declare his daughter 'dead'...well where did that leave me in his life? Who was I now?"

"So, then what happened?" Jonathan asked. "Was he going to dispose of you? Did you run away?"

"No, nothing like that," Mina replied. "If he wanted to do that he would have done so. Nevertheless, he didn't want me around any longer either because it would have been a painful reminder of what he had lost. So, he arranged for me to be sent away. He gave me money to get a place of my own and even helped me write a CV to apply for a job to help me begin a new life as my own person, 'Mina Radcliffe'. We still write to each other from time to time."

"Is that why you ended up here?"

"In a manner of speaking," Mina explained. "My father, or rather, 'Kenneth Steven', was a little naïve about the limited rights of clones in the outside world. I found it harder than most people to secure a decent job. I saw Arnold Tamworth's headquarters advertising for positions and tried my luck. I used to watch his live debates and reckoned if he had the gall to push through basic rights for clones then he should put his money where his mouth is and hire one."

"He seems alright on the surface," Jonathan said. "I imagine you are happy enough working for him?"

"On the whole, yes," Mina replied, with a slight chuckle. "He's been like a second father to me. My job is to help him with his administrative organisation. He despises paperwork and tries to avoid it if he can. Most of the time he delegates it to me. When I heard you were here, and why, I thought I would pop by, introduce myself and reassure you that you are not alone."

"Thanks," Jonathan replied as he helped himself to another sandwich. "It sounds like Cassy got in touch with the right man for the right job. Who better to look out for my interests than a clone-loving politician?"

Mina said nothing in reply and just smiled thoughtfully. Jonathan noticed her expression. She seemed to have found something amusing about what he had said and reacted almost as if she was hiding something, but he decided not to press her for the moment. He instead changed the subject entirely for the sake of just relaxing.

"So," he started, "are there any other clones working for Tamworth? I imagine the pay is good."

"There are one or two others," Mina replied, "and the pay is average. Our original owners, if we call them that for now, refused to take advantage of the new laws, which consequently prevented us from being able to open bank accounts in our name. Fortunately, Mr Tamworth created a joint account in his name for us to collectively use instead."

"Yes, about the new laws," said Jonathan. "I've always wondered about the *New Tamworth Manifesto*."

"You mean what it covers?" Mina asked.

"No, I mean why it's called that," replied Jonathan. "Whatever happened to the old one? Didn't it work out for him?"

"Oh no! Nothing like that!" Mina laughed. "I used to wonder that myself before I looked it up. It's called 'New' because there was already a Tamworth Manifesto back in 19th Century Britain."

"An ancestor of his?" Jonathan remarked.

"Not likely," Mina replied. "That one was named after a town in England."

"And probably not clone-related either," said Jonathan casually.

"Err...No!" said Mina with a smile.

Jonathan conversed with Mina for a little while longer until their dialogue was suddenly interrupted by the sound of frantic excitement outside the office. As the two of them turned to face the door, it flung open and in walked Tamworth, accompanied by another of his associates. Jonathan vaguely recognised the other man, known as Des, as the one who had helped to abduct him days earlier. The two of them were in mid-discussion as they entered the room.

"What's happening, Boss?" Mina inquired.

"Nothing to panic about," Tamworth replied excitedly. "At least not yet anyway."

"Just a bit of trouble with the natives, that's all," Des added, sarcastically.

Tamworth turned to face Jonathan directly. "Do you remember when you first got here, and I told you about waiting for your enemies to make the next move and that the ball was in their court?" he reminded him.

"I guess so," Jonathan replied. "It was something like that, anyway."

"Well then," Tamworth declared jubilantly, "I think it's time for kick-off."

"What do you mean?" asked Mina.

"I've just had a tip-off from down the road about police cars converging on our area," Tamworth explained. "Now why do you think they'd be coming here?"

"Police?" Mina exclaimed. She rose hastily to her feet as she spoke. "Are they armed?"

"Probably," Des answered as he cautiously peeked out through the Venetian blinds.

"We need to get Jonathan out of here, Boss," Mina suggested in a frantic panic. "We can hide him in one of our vehicles and sneak out of through the back."

"Hmph! First place they'd look!" Tamworth replied dismissively before putting into action his own plan. "I need to make a few quick calls while we still have a reception at this place. Mina, you take Jonathan upstairs, and Des, you keep the guards updated about our uninvited guests!"

"They're here!" Des announced as he backed away from the blinds.

"No way would they get a warrant out for us this quickly," Tamworth scoffed thoughtfully. "Something's wrong here."

Tamworth then signalled for Des to bring up the building's CCTV cameras. Des switched on the view-screen and began to flick through the various security cameras the premises had installed until he found the one where the police van had parked. Once he had done so he began to slowly zoom in for a better look.

"Couldn't have parked any more perfectly, Boss!" Des said with a smile. Tamworth and Des looked carefully as the van came to a halt and a man in uniform exited the passenger side. As they stared at the screen, something else caught Tamworth's eye – a minor detail but enough to rouse his suspicious instincts.

"Well, that's interesting," he muttered. "Jonathan, come over here and have a look at this. Let's see what you make of it."

Jonathan approached the screen and stared. Unfortunately, his own observational skills did not appear to be as finely tuned as those of Tamworth. As far as he could see, the screen clearly showed police officers in a marked vehicle. Nothing appeared out of the ordinary for officers conducting themselves in the line of duty.

"What am I supposed to be looking at?" he asked.

"Do you notice anything peculiar about them?" Tamworth asked. "Anything out of the ordinary?"

"No," Jonathan admitted.

"What about you, Des?"

"Nothing Boss," Des answered. "Just a police van with armed officers; albeit heavily armed. Were you not expecting them?"

"Look carefully at the blue stripe on the side of their vehicle," said Tamworth. He pointed towards the screen at what had caught his eye. "There are no words on it printed in white. It 'should' read *We protect and serve,* but theirs is blank!"

"Are you saying it's a fake car?" Des asked.

"And look at the weapon that officer is holding," Tamworth continued. "I don't think that's standard equipment for your usual friendly law enforcer. It's a bit heavy-looking, isn't it?"

"It's not!" Jonathan confirmed. "I have memories of those in the forces. They're ones associated with mercenaries and gangsters."

"So, they're not even real policemen?" Mina panicked. "Boss, we've gotta get him outta here. We can't let them take him away."

"Interesting," Tamworth muttered as he continued to look at the screen. "It looks like that one's getting back into the vehicle, while two others are approaching the gate."

"Do we let them in, Boss?" Des inquired. Tamworth paused for a minute as he thought about what to do next. When Des pressed his question again, he nodded, but also instructed that the men be requested to disarm beforehand. Tamworth then ordered Mina to take Jonathan upstairs into one of the spare rooms and wait with him. Jonathan, however, was reluctant to go with her.

"Mr Tamworth, with all due respect, I can help deal with these thugs!" he pleaded. "With my combat experiences, I can just as easily..."

"*Your* combat experiences?" Tamworth remarked. He scanned Jonathan up and down as he spoke. "You've probably never fought a battle in your life. That was the 'other' Jonathan Haughton."

"But don't forget I still have his memories!" Jonathan argued.

"But nevertheless," said Tamworth, "*you* have never fought. Having memories of combat and actually *being* in combat are two different things, my friend. Just because I watched 'Enter the Dragon' when I was younger doesn't suddenly make me a martial artist – nor does playing

'Tactical Ops' on the old computer box make me a SWAT-team professional."

"At least let me do *something!*" Jonathan pleaded. "If those men break through then it's all over."

"And they certainly *will* break through if anything untoward happens to our two visitors," Tamworth argued. "So, for the time being, you will do well to keep your head down and let me handle things! Mina! Take him upstairs and keep him there. Sit on him if you have to!"

As the others left the room, Tamworth continued to make his emergency calls but kept his eyes on the CCTV cameras as he did so. Eventually, he managed to get through to one of his contact's offices.

"Hello, Chicago News Forum," announced a secretarial voice over the speaker. "How may I help you?"

"Hello, can you put me through to Alice Beecham? Tell her it's Arnold Tamworth on the line and it's urgent!"

There was a minute or so of music coming from the speaker while he was put on hold and then a female voice could be heard over the line.

"Alice here! Long-time no-speak! How's my 'Mad Hatter' doing?"

"I'm fine, darling," Tamworth replied. "I just thought I'd give you the chance to peek through the rabbit hole and see what's going on in Wonderland."

"You have something for me?" asked Alice.

"Maybe," Tamworth replied, "but just a heads-up that I'm about to activate the camera at my end."

"You have a scoop?" Alice asked with keen interest. "Spill! Which political rival are you going to smash today?"

"This is something else, I'm afraid, Alice," said Tamworth. "I want you to monitor everything going on in my office for the next half-hour or so – at least until I call you back. It's really for my own protection. If you listen in and like what you hear then you are welcome to a piece of the action when it is all over."

"Would you at least tell me what it's about?" Alice asked.

"There's no time," Tamworth replied. "Just have the thing ready once I have activated it at my end. Also, make sure the audio is switched on. I can't go into it right now, but I assure you the situation is rather delicate."

"I'm looking forward to it already, Arnie," Alice cooed. "I'll get right onto it, but you owe me a scoop."

"Done! Tamworth out!"

Tamworth returned to his desk and relaxed back in his chair. Soon there was a knock at his door. When he called for them to come in, a servant poked his head around the door.

"Two policemen here to see you, sir," the servant announced.

"Oh?" Tamworth remarked with feigned surprise. "What the devil could they possibly want with me? Never mind, let them in."

The two officers from outside entered the office and the servant left, closing the door behind him.

"Mr Tamworth," said one of the officers. "I am from the Chicago Police department and would like to have a little talk with you about a cert..."

"How do you know it's me?" Tamworth boldly inquired. "There are several people living at these premises, you know."

"We err...we've seen you on the television, Mr Tamworth," replied the officer.

"Ah yes!" Tamworth remarked as he rolled his eyes up to the ceiling. "The burden of having a famous face."

The two men looked at each other unamused.

"As I was saying, Mr Tamworth," the officer continued, "we would like to have a little talk with you about a certain..."

"Drink?" Tamworth asked as he got up out of his chair and walked over to his cabinet. The officers politely declined.

"Oh yes of course," Tamworth replied, giving them a sarcastic wink. "Not while you're on duty!"

The officers turned to face Tamworth as he poured out a whisky for himself and slowly returned to his seat. The lead officer started again.

"As I was saying, Mr Tamworth..."

"Call me Arnold," quipped Tamworth. There was a brief and awkward pause, which followed his interruption.

"As I was saying...'Arnold'..." The man continued with a hint of increased frustration in his tone.

"Actually, scrap that idea," Tamworth quipped again with a mischievous smirk. "This looks like an official visit, so 'Mr Tamworth', if you please."

"Mr Tamworth!" the man growled. "We understand that you have a clone staying at your residence by the name of Jonathan Haughton."

"I might do?" Tamworth replied.

"Well, we are here to bring him in," the other man spoke.

"Ah, she speaks!" Tamworth said cheekily in reference to the other man, who, up until then had remained silent. "So not just a pretty face."

"Where is he?" the first man demanded as he leaned over the desk in a pitiful attempt to intimidate.

"Why do you want him anyway?" Tamworth replied. "He is in my care right now."

"We want to take him down to the station for questioning," said the first officer.

"What? All six of you?" Tamworth remarked. "And armed to the teeth? Is he dangerous?"

There was a quick pause of uncertainty as the two officers looked at each other.

"So, what's he done?" Tamworth then pressed.

"We have a warrant for his arrest, Mr Tamworth," said the second man as he fumbled about in his pocket.

"A warrant?" said Tamworth with raised eyebrows. "I would very much like to see this warrant if you don't mind."

The officer presented Tamworth with a detailed sheet of paper, which outlined their intention to bring in the 'felon' known as Jonathan Haughton. Tamworth took the document and looked at it carefully.

"You are aware that his original was recently reported as being alive, don't you?" he then told the men. "Have you arrested him also, just in case?"

"We are here for the clone, Mr Tamworth!" the first man bellowed. "Now are you going to take us to him, or will we need to arrest you for obstructing justice?"

"You don't want your political career plans to be marred with a criminal record," the other man added. "It would be quite a scandal."

Tamworth picked up the warrant again and examined it more thoroughly.

"Interesting warrant, this," he told them, "especially with how quickly you have put it together. Nevertheless, an authentic-looking document. I really must get in touch with your forger."

"You do understand that harbouring a fugitive is a federal offence!" the lead man pointed out. Tamworth rose from his chair with the confidence of a presidential candidate who had just swept the board from coast to coast.

"So is impersonating a police officer!" he replied sternly to the man. The so-called officers then glanced at each other to ascertain quietly which of them had just given the game away as Tamworth began to assert his control over their encounter.

"It was interesting that my recent tip-off didn't come from my connections at the station," he explained with a wink and a tap to his nose. "You also failed to introduce yourselves by name, but if I was to ask you now, I'd wager it would be something cringingly unoriginal like 'Smith' or 'Jones'. Also, that tattoo peeking out on your friend's wrist shows him to be a thuggish member of a political movement that would have instantly denied him entry into the force. Stop me if I'm wrong."

Immediately, the first man pulled out a hidden handgun and pointed it towards Tamworth's chest.

"The clone!" he demanded. "Give him to us!"

"No!" Tamworth valiantly replied. The man then cocked his pistol and raised it to Tamworth's head.

"We'll be taking him either way!" he threatened.

Tamworth smiled nervously and slowly backed towards his desk.

"You don't think I've thought of that?" he warned back. "I can assure you, my friend, that If I'm dead... *you're* dead; as will be the four men you left in your vehicle."

The man tilted his head slightly to await Tamworth's explanation of his risky and reckless behaviour.

"This is a political headquarters," Tamworth explained, "and like all rising politicians, I have armed guards patrolling the premises regularly and right now my own crack team have their sights trained on all four of your friends out there, with immediate orders to blow their ugly heads clean off if they don't hear from me in, ooh, the next five minutes?"

The men looked at each other and then back at Tamworth and attempted to ascertain whether or not he was bluffing. Tamworth then pressed a button on his speaker and spoke into it.

"Alice!" he then called down the microphone. "Tell me what you can see right now!"

"I see two men in your office," came the reply, followed by a very detailed and accurate description from Alice of what was going on in the room. Afterwards, Tamworth drew the men's attention towards the camera, which pointed down at them from the top of the room.

"That camera is linked to one of the top television studios in the city," he told them. "Right now, I have instructed my good friend, who has been watching this, to hold off broadcasting it live to the public, but no doubt she has contacted the 'real' police already. If you want to martyr me then so be it. You will not get what you came for and you will not get out of here alive!"

The men looked at each other one more time and humbly nodded. The armed man then lowered his pistol.

"You know, I could have you arrested," Tamworth warned them, "and possibly killed. With the footage we have on you we could make it look like self-defence in any case."

There was a slight pause before he calmed down and continued.

"However, I'm not going to go down that route; at least not today," he reassured them. "After all, you are just the goons, but I want you to take a message back to your employer...and back to the original Jonathan Haughton if he's in any way involved...don't try this again!"

"As you wish," the lead man replied. "Next time we will do it *your* way."

And with that, the men turned and sheepishly walked out of the door. They were greeted on the outside by three of Tamworth's assistants, who were also heavily armed. Tamworth instructed that the men be escorted back to their vehicle and then away from the area. Tamworth moved back towards his chair, collapsed back into it, and refilled his tumbler. The expression on his face was of a man who had won a glorious battle but with the full knowledge that the war had just begun. As he slowly sipped his drink his eyes stared across into nothingness while he pondered his, and his opponents' next moves. There was a crackle from the speaker, followed by the voice of the increasingly excited Alice.

"Holy molly, Arnold!" she exclaimed. "There's no way you can possibly expect me and my team to sit on our hands for this one...so spill it!"

10

The next day, Tamworth remained in his office all morning as he prepared for the inevitable legal battle that was coming. Meanwhile, the guards continued to patrol the grounds of the embassy and were on full alert for any repeat of the previous day's incident. As promised, Tamworth disclosed to Alice Beecham the basic details of the situation (i.e., his harbouring of a potentially illegal clone) but held back on the juicy details, such as the situation concerning the original Jonathan Haughton. In return for more later, Alice reluctantly agreed to Tamworth's insistence that the story is contained for the time being until he was more organised.

Meanwhile, Jonathan, Mina and Des relaxed and waited in the living room. As they waited for Tamworth to finish his work, they spent the morning reading magazines and flicking through the channels on the television. Understandably, Jonathan was unsettled throughout, and for him, the time passed very slowly. His discomfort was exasperated by Des' insistence he be sat far away from the windows so as not to present himself a target for any professional assassin who might take a chance. After many hours of work, Tamworth finally left his office and joined the others. He poured himself a glass of whisky, sat down with them and rested back in his seat.

"What news?" Mina asked him.

"News?" Tamworth remarked. "Thankfully there is *no* news right now. I managed to get Alice's network to sit on it for the time being but that's not going to last forever. Eventually, we'll need to throw her a bone."

"What about the police?" Jonathan asked. "And the courts?"

"All I was able to do was buy some time for us," Tamworth explained. "I was never expecting to get you citizenship rights like 'that'!" He snapped his fingers to emphasise his point before continuing. "If I could, then hundreds of other clones would be lining up outside trying to pull the same stunt."

"So, what *did* you get?" Jonathan asked.

"I got in touch with some of my connections at the Senate and the Supreme Court," Tamworth explained, "and I managed to secure for you some kind of temporary diplomatic immunity, including from arrest warrants, for as long as you are under my care...and provided you don't commit any direct felonies in the meantime."

"*Your* care?" Mina remarked with keen excitement. "Are you going to hire him?"

"Nothing like that," Tamworth replied with a tone of indifference. "This place is chronically overstaffed as it is. We just need to contact your Cassy and get her to temporarily sign your rights over to me – and I'm confident she will, considering the circumstances. As crude as it sounds, it's the best I can do for now, Mr Haughton. I had to pull in quite a lot of favours to get even *this* far without them hanging up on me."

"I appreciate the gesture, Mr Tamworth," said Jonathan. "I know what I am, and I know what I'm not. As a clone, I know that my rights are limited, but I am imbedded with the memories of the other Jonathan. It's not the best feeling in the world to have experienced the freedoms of our great nation through his eyes, only to have them snatched away."

"I certainly hope you *do* appreciate the gesture!" Tamworth sternly replied. "It wasn't easy!"

"So, what do we do now?" Des asked.

"Now, we sit quietly and wait," said Tamworth. "I hope to use the time granted to prepare a legal case for our clone-gentleman here. Winning citizenship might be a long shot but if we can get him some protection from the possibility of 'disposal' then that itself would be an accomplishment."

"Well, we had better get to work quickly, then," Mina commented. "The next visitor we get might have nothing to lose by pulling the trigger on us!"

"I still think you should have let me deal with them," Jonathan said suddenly in reference to the phoney policemen from the other day. "When I saw them on the screen, I had already dispatched with them in my head – a thousand times in a thousand different ways."

"A thousand eh?" said Tamworth in a questionable tone. "So, which method would you have gone for in the split second you would have had?"

Jonathan said nothing in reply. He didn't expect Tamworth's question and didn't immediately have an answer. After a few seconds, with his eyes rolled up to the right in thought, he began to answer but was cut off immediately by Tamworth's comeback.

"If it takes you this long to decide, I'd have been dead, along with yourself," he commented. "To quote that late, great, martial artist, Bruce Lee, '*I fear not the man who has practised 10,000 kicks once, but I fear the man who has practised one kick 10,000 times*' "

"What the hell is that supposed to mean?" Jonathan asked in slight bewilderment.

"It's pretty self-explanatory, Mr Haughton," Tamworth quickly answered. "Your problem is that you have all the knowledge up there in your head but none of the application; and whether you like it or not, all those conflicts you were involved in during 'your time' in the military...all those combat operations and drill training...that wasn't you. That was the other guy! So, don't think for a minute you would have just casually overpowered a couple of armed thugs because you happen to possess the memories of someone else playing soldier!"

Jonathan glared at Tamworth, perplexed and a little annoyed. He couldn't exactly argue with his guardian-to-be because he was right. Jonathan also noted the impatient tone in Tamworth's voice – almost as if Jonathan's presence had become a major inconvenience he could have done without. However, the man was prepared to come this far and even put his reputation on the line for him, so as far as Jonathan was concerned, he could afford him some leeway. Nevertheless, it still cut deep to be reminded that the memories he carried, which to him defined his entire life up to that point, were more 'inherited' than experienced.

"Back in the 20th Century," Tamworth began, "in the year 1955 of our nation's calendar, in the state of Alabama, a young African-American woman refused to give up her seat on a public bus. Back then our nation had been blighted by racial segregation and the law required that she vacate her seat when a white passenger got on. Consequently, she was arrested and charged."

"I've heard of that story," said Jonathan. "Rosa Parks, wasn't it?"

"Rosa Parks, yes," Tamworth agreed, "but she wasn't the first. A young lady by the name of Claudette Colvin did it also, a good nine months beforehand. However, while Parks' arrest was largely peaceful and non-confrontational, young Claudette was, shall we say, more resistant. It was easier for the authorities to focus on her resisting arrest, rather than her violation of their public transport segregation laws, as ridiculous as they were. Consequently, it was Rosa Parks' efforts that sparked the great Bus Boycott and propelled the Civil Rights movement that followed."

After he had finished his story, Tamworth turned back to face Jonathan to explain its relevance.

"You are already at a disadvantage simply by being a clone and being 'different' to the norm, Mr Haughton," he told him. "Taking the aggressive approach too early will not win you many friends and might alienate the public against you. To achieve your 'civil right' to exist, you yourself need to be civil. We need to play this one softly."

Jonathan nodded in acknowledgement and appreciation. For him, it was difficult enough being labelled 'different', especially when he had a vivid recollection of the time when he wasn't – a cruel design flaw in the preparation of replacement clones.

The four of them continued their civilised discussions about world affairs until they were interrupted by a loud ring tone coming from the phone on the other side of the room. Tamworth got up and answered it.

"Yes, what is it?" he asked.

"Hello, Mr Tamworth," spoke the voice of one of Tamworth's secretaries. "There is an Alice Beecham from the Chicago News Forum on the line for you. She says it's urgent!"

"Okay, put her through, thanks," replied Tamworth. His relaxed demeanour immediately faded back into 'work mode'. He tensed a little as he waited for the connection.

"Arnie? You there?"

"Yes, I'm here, Alice. What can I do for you?"

"You seeing what's happening on the television?"

"No, not really," Tamworth replied. He signalled Des to get the remote control.

"Turn to channel 48," Alice instructed. "I think the cat might be out of the bag!"

Tamworth nodded and signalled again to Des, who then prepared the channel. The four of them stared at the screen as the television tuned into ILNB (Illinois Local News Corporation) – a friendly rival to the network that Alice' Beecham worked for. They saw the image of a large crowd out on the streets and at the front was a man who faced them. He looked angry and determined as he riled up his audience. The four of them recognised him instantly.

"Tommy Dale!" Jonathan said, with a mixture of frustration and sarcasm. "Well, this is perfect! I wonder what *he* wants to talk about."

"I'm afraid I can't sit on this one any longer, Arnold," warned Alice apologetically down the phone. "I hope you understand."

"I understand," Tamworth acknowledged with a sigh as he ended the call. He placed the phone back down and stared at the television screen along with the others.

The news channel's anchor-man spoke about the crowd that had gathered and narrated a reminder about Tommy Dale and his views, occasionally quietening down in order to catch a few moments of the man's speech. Jonathan, Tamworth, Mina and Des watched and listened carefully as the man confidently and defiantly projected his controversial views to the crowd.

Tommy Dale was a well-known political extremist and troublemaker. He was once involved with a semi-militant populist movement, *Modern People's Party*, which advocated nationalistic views under slogans such as *Americans First and Always!* and *Western World is the Best in the World!* – but had now 'matured' his views (or so he claimed) to be more moderate and, consequently, acceptable to some. In recent times his policies had focused attention on alternative 'social scapegoats' – namely the replacement clones in society. This was made clear by the formation of his new group, the *Humans First* party – a name that was particularly anti-clone but also didn't win much support from animal rights campaign groups either. It was no secret that Tommy Dale's views towards clones were bigoted but at the time his ideology seemed more sensible sounding than those of the past when the status of fellow man was once determined by things like skin colour, gender, sexuality, religion, and nationality. One by one each category of bigotry had been neutralised by a series of progressive reforms and left very little to blame and be taken seriously...aside from the 'false humans' grown at the *Forever Together* clinic. Tommy Dale's views (and those of his party) largely consisted of ignorant age-old beliefs of clones 'stealing our jobs' and 'draining our resources' – both of which were easily debunked with a little sensible research (particularly when one considers that clones had limited choices when it came to employment and therefore would not be able to 'steal' jobs). However, beyond the misleading rhetoric lay a genuine concern about the misuse of cloning technology. For example, a fear of a totalitarian regime somewhere, enforcing its will using a cloned army, or one man remaining in power indefinitely through cloned descendants. It was because of these concerns, highlighted by people like Tommy Dale, which led to laws forbidding clones from military service, holding positions of authority, or even voting; effectively curtailing their basic rights. By that time, clones were not equal in society and many like Tommy Dale wanted to keep it that way.

Jonathan and the others listened carefully as the screen zoomed closer to Dale, who spoke to the crowd through a megaphone:

"When I began campaigning as a representative of *Humans First,*" Tommy began in his recognisable and charming manner, "my concerns for our welfare...the welfare of our fellow *true* humans, were as clear back then as they are now! Our ancestors fought hard to secure our freedoms and break away from overseas tyranny. African-Americans too went through terrible hardships over the years and campaigned hard and courageously for the freedoms and equal recognition that they have today!"

He paused briefly and allowed the crowd to applause in rapturous agreement. Afterwards, he continued:

"Now they expect human replicas, who have only been around for a few years – some even a few *weeks*, despite their adult appearance...now they expect what our ancestors laid down their lives for to simply be *given* to them? For free? Well, let me tell you...Freedom isn't free!"

Tommy Dale's audience roared and again applauded in delight. Jonathan and co. however, watched the screen with disgust and disapproval.

"What a cheap shot!" said Mina angrily. "To think he's actually using the American Revolution and the Civil Rights Movement to promote his own narrow-minded crackpot ideas!"

"Easy, tiger!" Tamworth remarked in a humorous response to Mina's rant.

"Of course, clones haven't laid down their lives for our nation, Tommy-boy!" Des commented at the screen. "Thanks to people like you, they can't join the army!"

The four of them quietened down as Tommy began to speak once again:

"Now a lot of people out there like to paint me with the old 'bigot brush' and label old Tommy Dale a 'racist' or a 'Nazi'," he continued. "Now, I am not a racialist! I have never once demanded the extermination of clones in any of my campaigns. I promote equal rights to all our American citizens, whether it be creed or colour. I... *love*...our great American people! But clones are not our citizens. They are, by definition, created not out of 'love', as the *Forever Together* programme claims, but rather a selfish desire by the rich to usurp the natural order in some forlorn attempt to avoid their inevitable death. It's madness!"

The crowd applauded again. Tamworth shook his head in a tutting motion.

"This is certainly one thing that Mr Dale fails to understand," he remarked. "If you feel you *have* to tell people that you are *not* a racist...then you probably are."

"Agreed!" Des nodded in response. As the crowd quietened down once again, Tommy Dale began to speak once more. At that point, there was a call put through to Arnold Tamworth informing him that a courier had arrived at the embassy with a parcel. Tamworth instructed that the parcel be examined at reception and brought to his office, while he sat with the others.

"Now, my friends," continued Tommy Dale. "I do not fear cloned people themselves. Many are genuinely nice people. They are here, and there is little we seem to be able to do about it. I opposed the passing of the so-called 'New Tamworth Manifesto', and I was defeated, but I accept that and truly believe the laws of this great nation should be upheld and respected!"

"Fat chance!" Jonathan scoffed.

"However," Dale then warned, "I make it my business to know the laws of this land, and like any true patriot I make it my responsibility to call out whenever our laws are being violated – and I have it on good authority, that there is a clone out there somewhere, being protected by influential people. And by law, he should not be here in the first place."

Jonathan and the others' eyes widened as they guessed immediately whom Tommy Dale referred. At that moment, the parcel from reception, a large brown envelope, was delivered into Tamworth's hands. He opened it and began to examine the contents as Tommy Dale continued.

"The rules are clear on clones that become 'unnecessary assets'," he went on, "as are the rules against having clones that are not for replacement purposes. Now, the original man is still alive, and from what I gather he says he doesn't need a clone. Does that not make the clone an 'unnecessary asset'? It does in my eyes! And yet the 'authorities', whom we pay and vote for, have given this clone some kind of diplomatic immunity! I tell you, my good friends...this cannot be!"

The crowd roared again as Jonathan and the others discussed their situation. Eventually, their attention turned to Tamworth, who had been sitting quietly as he read through the contents of the envelope.

"What have you got there, Boss?" Mina inquired.

"It's a message from Jonathan Haughton," Tamworth answered. "The 'other' Jonathan, that is. It appears he has decided to pursue legal action against his clone counterpart."

"You mean he's suing us?" Mina remarked.

"Not us. Just Jonathan," Tamworth replied. "The particulars being that he wants his life back, including what he had before his mysterious disappearance. He wants his house, his woman, his name and legal details, and so on and so forth."

Suddenly, the news footage on the television tuned out of Tommy Dale's rally and switched across to footage elsewhere of reporters that had surrounded two figures outside the courthouse. One of them was the original Jonathan Haughton and the other, his legal representative. It turned out that all news channels were starting to confirm Tommy Dale's story and had now tuned in to witness the 'real' Mr Haughton publicly launch his legal case. The four of them watched the screen as Jonathan and his lawyer answered the questions fired at them by the excited paparazzi. Jonathan's intentions echoed what was in Tamworth's documents. He sounded confident and determined – as did his young-looking lawyer. Deep down Tamworth was annoyed. His strategy had originally been to go through the courts in a civil and professional manner first and then bring the case out into the public eye, but on *his* terms. For now, he felt it was too early in the day for media attention, hence his move to stall Alice Beecham's own scoop on the story. However, this pre-emptive strike from the 'original' Haughton, coupled with Tommy Dale's unwanted interference, had now focused the spotlight onto the clone's opponents and completely pulled the rug from under him. His plans to use the media later was now reduced to little more than damage control. In any case, the cat truly was out of the bag.

11

Throughout the following day, things were busy at Tamworth's estate as he and Jonathan sat and discussed the subpoena that had been sent to them. Tamworth was naturally prepared to represent the clone in court but was under no illusion that it was going to be an uphill struggle. That said, he also relished the challenge and the chance to play a role more associated with the likes of Clarence Darrow or Atticus Finn.

The two of them also continued to watch the news channels to keep track of the reports. Tamworth was a little disappointed that Alice's *Chicago News Forum* was among the many channels covering the events that day. The network felt it could no longer contain the scoop and opted to jump on the bandwagon before it set off without them. However, the news they broadcasted was nothing different to what everybody else had reported and, thankfully, Alice's channel at least showed some restraint and seemed to portray a more balanced version of events.

As they continued to chat, Tamworth laid out his initial plans to Jonathan:

"As it stands, the original Jonathan holds most of the good cards," Tamworth admitted. "To many, your existence is in violation of several laws of this land. I seriously doubt that I could succeed in defending your right to an identity which he has had from birth and you have inherited, albeit too early, for only two years."

"So, what *can* you do?" Jonathan asked.

"As I have said before, my primary concern is your welfare," Tamworth explained. "Personally, I don't care who you are at the end of the day. I believe you have the right to live and that is what I am prepared to fight for on your behalf, and I'm sure your wife would agree with me on this matter. It was clear from speaking to her that she doesn't want to see you disposed of, particularly with you being Jack's true father. I would wager that she wouldn't care what you were called as long as you still live and breathe. After all, 'a rose by any other name' and all that."

"So, what are you suggesting?" Jonathan asked. "That I become somebody else?

"What I'm suggesting is that you remain yourself, at least in terms of personality," Tamworth answered. "I'm going to contact the other Jonathan's legal representative and see if we can push for getting you immunity from disposal so you can live your own separate life. For this, you may have to concede adopting an entirely new identity – as Mina had done instead of being 'Collette'. You may not like it but it's the only way out I can see."

Just then, a call came through from reception. Tamworth hit the button on his receiver and spoke into the microphone.

"Yes, what is it?"

"Mr Tamworth, this is reception here," the voice answered. "We have a young lady here to see Mr Jonathan Haughton. She says she is his wife?"

"Okay let her through," Tamworth instructed with a smile. He then turned back to Jonathan, who had overheard and was overjoyed.

"I took the liberty of inviting her over," he said. "I thought you could do with some cheering up while I look more into our opponents. She's being escorted into the reception room if you want to go and see her."

Jonathan said few words, other than Cassy's name, as he smiled and left Tamworth to his work. He dashed towards the reception area and there she stood, with little Jack in her arms. The young boy's face lit up in delight when he caught sight of his dad, who rushed over to greet them.

"Cassy! Jack!" Jonathan called out to them as he rushed over to embrace them both. "I've missed you so much. I've missed you both so very, very much!"

"We've missed you too, honey," Cassy replied between affectionate kisses. "When are you coming home?"

"I don't know," Jonathan replied, "but hopefully very soon, and when this is all over, I'll take you both away for a holiday! How does Florida sound, son? We've always wanted to go there!"

Jack giggled with glee as Jonathan gently stroked his cheek. At that point, Mina entered the room. Jonathan introduced her to Cassy and after a brief chat, he asked Mina to distract Jack for a few minutes while he got to talk to Cassy alone. At this point, Cassy could speak her true feelings to him.

"It's been so difficult," Cassy sobbed, "having to choose between the two of you like that."

"I can understand how hard it is," Jonathan answered. "When I first woke up back at the clinic, I thought *I* was the real Jonathan Haughton and thought of nothing else but to get back home to you and propose. That is what I... I mean 'he' wanted to do. Now that he's back..."

"I know, I know!" Cassy replied. "I loved him before he disappeared. Had he asked me to marry him I would have said 'yes'. We even thought of having kids as well."

"I know," Jonathan said quietly.

"When he came back home that night a lot of old feelings came back also. I... I didn't know..."

"Shhh, it's okay," Jonathan answered as he comforted Cassy.

"It's not okay for you though," said Cassy. Her voice trembled as she spoke. "You might die!"

"And I might not," said Jonathan. "It's going to the courts now and this Arnold Tamworth character thinks that there might be a way through this. It might, however..."

"Might what?" Cassy asked curiously.

"It might involve me giving up everything that I am," Jonathan explained. "Tamworth wants to appeal for my continued existence under a new name. As such, all the identity notes will be passed back to the original. I'll have to get used to a new name, but I'll be alive for you and Jack."

Cassy began to shake her head in sadness. Jonathan delicately lifted her chin so that he could look her in the eyes again. He could tell there was something else on her mind.

"What is it?" he asked.

"The other Jonathan came round to see me recently," Cassy explained. "He told me about the court case and what he wants. He told me he wants everything back. Everything that he believes should be his. His name, his house...me...and Jack."

"Jack?!" Jonathan exclaimed. "Jack is *my* boy, not his! He can't do that!"

As he spoke, Jonathan clenched his fists tightly and breathed rapidly as he battled the urge to punch the nearby wall.

"I know, and I agree," Cassy replied, taking Jonathan's hand into hers. "I want him to be happy also. After all, he has been through a lot as well. But I don't want Jack's real father to not see him. I tried to reason with him and already suggested the idea that you change your name and give his identity back but..."

"But what?"

"He feels that as long as you are still around, he will never have me back, regardless of who you are. He wants you out of the way!"

"So, he won't agree to Arnold's proposal?" Jonathan inquired.

"I highly doubt it," Cassy answered. She shook her head again. "I want to find a way around this which benefits the both of you. I don't want him to lose everything, but I don't want you to be disposed of either!"

"I'm afraid it will be for the courts to decide," Jonathan replied. "If I could speak to my counterpart again. Maybe try to reason with him. After all, he is me...and I am him. Surely, we must find some common ground. Or are we doomed to repel one another like magnets of similar poles?"

"He's different now, darling," said Cassy. "I guess his experience out there must have really messed him up somehow."

"I wish I had just gone out there and killed him when I had the chance!" Jonathan grumbled. "I'll tell you now, Cassy, if he tries that again I'll..."

"Oh, for goodness sake!" Cassy exclaimed in frustration. "Is this some pride thing? When there are more civilised ways to sort out our differences, all you want to do is butt heads. You men are all the same!"

No sooner had Cassy finished saying those words than she started to go red with embarrassment as she realised what she had just said. Jonathan gave her an ironic stare of *'was that supposed to be funny?'* – for surely her words in the current context constituted a pun.

For the next couple of hours, Jonathan, Cassy, and Jack spent time together. They played, chatted, and enjoyed each other's company. In the meantime, Tamworth busily researched his opponent's legal representative – a man by the name of Edmund Cottam. He was a mousy kind of man, with a geeky Buddy-Holly look about him that indicated a squeaky-clean persona. Not in a creepy way but with a genuine desire to please and impress. After doing some digging, and finding nothing of interest, Tamworth concluded the man to be a genuine and honest lawyer, at least up to this point. The original Jonathan Haughton had been clever not to formally align himself with Tommy Dale and his cronies but instead hire the wisdom of somebody who appeared to have his best interests at heart. Tamworth felt a little disappointed that he couldn't find any dirt on the man and a little sad that he may have to tear him to pieces in court – but that is the way it would have to be.

'Cottam doesn't need to worry about losing the case in the long run anyway,' Tamworth thought to himself. *'The way this story has been sensationalised he'll be remembered no matter what'.*

Nevertheless, Tamworth believed that it was still a good idea to try and reach a settlement, and with that in mind, he punched up Cottam's office contacts and dialled. Soon, he was put through to Edmund Cottam directly and the two faced each other for the first time on their respective view-screens.

"Ah, Mr Cottam, so lovely to meet you at last," Tamworth said. "Drink?"

"Err...no thank you," Cottam replied. "Unless you have the technology to fax me a dram?"

"Ah, no such luck!" Tamworth laughed in an attempt to lighten the mood a bit more.

"What can I do for you, sir?" Cottam said. "I take it the subpoena arrived safe and sound?"

"Oh, it did, thank you," Tamworth answered as he sat back in his chair. He kept a close eye on the screen as they interacted. "I also saw you and your client on the telly yesterday. A very interesting man you're working for, by the way. They must be in high demand...because I happen to have one myself."

"Indeed!" Came the reply from the unimpressed Cottam. "If we could get down to the particulars of this tribunal, we can..."

"You know it's very interesting how you addressed that subpoena directly to the clone," Tamworth interjected as he attempted to dominate proceedings. Cottam looked briefly perplexed but unfazed.

"Is he not the subject matter?" he answered. "My client is taking legal action against his clone and not anybody else. After all, the felony he has filed is no fault of yours or that of Ms Haughton."

"And what of the *Forever Together* clinic?" Tamworth asked.

"They will be dealt with as a separate issue," said Cottam. "And I am confident they *will* be dealt with. Not even you would oppose that, surely?"

"But surely, Mr Cottam, by addressing the subpoena to my client, are you and *your* client not technically recognising him as an 'individual'," Tamworth pointed out, "and thus providing him access to certain liberties?"

Cottam grinned at the suggestion. He wasn't stupid and could see through Tamworth's attempts to faze him.

"Not at all, Mr Tamworth," he answered calmly. "The wording of those documents is courteous at best. I see no reason to be overly nasty in our proceedings."

"But you could have addressed them to me, his guardian and technical owner just now? Instead, you addressed them to him directly...as a person."

"Interesting choice of words to refer to yourself as his owner, Mr Tamworth," Cottam quipped suddenly. "Your words, not mine."

"No, no you are missing the point," Tamworth replied. "I am merely pointing out that you have already recognised my client as a..."

"Actually, Mr Tamworth, I believe it is *you* who has missed the point," Cottam interrupted. "The point of those documents was to make clear, in no uncertain terms who or what was on trial, but don't think for a minute that our request of his presence should be mistaken for an extension of privilege. History is full of examples of defendants taking unusual forms. In 1661, the corpse of Oliver Cromwell was posthumously tried and executed in England. And there are many examples of other defendants being animals. Did *they* have the same legal standing?"

Tamworth's face dropped slightly as he began to take note of the man he was up against. A rising star in the legal world and clearly not a man to underestimate. Tamworth smiled mischievously at the thought of meeting his match – not in the same way that their respective clients would – but nevertheless, he knew he was going to enjoy himself.

"Point taken," Tamworth conceded, "but then they never had *me* on those particular cases now, did they?"

"Are you that confident, Mr Tamworth?"

"What about you, Mr Cottam? Are you, yourself, good?"

"I like to believe so, sir," Cottam answered, "as do the clients whom I represent."

"I can sense you are a good man of sorts," said Tamworth. "So, tell me, are you the kind of lawyer who wants what is right? No matter what?"

"My role is to represent my client to the best of my ability, Mr Tamworth," Cottam answered quickly and confidently. "And yes, I firmly believe in my client's right to have his name and identity restored to him – that which had been given to him by birthright."

"Well, are you prepared to entertain the possibility of..."

"A settlement? Not a chance," Cottam replied forcefully, "And I advise you to save your energy for the courts."

"But I had hoped to talk to you and your client about the possibility of granting your wishes," Tamworth suggested. "I believe I can persuade my client to relinquish his rights to Jonathan Haughton's identity in exchange for his own right to exist."

"I'm sorry Mr Tamworth, but instructions from my client are perfectly clear – as are the laws of this land," Cottam warned. "To negotiate on your terms would run the risk of overturning many of those laws."

"Well, maybe it's about time those laws were overturned!" Tamworth argued.

"Again, that will be for the courts to decide, Mr Tamworth," Cottam concluded, "and as such, I advise you to get some rest. It appears tomorrow is going to be a long day for you."

Tamworth and Cottam amicably ended their transmission, but as the screen went blank Tamworth let out a frustrated tirade of expletives.

"Damn! He's good!" he cursed under his breath. He then moved over to his drinks cabinet and poured himself another whisky. At this point, Jonathan walked into the room. His time with Cassy and Jack was over for the day and they had now left for home.

"How did the negotiations go?" Jonathan asked.

"Not good," Tamworth confessed, taking large gulps from his glass. "Your counterpart seems to have got himself a good lawyer...a *very* good one."

"As good as you?" Jonathan asked.

"No chance!" Tamworth joked. He offered a glass to Haughton, who opted for one of the beers instead."

"I spoke to Cassy about your settlement option," Jonathan told him, "but she told me she had spoken to my counterpart already and he doesn't want that...and neither do I. So, I have decided to fight him head-on."

Tamworth looked at him in astonishment.

"Have you taken leave of your senses?" he shouted. "You cannot begin to challenge his birthrights!"

"It's not about birthrights, Arnold!" Jonathan argued. "He wants to take everything from me! He wants to take more than what he had before. He knows full well I won't stand for that! As long as I'm alive he'll never have it all. He'll never have Cassy and he sure as hell will never have Jack! He wants me out for the picture for good!"

For the rest of the evening, the two of them settled and talked more over more beers, and eventually, the coffee table was filled with empty bottles. Tamworth sat back on the sofa and sighed.

"You have a dark side to yourself which you obviously didn't realise, eh, Mr Haughton?" Tamworth commented, in reference to the other Jonathan.

"He never used to be like that," said Jonathan reflectively. "Believe me, I know. He's noticeably changed in recent times."

"In what way?" Tamworth inquired.

"Well for a start his attitude towards clones appears to have hardened."

"Well, to *one* clone anyway," Tamworth joked.

"He also appears to be more unhinged and erratic," Jonathan continued. "I could tell be the way he spoke to me that day. His head seemed to be all over the place, shaky, like a crazy man. I guess the past two years must have taken their toll on him. I don't completely blame him though. No doubt I would have turned out the same. He and I are, after all, the same."

"Don't be so sure, Mr Haughton," Tamworth assured him. "If you ask me, the past two years are what has defined you both as 'different' individuals. You have lived a relatively happy family life, while he has no doubt been through hell in hostile territory. Consequently, two very different lives. Had you been identical twins in those circumstances you would have been regarded as two different people. Just because he's a good soldier doesn't necessarily mean you would be. But in the same manner, he can't expect to be a good husband and father simply because you happen to be."

"It's just a shame this tribunal isn't to determine who the 'better' Jonathan Haughton is," Jonathan joked. "I'd probably win hands down. I think I'm turning out to be more laid back than he is. He's certainly not the man he used to be. If anything, I'm more of 'old' Jonathan than he is."

When Tamworth heard those words, he paused for a moment as an important realisation slowly, but gradually began to develop in his mind.

"What did you say?" he then said. He scrunched his face slightly as he sat up more alert.

"Oh nothing," Jonathan replied as he took another sip of beer from his bottle. "I was just saying how different the other Jonathan is now, compared to how he was before his disappearance. If he hadn't gone on that mission, he probably would have been exactly like me – married and the father of Jack."

"But he's not," Tamworth replied, "and that's not what I'm getting at, either!"

Jonathan looked bemused as Tamworth quickly rose from his seat and began to pace up and down the office as he psyched himself up for work again. He stopped for a moment and looked at Jonathan with a sudden rejuvenated smile. It was a eureka moment for them both.

"You," he declared with excitement, "are a genius! And when I say *you*... I really mean *me*!"

Afterwards, Tamworth resumed his pacing and began to get himself organised. Jonathan began to sober himself up and take more notice of his lawyer's sudden change in mood.

"What is it?" he asked curiously.

"I think I have it," Tamworth joyfully declared. "If the other Jonathan wants a fight...and if *you* want a fight...then let's have a fight!"

"You mean...actually fight?" Jonathan inquired, with a slight look of confusion.

"Oh goodness, no! Nothing that crude!" Tamworth replied. "They think they've got this tribunal in the bag already...but I think we might have a chance if we play this right!"

Tamworth grabbed his laptop, sat back down, and cleared the table to make space. He then got onto the phone to reception and ordered up copious amounts of coffee for them both.

"Now, Mr Haughton," he said gleefully, "you are going to tell me everything I need to know about Jonathan Haughton, both yourself and the original, no matter how trivial."

"What specifically do you need to know?" asked Jonathan.

"Everything, Mr Haughton," Tamworth insisted. He cracked his knuckles with excitement and prepared himself for the rapid typing ahead. "Every personal preference, every funny anecdote. I want to know your academic history and medical history! Everything! Do you understand?"

"I'll give it my best shot," Jonathan replied. He sat up and leaned forward towards the laptop.

"This is going to be a very long night, Mr Haughton," Tamworth warned reassuringly, accompanied by a sly confident wink. "But I assure you it's going to be worth it!"

12

It was the morning of the first day of the tribunal and everything was hectic. As Jonathan, Mina and Des sat down to breakfast, Tamworth sieved through the news channels and saw that all of them were reporting on the same thing – the upcoming hearing of 'Man vs Clone' – at least that was how one of the tabloid newspaper headlines described it.

"Man vs Clone," Mina commented when she saw the title. "That doesn't sound fair! They're making it out to be some kind of low-budget B-movie!"

"Is it?" Tamworth remarked with a cheeky smile. "Well, by the time we're through, they're going to read 'Clone vs Man!' – much more threatening!"

Mina turned her attention to Jonathan, who was sat at the table in the smart and clean court-friendly clothes, which Cassy had dropped off earlier. He did not look at her initially but sat there and motionlessly stared into his black coffee. Mina could tell he was apprehensive – not necessarily at the thought of disposal but more of a soldier preparing for a covert mission deep within enemy territory.

"And how do you feel, Jonathan?" she finally asked with a comforting smile. Jonathan didn't answer quickly. He heard Mina speak to him, but the question took a few seconds to register. Eventually, he turned to her and said with a smile, "I feel ready for battle, at least, and a little tired."

"A little?" Des laughed.

"Mr Haughton and I spent the evening together, Mina," Tamworth joked with a non-serious wink. "The folks at the courthouse didn't leave us much time to put our arguments together, but we just about managed it."

"Any idea who the judge is going to be?" Mina asked.

"Assuming there are no sudden changes, the case will apparently be overseen by Avery Taylor-Beckett," Tamworth answered. "An interesting man."

"Is that good?" Jonathan asked.

"It's fair," said Tamworth with a satisfied expression. "I've met the man a few times and his reputation holds up well. I'm not sure what his own stance on replacement clones is but that would be a good thing. Pro-clones don't tend to be quite so vocal in these political waters."

"I'm really nervous, Boss," Mina declared. "This has already gotten out of hand with all these negative vibes."

"Why should *you* be nervous?" Tamworth shrugged. "It's not you who is on trial here. *He* his."

"What I mean is," Mina clarified, "I'm worried that if he loses, he will be disposed of. Why not avoid the trial altogether and arrange for him go into hiding?"

"Because if I do that, I lose everything!" Jonathan remarked. "I lose my identity...my home...Cassy and Jack. I know my 'other' self won't stop pursuing me until I am out of the way entirely, one way or the other. At least this way we force him to the debating table."

"Which neither of them is particularly good at, according to our Jonathan," Tamworth added. "While our opponents out there will likely argue why Jonathan here should be lawfully disposed of as an 'unnecessary asset', *we* will argue that the law only applies to un-activated clones and needs clarification for an unusual case such as this."

"I'm sure the original me is just as interested as I am on how this will pan out," Jonathan said. "I have memories of facing many opponents in my lifetime, from school bullies to street thugs, friendly rivals in boxing matches and martial arts tournaments, but there were always those subtle differences that set them apart from me. Today I get to face off against myself...my *exact* self. It will be like seeing what would happen when an unstoppable force hits an immovable object."

"In any case," said Tamworth, "we will need to finish this conversation on the way. Des, get the car ready out the back!"

"Righto, Boss!" Des answered. As he disappeared out of the room, the others gathered their belongings and prepared to head out also. They waited outside the building while Des pulled the car round to them, and once they were in, they headed off into the city and towards the courthouse.

When they arrived at the courthouse, they exited the vehicle and made their way up the iconic stone steps. They quickly found themselves surrounded by eager photographers hoping to catch a quick interview with the infamous clone.

"Mr Haughton! Mr Haughton! How do you feel having to go to court today?" asked one journalist, but before Jonathan could form an answer, other questions were thrown to him from all sides, which ranged from reasonable to controversial. At each attempt for a story, their efforts were blocked by Tamworth, Des, and Mina, who all flanked the anxious Jonathan. Jonathan looked around for a friendlier face in the crowd, but he could see none – and to make things worse he caught a glimpse at the entrance of a couple of skin-headed troublemakers positioned near the top of the stairs. They were waving uncomplimentary placards and staring menacingly at him.

'*We already have one Haughton, we don't need another!*' read one of the signs, while another read '*Send him back!*'

Once at the top of the steps, Tamworth and the others shuffled Jonathan through the revolving doors and into the reception area, where they were greeted by one of the security guards.

"Passes, please?" he asked them. Tamworth, Mina and Des showed him their passes. The security guard looked at the clone impatiently.

"His err...pass...is in these documents right here, officer," Tamworth said. "He's due in the chamber in about fifteen minutes."

The guard turned again and looked at Jonathan.

"And is this Mr Haughton 'the man' or Mr Haughton 'the clone?'" he then asked.

Tamworth's face lit up with interest at the question.

"Hmm!" he remarked to the others. "Evidently we've arrived first." He then nudged Jonathan slightly before saying, "Well, show him, then!"

Jonathan rolled up his sleeve and turned his hand over for the guard to examine the *Forever Together* barcode. The guard quickly scanned the barcode with a special scanner, after which he guided Jonathan, Tamworth, and Mina through the reception area. Des, meanwhile, waited near the car as ordered. As the other three headed down to the waiting room, they were greeted by a familiar and friendly face – familiar that is, to Tamworth, at least.

"Hey, Alice!" he shouted as she ran towards them. "Glad you could make it today!"

"Indeed, Arnie," Alice replied. "This story has been bigged up somewhat, so I thought it better for the network to send over their best reporter and editor. So, here I am!"

"Miss Alice Beecham, may I introduce you to my secretary, Mina...and my client, Mr Jonathan Haughton, the clone."

"Pleased to meet you," said Alice, shaking Jonathan's hand as she spoke. "And may I also congratulate you on being the talk of the town."

"If it's all the same, Miss Beecham," Jonathan replied, "I would rather not be here at all if it could be helped."

"I understand, Mr Haughton," Alice remarked. "I am aware that so far the media hasn't been too kind to you, what with the other Mr Haughton's public plea for support and Tommy Dale's recent interest in the upcoming case."

"You've got that right!" Jonathan replied. "This all seems like a show trial to me, and I've already been torn to shreds by the tabloids, thanks to him!"

"I guess fear is a powerful weapon, Mr Haughton," Alice began to theorise. "After all, you are the first case of a replacement clone being alive and active before the original's death. I guess if there is any chance of you winning...where would it lead?"

"Well, what you think?" Jonathan asked her, almost defensively. "What's *your* take on all of this?

"Mr Haughton," Alice responded tactfully. "Presently I don't know *what* to think, but I see the one-sidedness of the rest of the press and I believe that my network can offer a more balanced approach – especially if I can get an exclusive interview with you?"

"Perhaps some other time, Alice," Tamworth interjected as he strategically placed himself between the two of them. "My client and I have some last-minute preparations before proceedings, but if you stick around and are still here at the end of the day, then yes, I believe an exclusive interview is on the cards if my client is in the mood for one."

Tamworth ended the conversation and instructed Mina to escort Alice to the main courtroom and sit with her, while he and Jonathan psyched themselves up for their initial performance. Soon they were called up and they made their way out of their waiting room, escorted by a security guard to where everyone else waited. As they entered the courtroom, all was quiet, and all eyes were focused on the conspicuous clone. This was no surprise for Jonathan. He expected as much. Standing straight and proud, Jonathan and Tamworth defiantly made their way towards the defendants' area and took their seats. Jonathan noticed his counterpart, the 'original' Jonathan, staring at him from the opposite side of the room and readying himself in his own mind for battle. Likewise, Tamworth noticed his legal opponent, the unfazed Edmund Cottam sitting across from him. They gave each other respectful nods of acknowledgement as Tamworth took his seat. During the final minutes of waiting for the judge-advocate, both Jonathans were engaged in whispering dialogues with their respective lawyers, until an authoritative voice brought the courtroom to complete silence.

"All rise for Judge Taylor-Beckett!" it boomed. All rose and were seated again when Judge Avery Taylor-Beckett reached his chair and sat down. They then waited as he skimmed once again through the documents in his possession. Afterwards, he looked across to both the plaintiff and the defendant and began to address the plaintiff first.

"Are you, Mr Jonathan Kenzie Haughton, born August 11th, 2085?" he asked.

"I am," replied the plaintiff.

"As am I!" the defendant (the clone) interrupted. The Judge turned to face the clone and gave him an impatient look.

"With respect to you, sir," he began, "assuming you are the clone replacement of Mr Jonathan Kenzie Haughton, it is my understanding that you were not born in the conventional sense but created and developed more recently and over a much shorter space of time. For my own records, and for the benefit of the court, I am addressing and clarifying the holder of the title 'Jonathan Haughton' for these proceedings."

"Your Honour," Tamworth spoke as he quickly rose from his seat. "May I ask the court to consider our recent request submitted just this morning regarding these proceedings – particularly with regards to how my client will be identified in the official recordings?"

"Ah yes!" Taylor-Beckett smiled. "You have requested that, for the purpose of these proceedings, your client be referred to as 'John' Haughton, instead of 'Jonathan'. Is that right?"

"That is correct, Your Honour," Tamworth nodded.

"Erm, if it may please the court, Your Honour," Cottam suddenly interrupted, rising from his own seat in the process. "May I take a brief moment of this time to query my learned friend on the choice of this temporary name?"

The judge nodded and granted the request.

"It is simply to aid record-keeping," Tamworth answered. "I would like these proceedings to run as smoothly as possible, without any mistakes on who said what. I merely did not wish to 'confuse' the two Jonathans in our presence."

"But do you not think 'John' to be a rather provocative choice, in light of the circumstances?" Cottam inquired. "Surely something less similar to that of the plaintiff would be better if we are to go down this route?"

"Oh, you mean a different name entirely. A different identity?" Tamworth replied with confident sarcasm in his tone. "You had your chance for that not too long ago, so don't come crying to me now!" He then turned to face the judge again and continued to speak:

"It is my opinion that my client's willingness to settle for any diversion from his name during these proceedings should be interpreted as a willingness to compromise, without conceding defeat before we even get underway."

Judge Taylor-Beckett smiled and gave a thoughtful nod of approval.

"For the time being, I am happy to move with your request," he declared. "May the records show that for the duration of these hearings the defendant, known currently as Jonathan 'the clone' Haughton, will be referred to as 'John' Haughton, both verbally and in our official documentation. But also note that this is purely for the sake of complication and it does not affect the clone's legal standing in this matter.

"What legal standing?" whispered the 'original' to his lawyer.

"Mr Cottam, have you prepared a statement on behalf of your client?" the judge then asked. "And if so, you may begin the proceedings in your own time."

Edmund Cottam rose from his seat and began to address the court. He moved around the room with the confidence of a man who was tasked with proving that two-plus-two was equal to four. The court listened as he laid out his argument on Jonathan's behalf – the fact that Jonathan Haughton was born, that it was *he* who was educated at the school and subsequent colleges, that it was *he* who joined the army and fought bravely for this great nation, and that it was *he* who arranged for the creation of the clone now identified as 'John'.

John and Tamworth sat and listened as Cottam continued his persuasive opening statement. Admittedly he was quite convincing and none of his facts was false from a legal standpoint. For Cottam, this was an open and shut case. After all, Jonathan's birth, education, and life before the clone's activation were well documented. It would not be right for 'John' to steal those achievements and claim them as his own. Before closing his speech, Cottam also threw out a cheeky below-the-belt shot by suggesting that John's so-called military experience were akin to the 'Walter Mittys' of the world – deluded people who pretend they were in the armed forces, who don medals they did not earn and march in parades with comrades they never fought alongside. Had the clone been guilty of such behaviour, he would have fallen foul of the nation's *Stolen Valour Act*.

"And with that," Cottam began to conclude theatrically, "it is clear that the clone...this substitute of a man...should step down – for my client, the real Mr Haughton, is not yet finished!"

This last part of the speech did annoy John very much. He wasn't out to 'steal' Jonathan's past, but at the same time, he possessed the memories of those events – memories so vivid he may as well have been there; because as far as he believed, he was. He knew he really wasn't, but he did not like to be reminded. That said, in the two years of his official existence, he had never spoken about those times in the army – not to anyone – and to suggest otherwise was tantamount to slander. Nevertheless, John remained as calm and restraint as he could, to give Tamworth the chance to flex his own muscles in the courtroom.

When it came to Tamworth's opening statement, he waltzed onto his stage with the confidence and flamboyance of an actor who knew the Oscars were rigged in his favour. He was not fazed one bit by Cottam's speech. As a politician, he had been grilled at select committees in the past and had, himself, made occasional court appearances on both sides of the room. In each case, however, whenever it was Tamworth's time to speak...the floor became his property – a stage for his show-stealing performance. Had he been an actor in a play, they would have renamed the theatre after him by the time he was finished – such was the confidence he had in himself.

"My dear friends," he began. "I believe my client has been at a legal disadvantage long before these proceedings even started. Sure, there are people out there, bigoted people, who believe he is lucky to even be given this opportunity, but I believe his presence here is an important one, and not just for clearing his name."

The court listened intently as Tamworth strutted around confidently as he spoke.

"The story of his circumstances is simple enough," he continued. "It was believed that Jonathan Haughton was dead – killed while on a mission, and consequently his clone, my client, was activated and released. At the time, all this was in accordance with the law. It is not John's fault that his predecessor was still alive, nor is it his fault that it took two years for him to come home. In fact, there isn't much here that *is* John's fault – and yet here he is being treated like a criminal."

The courtroom quietened further as Tamworth continued his statement.

"My client is fighting for his life...literally. The law 'appears' to suggest that clones declared an 'unnecessary asset' are to be disposed of. There are other laws forbidding the creation of clones that are not 'replacements' - but I say these laws only apply to the activation of clones, and at no point was my client ever declared an 'unnecessary asset' prior to his activation. I put it to you all that it would be wrong to do so in retrospect and sentence an innocent man to death. Surely our laws cannot be so draconian in practice?"

Tamworth paused for theatrical effect, before turning to face his audience once again, particularly towards Jonathan.

"That said," he went on, "I also put it to you that there are other ulterior motives behind Jonathan Haughton's misguided decision to bring my client to court. We tried to reason with him, but he would not listen. We asked for clemency but there was none. We tried to negotiate, even to the point of granting his wishes, but it became clear that as long as my client was still around, Jonathan Haughton would never really have his life back. But does he really believe that his counterpart will simply give up all he has built without a chance to defend himself? He should know him far better than that, surely! Hence our counter-suit."

There was a chorus of mumbling around the courtroom as people wondered what Tamworth meant by this.

"Allow me to clarify to the court today," Tamworth announced, "that this is more than John's right to exist. It is about his right to exist as he always has – as Jonathan Haughton. My learned friend across the room wishes to get back his client's identity, his legal status and everything else, including all that *my* client has personally build up over the past two years. Our argument, on the other hand, is that my client is, in fact, the *true* Jonathan Haughton."

Tamworth paused momentarily as the room began to erupt with sounds of astonishment from the audience. Jonathan and Cottam meanwhile, who were both initially relaxed during much of Tamworth's statement, now sat up straight and looked at one another as if they were about to have the rug pulled out from under their feet.

Taylor-Beckett banged his gavel repeatedly to restore order and signalled Tamworth to continue, but also clarify his outrageous claim.

"I am under no illusion as to what is what," Tamworth went on, "nor am I under any illusion as to who is who – and *that* is the real question we face today. What truly makes a person? During his opening 'diatribe', my learned friend humorously demanded my client make way for the return of the 'real Mr Haughton'. However, we wish to present the counterargument that the clone, my client, is far closer to being the 'original' Jonathan Haughton...than the so-called 'original'.

Ever-increasing murmurings of excitement filled the room as Tamworth stretched out his hand towards where his client was seated.

"And, to that effect," he concluded, "regardless of what we may call him for now, may I present to you, my client, John Haughton – the *real* Mr Haughton!"

As Tamworth closed his statement the people in the room looked around in excitement at what had been said. The journalists nearby began to prepare their cameras, itching for an interview the moment the court was adjourned for the day. Jonathan and John both looked across at each other with respectful disdain. John was no longer defending his own right to live. He was now formally challenging his original. It was a challenge that both Haughtons understood well. It was going to be all or nothing. Game on!

While Cottam and Jonathan quietly spoke to each other about how to respond to this challenge, Judge Taylor-Beckett banged his gavel again to silence the room and began to address the rest of the courtroom.

"I must say," he began, with a tone that expressed a feeling of great interest and curiosity, "never in my forty years of service to our nation have I ever encountered a case like this. This extraordinary tribunal was caused by extraordinary circumstances, and it is folly to believe that all laws are infallible. Clearly, the clarification of our laws will be one outcome of these proceedings. The man we call Jonathan Haughton arrived today to demand back all the titles and materials associated with the name, from a clone that has lived with them since his activation. However, I am intrigued, and impressed, by this unusual counterclaim from the defence, and as such, I want to hear more. The court will recess until Friday when we will begin to hear these compelling arguments."

At the final bang of his gavel, the judge got up and made his way out of the side door. As he did so, the courtroom erupted in loud excitement once again. Tamworth paid attention to what he was hearing and for the first time, he could hear the balance of opinion. Yes, there were 'boos' and heckles from some of the crowd, no doubt insulted by the suggestion that a 'clone' be considered more a person than a conventional human, but Tamworth also picked up on the sounds of applause coming from the stands as well. His challenge was unexpected, to say the least, and a clear broadside warning to Jonathan and his lawyer that the outcome of this was far from clear cut. As the two Haughtons were escorted out of the room via different exit points, Cottam approached Tamworth with the look of a man who had been caught with his trousers down.

"What the devil do you think you're playing at, Tamworth?" he hissed.

"Just a little taster of what's to come, my friend," Tamworth chuckled. "With the greatest respect, of course."

"You do realise there is no way you can possibly win this ridiculous counterclaim," Cottam said sternly. "Even you must know that!"

"On the contrary," Tamworth replied with a confident smile, "I believe this is as good an opportunity as any for us to reflect on the rights of clones in our society."

"Spoken like a true politician," Cottam answered back. His facial expression slowly changed from an initial scowl to an acknowledging grin, which signalled: 'challenge accepted'.

"We shall see!" was his response.

13

The tribunal adjourned for the rest of the day to give the authorities time to properly process Arnold Tamworth's sudden and unorthodox counterclaim. Jonathan and Cottam left first, possibly to prepare for their first assault, while Tamworth ordered 'John' back to their headquarters with Mina and Des to catch up on the media coverage of the day's events. Ideally, Tamworth would have wanted to celebrate by eating out, but instead, he chose to remain cautious for the time being and save any external celebrations for a time when he had a clear and unquestionable advantage.

After the tribunal, Judge Avery Taylor-Beckett withdrew to his office to continue his work. No more than an hour later there was a knock at his door; one he had been expecting. He rose from his seat and answered it.

"Ah, Arnold, come in. I'm glad you could find the time," he greeted.

Arnold Tamworth entered the room and was guided to a seat.

"Are we being formal or informal, today?" asked Tamworth.

"This meeting is not going to be on the record, if that's what you're wondering," Taylor-Beckett answered. "Can I get you something to drink? Your usual, maybe?"

"Please!" Tamworth said with a smile as Taylor-Beckett approached his decanters.

"Well, this is a very interesting case you've got yourself into," he said and as he began to pour out a whisky. "So, what do you think of your opponent?"

"Who? Edmund Cottam?" replied Tamworth.

"Yes," said Taylor-Beckett with a nod.

"He comes across as a little too sure of himself," Tamworth commented humorously. "A typical trait for a young pup."

"Much like somebody else I know," Taylor-Beckett quipped as he placed the whisky glass into Tamworth's waiting hands. "But don't get too complacent, my friend. I hear he's rather good. His mind's certainly sharp enough."

"So, you've spoken to him recently?" Tamworth guessed.

"We had an informal chat earlier, yes," Taylor-Beckett nodded, "which brings me back onto the main issue of why you are here."

"You invited me," said Tamworth in a matter-of-fact way.

"Of course, I invited you," Taylor-Becket confirmed sternly. "And maybe for more than just the kindness of my heart."

"About the upcoming case, I imagine," guessed Tamworth.

"Or more specifically," Taylor-Beckett began to elaborate, "your proposed counterclaim."

"I see!" Tamworth quipped quietly as he stared down towards his tumbler.

"The real Mr Haughton…" Taylor-Beckett commented thoughtfully. "It certainly has an interesting catchiness to it, I must say."

"Yes, remind me to thank Mr Cottam for that one at some point," Tamworth concurred with a smirk and a chuckle. "I think that was supposed to be his promotional tagline to the media."

"I meant what I said though, Arnold," Taylor-Beckett began to press as he returned to the subject at hand. "Your little theory today has got to be one of the most extraordinary things I have ever heard. This absurd idea that the clone is more original than the plaintiff. So, what *are* you playing at?"

Before he answered, Tamworth re-positioned himself in his chair so that he was more relaxed, and when he finally did start to answer, it was by means of his usual profound illustration.

"Have you ever heard of *Stranger in a Strange Land*, Avery?" he began.

"Not beyond the biblical reference, no," Taylor-Beckett replied.

"It was a popular fictional novel from the 20th Century," Tamworth explained. "When it was first written, the author, Robert Heinlein, was advised by his publisher to trim it down or it wouldn't see the light of day. By the time it was released, it had been cut down by around sixty-thousand words."

Taylor-Beckett whistled slightly upon hearing of the arduous undertaking.

"Wow!" he then commented. "That's quite a reduction. I bet that hurt."

"Approximately thirty years later, the longer, uncut version of the novel was released," Tamworth then added.

"So, what are you driving at?" Taylor-Beckett asked in an attempt to keep up.

"My point is," said Tamworth, "in this instance the 'first edition' is not necessarily the 'original', whereas the 'new' edition...is. Comparatively, they both tell the same story, but which one do we consider to be *the* novel? The one that was *published* first or the one that was *written* first?"

Judge Talyor-Beckett let out a sigh and gave Tamworth a brief analytical stare before responding.

"I like to think I'm sensible enough to be immune to your profound logic, Arnold, but I'll bite," he then remarked. "While on the surface your reasoning has merit, it is also flawed...and not as rare you think. The same could be said about certain movies that roll out a theatrical version, to begin, with and later an extended version, a director's cut, or a final cut. Some movies have all of them and still no clear indication on which one is the best."

"But I'm not trying to argue that my client is the *best,* Avery," Tamworth pointed out. "I'm suggesting that he is the original and *truer* version."

"But you are not dealing with a fictional story either!" said Taylor-Beckett sternly. "This is real life, involving real people, which will have real impacts. I just want peace of mind that you know what you're getting yourself into; not necessarily for *your* sake, but also for *his.*"

"His?"

"Are you sure you have your client's best interests in mind, Arnold? It wouldn't be right if his predicament turned out to be little more than a pet project of yours. What exactly are *you* wanting out of this?"

"I have to say I'm a little insulted, Avery," Tamworth replied. "Why would you think such a thing?"

"Because I know you, Arnold," said Taylor-Beckett, "and you have a habit of inflating the situation when it suits you. I'd have happily entertained your attempts to suspend the clone's disposal but the route you ended up going down today is very ambitious, even by *your* standards. Surely you must know that you probably won't win this for him; not with what you are proposing."

"Well, that'll be for the courts to decide, Avery," said Tamworth confidently. "I assure you my client's claim is sound."

"But this isn't exactly the 'chicken or the egg' Arnold!" retorted Taylor-Beckett. "I cannot see how you will be able to successfully argue that the plaintiff, who has existed as 'Jonathan Haughton' for longer, is *not* that person!"

"Ah! But you are curious nevertheless," Tamworth replied. "Otherwise you wouldn't have allowed me to be heard."

"I allowed your counterclaim to be heard more as a favour to you, Arnold; as dare say I owe you a few," said Taylor-Beckett. "I also did it because I believe your client deserves a fair hearing, clone or not. But for the rest of it, I will be doing this by the book."

"I expect nothing less," Tamworth acknowledged.

"So, I will tell you now," Taylor-Beckett warned, "whatever you're planning...whatever trick you've got up your sleeve...do not make a mockery of this court!"

14

While Tamworth was meeting with Judge Taylor-Beckett, John, Mina and Des made their way back to headquarters. As promised, Alice Beecham and her news network had been granted a quick interview with the clone beforehand, and it was this interview that they searched for on the television when they got back. Tamworth returned not long after and joined them.

The four of them watched the broadcast of the interview with interest. John had done well to keep himself composed for his first time on national television. After all, his memories in the military had developed him into a more private and secretive individual – and more so now, being a clone. Alice's questioning was probing at times but remained diplomatic. John kept his answers short most of the time as he explained the recent events from his perspective and tried to garner sympathy from the national audience. Tamworth however, in a rather unusual move for him, had remained off-screen for the entire interview.

"How come you weren't there to support him, Boss?" Mina asked him.

"I was busy elsewhere, my dear," Tamworth answered, "but it was also part of my overall strategy."

"What do you mean?" Mina then asked.

"Well, everyone knows who *I* am," said Tamworth, "and I wanted to make sure that this interview was all about our John, here." He looked at Mina with a sly smile before adding, "Didn't want to upstage the fellow on his debut outing."

"I wouldn't have thought so," Des then remarked. "I saw the other Haughton being interviewed on one of the other channels and he had *his* lawyer beside him."

"Yes, and did you notice Mr Cottam doing most of the talking?" said Tamworth.

"Actually, yeah!" Des answered thoughtfully. "Come to think of it, when Jonathan Haughton *was* talking, it was either a gesture of agreement with whatever Cottam had said or a reading from a pre-prepared statement."

"Which is precisely why I left *our* John in Alice's capable hands," Tamworth explained. "If we're going to get him his human rights then we need to start from the bottom and show off the more human side of him as often as we can."

"What do you mean?" John asked curiously.

"If you watch and compare the two interviews," Tamworth began to explain, "you will see the other Jonathan being told what to say...while our clone was allowed to decide for himself what to say. I don't know about you, but first impressions are important in a case like this, and the latter will be viewed as the more confident individual. It'll be like Nixon and Kennedy all over again."

"Oh, you mean the speech thing?" Mina remarked, after which Tamworth turned to her and gave her a slight look of confusion.

"I'm not sure what speech you are thinking of," he replied, "but I'm talking about their presidential race back in the 20th Century."

"That's what I meant, Boss!" Mina laughed. "They debated on television together...and Kennedy won?"

"He certainly won the presidency," Tamworth agreed, "but determining the winner of the debate itself became...a matter of debate."

"How do you mean?" asked John.

"You see, while politicians today thrive on the opportunity to be seen on television," Tamworth explained, "the debate between Richard Nixon and John F Kennedy was the first of its kind and produced some rather startling results in the process."

"In what way?" Des asked.

"Several polls were taken afterwards to ascertain who had won," Tamworth continued. "According to polls from those who saw the debate on television, Kennedy had won it hands down, but according to those who had merely listened to it on the radio, Nixon was the victor! It would seem that on telly, the viewers disliked Nixon's sweaty and nervous demeanour compared to Kennedy's confident charismatic charms, but those using the radio didn't get to see those flaws and instead listened more to the policies. In the end, it was what the people *saw* that swung it."

"Ah, I see," Mina concluded. "The people will prefer the look of the 'stronger' John compared to the seemingly 'weaker' Jonathan?"

"In theory, anyway," Tamworth nodded. "At the end of the day, the courts will ultimately decide on the matter. We just need to convince enough people out there that our clone is not something to be afraid of. That way, if we do lose the case, we might be able to sway enough public opinion to keep him alive."

"And I suppose I'll need it considering all the opposition I'm up against," John remarked in a defeatist tone.

"Oh, don't be like that, John," Mina responded. She then moved next to where he was sitting and put a comforting arm around him as she continued to try and reassure him. "You did beautifully in the interview. I'm sure the people at home will be on our side, just like Arnold said."

"Yeah, right! Tell that to the protesters outside the courthouse today," John remarked, "and the crowd that harassed us in the car on the way home!"

"And the current opinion polls," Des added. He drew attention to the websites he had been tracking on his computer and flashed the images up on the main screen for all to see. Most of the polls rolled out during the day appeared to show support for the other Jonathan Haughton. The *Chicago Echo* was quite damning with its poll, which showed 82% in favour of forcing the clone to relinquish his identity back to the original, while another poll conducted in Washington had the clone's odds of winning the case down to 17%. A more 'comforting' poll in the area came from Alice's network, with the numbers favouring Jonathan Haughton over the clone as low as 52% - lower than most others but still not in John's favour. The only positive result came from one conducted in Baltimore, where the notion of 'compulsory disposal' of the clone was rejected by 55% of those surveyed, but even then, the context of the question implied the clone's inevitable defeat.

"The whole nation is against me, right now!" John groaned in exhausted despair as he sank further down in his seat.

"For now, maybe," Tamworth reassured him, "but History and literature are both loaded with examples of underdogs overcoming great odds. It's what makes their stories so memorable. Think of the *12 Angry Men*, for example."

"That's a classic!" Des commented. "One of my favourites, actually."

"Mine too," Tamworth agreed, "and it's apparently up there on Cottam's list from what I've gathered."

He then turned his head towards John.

"I'm not going to lie to you, John," he said to him. "Our fight is going to be an uphill struggle, but big changes, social or political, have often spawned from the most trivial origins. I imagine our situation to be no different."

15

When Friday came, the journey to the courthouse was a similar experience for Tamworth and co. to the last time they were there but there were a few differences also. Firstly, there appeared to be fewer friendly faces greeting them at the front steps and instead, a thicker crowd of anti-clone protesters; no doubt fuelled by the encouragement from Tommy Dale's attempts to involve himself in the proceedings. The authorities had also started to take the case more seriously and had stepped up security for John and his team as they arrived, but this provided little comfort for them as they made their way up the steps. They soon made it into the foyer and were escorted to the main tribunal room, to find Jonathan Haughton and Edmund Cottam already waiting for them, along with other officials and public spectators.

John and Tamworth were shown to their allocated seats and sat down, while Mina and Des were directed to the public chamber. All silently awaited the arrival of Judge Taylor-Beckett. All rose respectfully when he finally entered through the side door and took his seat. He then signalled for all to be seated and, as he quickly rifled through his notes and discussed formalities, he signalled for Cottam to present his case.

Cottam rose to his feet and began to address the room. The case he put forward was, on the surface, a particularly strong and obvious one. The tone of his voice expressed not only his confidence but also his frustration at why they were even bothering with the tribunal. He went into detail on the origins of Jonathan, the man, and compared it to that of 'John', the clone. He reminded the assembly that Jonathan Haughton had been around for longer, had been given the name by his biological parents and had forged his identity with every passing day that he had existed. John, he argued, had merely inherited this man's life experience, reducing what *he* had to little more than a collection of memories – a living, breathing memoir. Cottam presented birth certificates, school diplomas and other exhibits that supported his client's claims and questioned key witnesses who knew Jonathan Haughton personally. To reinforce his point, Cottam ended each interview the same way, by instructing each of them to 'point' to the man in the room whom they identified to be Jonathan Kenzie Haughton. All of them pointed to his client, who sat there gleaming and nodding with satisfaction.

All seemed to be going poorly so far for Tamworth and his clone client, but it was particularly difficult for them when Cottam used the opportunity to call his final key witness for the day.

"I call to the stand, Ms Casandra Eleanor...Haughton!" he announced. There was a sound of low-level muttering as Cassy, who was sitting among the crowd, uncomfortably looked around the room, stood up and slowly made her way to the stand. John looked towards Tamworth in annoyance and leaned across towards him.

"Can he do that?" he whispered desperately. "Is he that low as to try and use my own wife against me and..."

He was quickly cut off by Tamworth's silent gesture for him to keep quiet.

"He's entitled to question anyone he likes, within reason," Tamworth said silently. "I say let him."

John sat back in his chair and folded his arms in frustration. Tamworth scribbled some notes on a sheet of paper, leaned again towards John and quietly spoke to him. "Cassy's refusal to testify would serve no useful purpose," he said softly. "Let the man have his moment and see what he says."

They looked towards where Cassy stood as Cottam began his questioning.

"Could you please state your name for the records, Ms Haughton?" he instructed.

"Mrs Casandra Eleanor Haught..." she began, before being cut-off mid-sentence.

"I'm sorry...*Mrs?*" Cottam inquired, drawing emphasis on her title. There was a brief but awkward pause before Cottam continued. "Your *original* name, if you please?" he insisted.

"My name is...was..." Cassy replied slowly, "Casandra Eleanor Summers."

"My apologies," Cottam remarked with a slight gloat in his tone that was masked by his feigned expression of surprise. "I am under the impression that you referred to yourself as *Mrs* beforehand. Had I misheard?"

"I err...I am, in a way," Cassy answered.

"In what way?" Cottam asked.

"In the way that I took my husband's name," Cassy replied with a confused tone, "so to speak."

"Your husband being 'John' Haughton," Cottam clarified. "Is that correct?"

Cassy nodded. "Yes!"

"But you aren't married in the legal sense, though?" Cottam went on. "There are currently no legal grounds in our nation to recognise marriages between clones and... non-clones...in an official capacity?"

"Not yet," Cassy argued, "but I don't see how this question is relevant. If you're going to ask me to point out my husband in the room, then I know who I'll be pointing to."

As she spoke those words she looked towards John and gave him a loving smile of assurance.

"Of course," Cottam remarked with feigned delicacy. Suddenly, Tamworth rose up and interjected.

"Objection, Your Honour!" he protested. "I also fail to see how this line of questioning is of any relevance to the main issue. How my client and Ms Haughton refer to each other privately is not on trial here!"

"Objection noted," Taylor-Beckett agreed. Afterwards, he turned to Cottam and added, "Mr Cottam, I must advise you to make your point quickly or excuse the witness."

"Certainly, Your Honour," Cottam replied, before turning back to conclude his examination of Cassy.

"I have no issue at all with how you see yourself, Ms Haughton," he went on. "However, it is true that you willingly took the name 'Haughton'. Is that correct?"

"Yes," Cassy nodded.

"And were you aware at the time 'John' proposed to you, that his original had similar plans before his disappearance?"

"I suppose so..." Cassy answered, before adding a "Yes" to confirm.

"And that is why you said 'Yes' to the proposal?" Cottam began to lead, "because of your feelings for Jonathan

Haughton? Feelings that you had for him and he had for you, for many years?"

He then pointed indicatively to where his client sat. Cassy said nothing. She grew more aware of the trap being set but felt no way out.

"So, we could say," Cottam continued to press, "that 'John' Haughton, the clone replacement, asked you to marry him out of respect for Jonathan's wishes, from the memories artificially implanted?"

Again, Cassy said nothing.

"And this man, whose name and details you arranged to be transferred into the mind of this clone," Cottam concluded, "can you point him out to us, today? The man who actually 'lived' those memories with you? The man whose memories and experiences you sought to keep alive?"

"Objection, Your Honour!" Tamworth interjected again as he defiantly rose to his feet once more.

"Objection noted," Taylor-Becket acknowledged with a nod. "I think we get the point, Mr Cottam. You may excuse your witness, for now."

Cassy was escorted down, visibly distressed by Cottam's line of questioning. As she moved towards the back of the room she glanced towards Jonathan, who stared motionless back at her and then back towards John, who gave her a comforting smile and a nod.

After Cottam had finished his examination of Cassy, Judge Taylor-Becket called for a short recess. Most of the people involved remained in the room. John turned to speak to Tamworth in preparation for his own case.

"That was unnecessary of him, don't you think?" he said to him. Tamworth raised his eyebrows and nodded in agreement.

"Yep!" he quipped. "It's a mistake that a lot of young hot-headed lawyers tend to make when they're out to make a name for themselves and that Cottam fellow is one aggressive son of a bitch!"

"And you?" John asked.

"I'm worse, I assure you," Tamworth chuckled lightly.

"So why *did* he call Cassy out like that?"

"I expect it was an attempt to psych us out," Tamworth guessed. "Perhaps to try and inflict some initial damage by causing a rift in our camp – maybe get Ms Haughton to doubt herself...and then you."

"You mean like...divide and conquer?"

"Something like that...but as you can see, such actions are not without risk."

Tamworth pointed towards Jonathan, who was sitting at the other side of the room. His facial expression showed many mixed feelings. On the one hand, he still seemed confident of his case, but by the way he looked at Cottam, he also seemed annoyed by the stunt his lawyer had pulled with Cassy. He still loved her, deep down, and didn't appear to appreciate her being used as a pawn for his own gains.

"I think there's some rift forming in *their* camp," Tamworth chuckled again. "Cottam had better not try anything like that again lest his client decides to throttle him."

"That's certainly what *I* feel like doing," John remarked.

"And therefore, something he is probably considering also," Tamworth added.

Soon after, the recess was over, and Judge Taylor-Beckett returned to his seat.

"Arnold Tamworth!" he called. "Would you like to present your defence of this clone...and your so-called counterclaim?"

Tamworth rose to his feet and approached the centre of the room.

"People of this tribunal," he began theatrically. "We are here today for various reasons but mainly to determine which of these men sitting before us claims the right to the name 'Jonathan Kenzie Haughton'. Sure, it would be simple if it was 'just' a name, what with the millions of 'John Smiths' we have had in our time. However, this seems *not* to be about ownership of the name, but rather the ownership of a very specific and unique aspect of Jonathan Haughton...his very identity."

Many people in the room nodded in agreement to Tamworth's point.

"On top of that," Tamworth continued, "my client is also fighting for his life. Is it right that he be sacrificed in such a way when he has committed no crime? Surely such a move would be tantamount to a public execution!"

"Objection, Your Honour!" Cottam called out. "My learned friend risks confusing the committee. Should we not be dealing with one aspect at a time?"

"Objection noted!" Taylor-Beckett replied and instructed Tamworth to focus on one aspect for the time being – either John's right to the name or his right to live.

"I tip my cap to my colleague," Tamworth appeared to concede, "but at the same time it does seem to me that if my client can win his right to the name...he also wins the right to exist?"

Taylor-Beckett began to ponder in consideration, while Tamworth turned to face Jonathan and his lawyer.

"Mr Haughton...*Jonathan,*" he began. "During his opening statement, your lawyer used the clones' origins against him and effectively argued that he is less important because he was created in a laboratory. May I ask what your own views are on that, sir?"

Jonathan looked at his lawyer before answering and, after receiving a silent nod from Cottam, he turned back to respond.

"Well..." he began to explain, "my lawyer's views do reflect my own. The way I see it, he was grown and engineered at an unnatural rate. I was not. He was created for the sole purpose of replacing me upon my death, whereas I was created as an expression of love between my parents, who wanted to have a family."

"Interesting point you make there, Jonathan," Tamworth remarked, "but surely, in a similar sense, the clone...my client...was created as an expression of love also – the love that you and Ms Haughton once shared?"

"In a way, but..."

"And according to official records," Tamworth continued, "you aren't exactly a natural product yourself, Jonathan. Your parents, Charles and Mary Haughton, tried for years before eventually being granted the funds for IVF treatment. So, by that logic, were you not also 'produced in a lab'?"

"But that's different and you know it!" Jonathan sternly replied. "IVF is different from cloning. Everybody knows that. Without *me,* there would never be a Jonathan Haughton to speak of. I am the original and he is, by definition, a copy."

Tamworth paused and smiled slightly. "Ah, now that's a very interesting choice of words," he pressed. "In what manner are you the 'original'?"

Jonathan looked confused at the seemingly obvious question.

"To the extent that *he* came from *me*!" he said with a laugh. He wasn't the only one who found the question amusing, as sounds of chuckling could be heard from others around the room. Taylor-Beckett, however, wasn't impressed and banged his gavel to silence the room.

"Mr Tamworth," he said. "You had better be going somewhere with this!"

"I am, Your Honour," Tamworth replied reassuringly. "The point I am raising is one that has been debated and pondered by philosophers for hundreds of years – this concept of identity."

He then turned to face everybody else in the room.

"Has anybody here ever heard of the ancient paradox of Theseus' Ship?" he asked them. He looked around at the many puzzled faces in the room; before he started to explain the concept:

"Greek historian, Plutarch, asked us to imagine the great ship of Theseus on display in Athens as a permanent museum to honour their hero's deeds. As the years pass by, several parts of the ship start to decay and are gradually replaced. A plank here...an oar there, etc. Now, let's imagine that this continues through the decades until eventually, piece by piece, every part of that ship is replaced with a new part. This then raises the question...is it still the same ship? Many might think it is, but if you were to gather up all the discarded rotten parts and put them back together to make an identical ship...is *that* not the actual ship? And what if you had two separate ships, each containing some parts of the original? Would they *both* identify as Theseus' ship?

"Where are you going with this, Mr Tamworth?" Taylor-Beckett asked suddenly, and more impatiently. Tamworth raised his hands demonstratively before answering.

"I believe that the same concept regarding Theseus' Ship also applies to us today," he began to explain, "and certainly applies to our two Haughtons."

He approached Jonathan again and continued his examination.

"According to your medical records, Mr Haughton, you have had quite a few visits to casualty in your lifetime," he revealed. "Is that correct?"

"It's part of the job," Jonathan answered with a slightly sarcastic tone.

"I agree," Tamworth acknowledged. "I look at your face and I can already see the odd scars here and there. And as you say, what else would we expect from a decorated soldier? But nevertheless, you have also had more life-threatening injuries in your time. Would you care to explain some of those?"

Jonathan looked at Cottam but, sensing a trap, he remained silent.

"Well, do you mind if *I* list them?" Tamworth then asked.

"Go right ahead," Jonathan permitted with a shrug of indifference.

In response, Tamworth listed off some notable examples of Jonathan's past surgeries. They included skin grafts, blood transfusions and a transplant of a kidney and a lung. Jonathan sat and listened. He seemed unfazed by the list and in a sense pleased with himself as he reflected on his 'achievements'.

"So, all in all, you've done well to still be here today, Mr Haughton," Tamworth joked, "and for that, I salute you."

"So, what's your point?" Jonathan then asked.

"My point is this, Mr Haughton," Tamworth began. "You sit here today in a body that, through transplants and surgeries, is also made up of other people's organs – your 'replacement parts', so to speak. On the other hand, your clone counterpart sits over there with all of his body parts still intact, and with a DNA trail leading back to the original genetic code that created him – a code that identifies as Jonathan Haughton. While Jonathan the 'human' is about, say, 90-95% there...the clone is 100% made from the original – and by that logic, surely, *he* is more 'Jonathan Haughton' than the so-called original, quantitively speaking.

As the audience in the public chamber erupted with expressions of surprise, with some shouting in anger while others applauded in delight, Cottam rose to his feet to voice his objections.

"Your Honour!" he cried out. "Surely you cannot take this ridiculous argument so seriously! It's madness!"

"And yet intriguing at the same time isn't it?" said Tamworth as he sat back down. Now it was *his* turn to feel pleased with himself. John also gave a look of surprise, mixed with relief. Initially, he had been as doubtful of Tamworth's strategy as the judge had been, but now he started to have faith and sat back in his chair, more relaxed than he had been at the beginning. Jonathan on the other hand became less relaxed and more tensed.

Judge Taylor-Beckett banged his gavel again to restore order. He then signalled for the tribunal to recess for the rest of the day to allow time for Jonathan and his team to prepare a rebuke to Tamworth's compelling argument. The press and the media, however, were already lapping it up, just as Tamworth had wanted...and that was just the beginning.

16

Following the day's turbulent events, Tamworth and John returned to headquarters to recuperate and prepare for their next offensive. Later that evening, John paid a visit to Tamworth in his office. As he approached the room, he noticed that its main lights were out and the door halfway open. He looked through and observed the solitude and silhouette-like Tamworth sitting back in his chair, pondering quietly as he cradled his tumbler of whisky with one hand and thoughtfully tapped at the edge of the glass with the other. The only light in the room came from a small lamp beside where Tamworth was sitting and the faint image that glowed from the television screen. John stood at the doorway and knocked slowly. Tamworth took notice and sat up slightly.

"Ah, Mr Haughton!" he said with a smile. "Come and join me!"

John sat down quietly as Tamworth pointed eagerly towards his cabinet.

"Drink?" he offered.

"No thank you," John declined.

"Are you sure?" Tamworth replied. "I have a whisky here all the way from Scotland, you know. Nothing but the best in this place!"

John said nothing and shook his head. Tamworth shrugged lightly in response.

"Well do you mind if *I* have a drink, then?" he said, making no effort to hide the glass in his hand. John looked at him slightly perplexed.

"But you already have one," he commented.

"Ah, so I do," replied Tamworth with a mild chuckle. "Always one step ahead, me! But anyway, enough of that. How do you think today went? Good start or what?"

"Um, I guess so," said John. "I just wish they hadn't pulled that stunt with Cassy, that's all."

"Any why not?" said Tamworth. "You've nothing to hide, after all."

"Yeah but...you know...isn't there a law for this?" asked John. "I mean, isn't there supposed to be some kind of rule about not having to testify against your partner?"

"You mean the Spousal Communications Privilege?" Tamworth acknowledged, followed by a doubtful shake of the head. "That would only have applied if your marriage to Ms Haughton was lawfully recognised but unfortunately, it's not."

"Oh!" remarked John; and with a sigh, Tamworth began to elaborate further on his plans for them.

"As I said already, Cassy's refusal to testify would have served us no purpose whatsoever," he went on. "If anything, it might actually have harmed our position."

"How?" asked John, curiously.

"I want to present our case as openly as possible, Mr Haughton," Tamworth explained. "So far, I've gone to tremendous effort to publicise your predicament to prevent it from becoming some back-door secrecy nonsense that would likely sink us. It won't look good for our image if we start being difficult with the opposition's evidence and witnesses. It would look as though you have something to hide."

"But I don't have anything to hide," John remarked.

"Precisely!" replied Tamworth. "So why give them the opportunity? It makes more sense if our part in this tribunal is as open and as honest as possible, and on that note, you will neither oppose nor deny any future witnesses nor will you plead the Fifth! You got it?"

"Yeah!" John acknowledged and nodded in agreement. He sat there in silence with a solemn preoccupied look in his eyes. Tamworth clocked it immediately.

"Something else on your mind, chap?" he then asked.

"Yeah!" John answered. "Be honest with me, Arnold. What are my chances? I mean...do you really think I can win this case? After all, we can't exactly prove that my counterpart is *not* Jonathan Haughton."

"Nor can *he* disprove *your* claim," Tamworth replied reassuringly.

"Yes, but the difference is if I lose the case, it'll be the end of me!" said John solemnly. "That'll be me done – possibly and probably disposed of. It's not as if my victory would lead to *his* disposal instead."

Tamworth laughed at the suggestion and shook his head.

"It's funny you should say that," he said. "There have been a fair few trash articles on the web which, in light of today, have raised that very possibility – that Jonathan be disposed of instead of the clone."

"Is that what you are arguing for?"

"Oh goodness no!" Tamworth remarked. "There is no way that the laws of the land would stretch *that* far, and no right-minded jury or judge would ever allow for it."

Tamworth paused briefly and looked toward John for comment, but John remained silent and lost in thought.

"So, what do *you* think, Mr Haughton?" Tamworth then asked him. "Do you think it's fair? The fact that he can't be disposed of, whereas you can?"

"No!" John answered boldly. "No, it's not fair. It's not fair on any of us clones."

"Furthermore," Tamworth continued, "do you think it is fair that you should be in the dock and constantly defending your right to an identity that you have had from the day you were activated? Why should you be the only one on trial here?"

John pondered this for a moment while Tamworth continued to speak.

"Have you ever heard of the case of *Griff vs Gravity*?" he asked him.

"Kind of," replied John.

"Axel Griff was a member of a hard-rock band known as *Dilute Gravity* - 'was' being the important word here," Tamworth began to recall. "As it was with many bands, Dilute Gravity had a somewhat high turnover of talent. Many members came and went in its time, but one thing remained constant...Axel Griff. That is, until his own departure. Do you know why he left the band?

"Not really," said John.

"Creative differences with their new record label and the rest of the band forced him out," Tamworth explained. "Axel Griff was effectively kicked out of his own band, which he founded, and for the first time in its history the band toured without any of its original members."

"So, what happened next?" asked John, curiously.

"In an attempted 'middle finger' to his former band, Axel reunited with other former members and tried to tour the country as *Dilute Gravity*," Tamworth went on. "He was sued for it, of course...and lost; after which his band continued to tour and perform their old hits but under a different name...forever a tribute act to themselves."

There was another brief silence in the room as two of them looked thoughtfully into the distance. Eventually, John spoke up.

"So why are you telling me this?" he asked.

"I believe that your counterpart, in a way, is very much like Axel Griff," said Tamworth. "He wants to continue touring, but right now...you're the new band."

"But it's not like he's going to settle with a new name anytime though," John pointed out, "not when I haven't, either."

"Which brings me to a rather interesting paradox I hit on during these proceedings," Tamworth revealed. "A real Haughton-Dilemma, so to speak."

"What is?" asked John.

"He is Jonathan Kenzie Haughton...but in your mind so are you. You are both Jonathan Kenzie Haughton! Identical in practically every way...and yet very different at the same time," Tamworth said. "To secure your identity I have to prove that you are Jonathan Haughton, but to secure your continued existence I must also argue that you are a different person."

"I'm confused," John confessed.

"So am I, if I say so myself," Tamworth replied. "So how do we get around this dilemma?"

"I don't know," said John, still confused.

"I'll tell you how," Tamworth answered. "Nobody is debating the life of and times of Jonathan Haughton up to the time of his disappearance, but what matters right now is the most recent two years and which version we consider canon – your version or his version? So, instead of trying to convince the world that you are really Jonathan Haughton...what we need to do is convince the world that Jonathan Haughton is really you – and that it is *your* life story that counts."

Tamworth put down his drink and leaned forward across the table so that he and John were eye to eye.

"Tell me something," he began to ask him. "Are you Jonathan Kenzie Haughton? Is that your name? Are you the husband of Cassy and the father of Jack?"

"Of course, I am!" replied John with a frantic nod. "Yes, to all of those things!"

"Then we shall fight to keep it that way," said Tamworth confidently. He then sat down again and leaned back in his chair."

"Don't think my counterpart won't go without a fight," John warned.

"I don't think that at all," said Tamworth. "He and his puppy lawyer tried to be smart today and got knocked down a few pegs. So, my guess is they'll go home tonight, lick their wounds, and come back tomorrow with a more cautious strategy. They'll more likely focus on the raw facts."

"And you?" asked John. "Is that what you're going to do?"

"Of course not!" replied Tamworth with a sly wink and a mischievous chuckle as he raised his glass into the air. "Sharp and smart all the way, my friend! Sharp and smart!"

17

When the tribunal resumed the following day, the prosecution continued their relentless offensive against the clone; and just as Tamworth had predicted, they steered away from the underhanded baiting tactics and stuck mainly to the raw facts of the case. Cottam continued to broadcast his client's past achievements and used clear documents and certificates to back up his claim. His argument was clear – that this was Jonathan's life so far and not that of the clone. It was a solid argument but one that was starting to get old and overused.

Eventually, it was Tamworth's turn to counter once again on behalf of the clone. He got up and immediately called Jonathan Haughton to the stand, to which Jonathan obliged. Tamworth took hold of several documents that had been lying on his desk and held them while he talked.

"Mr Haughton," he began. "According to my client's testimony, and backed up by that of Ms Haughton, on the night you returned and first encountered your clone, you had offered him a way out. Do you remember that, at all?"

"I'm...I'm not really sure," replied Jonathan as he attempted to recall.

"Well, allow me to jog your memory," said Tamworth. He rummaged through his loose sheets of paper as he spoke until he found the relevant documents. "Do you remember saying something along the lines of his services no longer being needed?"

"Maybe," Jonathan began to recall, "but I don't re..."

"And in that same conversation, you told him that this *wasn't personal*...and that it made no difference to you if he went back to the clinic or emigrated?"

"I er..." Jonathan stammered.

"So why the change of heart?" asked Tamworth provocatively. "I mean, the laws concerning his existence obviously didn't matter to you at the time, did it? Otherwise, you wouldn't have given him the option to just leave."

"I don't really recall," said Jonathan, "but if I did say that, I might not have been thinking straight. I had just come home after all!"

"Maybe you expected your clone to take up your offer and step aside for you," Tamworth then suggested. "Maybe you expected Ms Haughton to come running into your arms when you got through the door, but when neither of those things happened it suddenly became a problem...and became personal."

"Objection, Your Honour!" Cottam protested. "My learned friend here is dealing in speculation which has no bearing on the current laws of the land!"

The Judge agreed. "Mr Tamworth," he then instructed. "Your inquiry *will* have some legal bearing from now on if you don't mind."

"It will, Your Honour," Tamworth conceded. He took the papers that were still in his hand and placed them down in front of Jonathan for him to look through.

"Mr Haughton," he resumed. "Do you recognise those documents, at all?"

Jonathan picked up the various sheets, quickly skimmed through the pages and quietly shook his head.

"They are official documents that show various transactions, insurance policies, and other financial arrangements...all signed in part by a 'Mr Jonathan Haughton'. Look, you can see the signature, right there."

Jonathan looked again and indeed saw that the signature on each of the documents was his own.

"Do you recognise them now?" Tamworth then asked. Again, Jonathan shook his head.

"I don't blame you, Mr Haughton," Tamworth began to explain, "for these arrangements were signed off by your counterpart. They are two-years-worth of a life that didn't involve you at all."

"What's your point?" Jonathan asked impatiently.

"My point is, Mr Haughton," replied Tamworth, "that while you argue that my client has no claim to the life you have lived so far...in the same way you have no claim to the life that *he* has led. These past two years...every decision on the house, the money, the job...that's all been him. What right have you to suddenly lay claim?"

"But it was my money and my assets!" Jonathan protested.

"All but the last two years, maybe," argued Tamworth, "but everything else is John's, surely?"

"No!" replied Jonathan sternly.

"No?" Tamworth remarked with raised eyebrows. "Well, I hardly find that fair – you, taking credit for all of John's hard work."

"It should all have been mine!" Jonathan protested again.

"But it's not, though!" said Tamworth. "You may have you pound of flesh, sir, but nothing more!"

Tamworth quickly produced another single sheet and held it up for all to see.

"Which now brings me onto the most sinister thing part of this whole tribunal!" he announced. He then placed the sheet forcefully onto the table in front of Jonathan's eyes.

"That, Mr Haughton, is the birth certificate of baby Jack Haughton," he declared. "Again, this reads as your name and signature...but you didn't sign it did you, Mr Haughton?"

"No, I..."

"But then again there is no reason for you to do so. After all, you are not the father."

"But I can be..."

"I am not questioning your potential parenting skills, Mr Haughton," Tamworth interrupted, "but rather your right to claim this particular child as your own. He is not property. He is a human being who has the right for his father to not be taken from him. His father being my client, John."

"Objection!" Cottam protested again as he rose from his seat.

"Overruled!" came the reply from Taylor-Beckett, who gestured for Cottam to remain seated. He then nodded lightly to Tamworth for him to continue his line of questioning.

"Thank you, Your Honour," said Tamworth as he continued. "And yes, I will move quickly to my point. You see, while there is no legal precedent in place that recognises marriages between clones and, shall we say, non-clones, it has certainly never been illegal for them to form relationships or have children. What worries me is that any ruling that removes custody of young Jack from my client could signal a wider restriction on other clones being parents. Is that the intention of this court?

"Objection again, Your Honour!" shouted Cottam again.

"Sustained!" Taylor-Beckett agreed sternly. "Mr Tamworth, please do not assume to know the intentions of this court. We'll decide that if you don't mind!"

"My apologies, Your Honour," Tamworth conceded. "So, coming back to my original point, Mr Haughton, would it be out of line to suggest that the real reason we are here today is more to do with Ms Haughton's refusal to part with the clone and that you are now trying to force the issue and get him out of the way for good?"

"That's not true!" Jonathan began to argue back.

"I mean, you're a soldier. You could have dealt with him yourself already. So why the charade of this tribunal?"

"I...I..." Jonathan stammered again as he continued to squirm uncomfortably in his seat.

"I'll tell you why!" said Tamworth accusingly as he leaned forward towards his opponent. "You want to keep it all clean and above board. You want the State to do your dirty work for you. That's why you are so keen to push for his disposal. You probably reckon that if you killed him yourself, Ms Haughton would never take you back!"

Again, Jonathan stammered and spluttered in protest. No sooner had Tamworth finished than Jonathan leapt out of his seat in a rage, almost as if he was going to throttle the wily lawyer. Tamworth stepped back and out of the way as the porters and Cottam attempted to restrain the agitated Jonathan. At the same time, Taylor-Becket hammered his gavel furiously in a bid to maintain order.

"We will have order here!" he demanded. "And Mr Tamworth, you go too far! You will...I repeat *will* retract your statement or I will hold you in contempt!"

Immediately, Tamworth took a deep breath and began to calm himself down; after which he backed down to Taylor-Becket's demands and retracted his statement. He turned again towards Jonathan, who had also started to compose himself again.

"Your pound of flesh..." Tamworth concluded to him, "and nothing more!"

Immediately Taylor-Beckett announced a formal recess of the proceedings and once he had left the courtroom, everybody else began to gather their belongings and filter out of the room. At this point, both John and Jonathan locked eyes and stared at one another with contempt and determination. Eventually, Jonathan broke their non-verbal standoff and spoke up first.

"You really should have left when you had the chance, you lab-rat freak!" he hissed. John immediately responded and began to move provocatively towards his nemesis. He was just about to respond when Tamworth put his arm across him and began to guide him back.

"Don't rise to it, Mr Haughton," he advised.

"Yeah, that's right! You hide behind your lawyer!" Jonathan went on as he continued to try and bait the clone. At this point, Jonathan's own lawyer, Edmund Cottam, also intervened and began to guide him away from the clone.

"Mr Haughton," he cautioned him. "This is not what we are here for. Remember that we need to maintain the moral high ground in this case."

Although he spoke those words to Jonathan, Cottam made sure that he was loud enough for John and Tamworth to hear in a subtle attempt to bait them himself. He almost succeeded when John moved forwards again to reply.

"Moral high ground?!" he rebuked loudly. He focused his gaze on Jonathan once again.

"You know, I feel sorry for you," he said to him. "I remember the person you used to be, and you were never like this. Whatever happened to you out there in the wilderness...I can safely say you are no longer the man you used to be. *I* am!"

Jonathan rose to the challenge. "Oh really?" he scoffed. "Well, I feel sorry for *you*! You have this delusion that you can just take over my life and all you have is this mindless nutter backing you up!" Jonathan pointed towards Tamworth to emphasise his point. Tamworth himself was indifferent to the gesture.

"He's run rings around you and *your* lawyer so far!" John barked back. "If anything, it's your lawyer I feel sorry for!"

At this point, both Cottam and Tamworth positioned themselves between the two Haughtons and persuasively guided them away from one another in opposite directions.

"Well, now that we've finished feeling sorry for one another, I suggest we all retire and regroup," said Tamworth sarcastically.

"Agreed!" Cottam added; and with that the, two parties prepared to depart from different exits, but as they started to head out, Cottam quickly caught John by the sleeve and stopped him for a brief and quiet word.

"You know, it is actually *you* who I feel sorry for," he told him, quietly. "I mean, on the surface, you appear to be fighting a moral and respectable case here, misguided as it may be. It's just a shame how you've allowed it to be hijacked by his shenanigans."

As he spoke, Cottam flicked his head lightly in the direction of whom he was referring, making it clear to John that he was talking about Tamworth.

"What do you mean?" John asked.

"Well," Cottam went on, choosing his words carefully, "if I were you, I'd watch myself, you know. Remember that *your* tribunal will affect *your* life, so just..."

Tamworth, at this point, became aware of the conversation when he noticed the two of them talking out of the corner of his eye. Curiously, he turned and walked towards them. The fact that Cottam's chat had come to an abrupt halt when they saw him coming did not go unnoticed.

"I hope you're not badgering my client, Mr Cottam," Tamworth jokingly warned as he butted in.

"Nothing of the kind, Mr Tamworth," Cottam replied politely. "Just giving him some friendly advice, that's all."

"Oh, I see!" said Tamworth boldly. "Trying to reach a settlement with him already?" He then leaned in closer towards Cottam and slyly remarked, "Got you running scared, have I?"

Despite Tamworth's posturing, Cottam remained calm, collected and above all, professional. He smiled indifferently at Tamworth as the conversation continued.

"With respect, Mr Tamworth, I was merely ensuring that we all have our client's best interests at heart," he said. "I wouldn't want your clone to become another celebrity guest on the Arnold Tamworth Show...or what I call the *Billy Reece Fan Club*."

For a few seconds, that remark alone appeared to stop everyone in their tracks, particularly Tamworth. While John was merely confused and curious about Cottam's choice of words, Tamworth's facial expression, brief at it was, displayed immediate discomfort. His eyes twitched slightly, and his mouth made a great effort not to quiver. After a few seconds, he coughed loudly in a feigned clearing of the throat, as if to quickly change the subject.

"Nice try, Cottam," he then told him. "But 'with respect'? Since when did you start *respecting* my client?"

Cottam said nothing in reply as Tamworth went on.

"If you want to lecture me on respect and the best interests of my clone then answer me this...during that little discussion you had with him just then, how many times, if at all, did you refer to him as Mr Haughton? Eh?"

Again, Cottam said nothing. Under his annoyance, Tamworth forced a slow smile.

"I thought so," he then commented. "So, with *no* due respect, I advise you to leave him alone!"

Cottam knew he had almost baited his nemesis and wanted him to know it too, and with a wink and a smile, he turned around and walked the other way to catch up with Jonathan and the rest of his team, leaving Tamworth and John alone in the courtroom.

"So, what was all that about?" asked John. "Anything I need to know?"

"Huh?" Tamworth remarked before answering properly. "No, nothing really. Just him trying to be underhanded, that's all. Didn't work...and doesn't really suit him if I'm honest."

"So, who's Billy Reece?" John then asked.

"Nothing connected to the case, that's for sure," replied Tamworth. "And therefore nothing you need concern yourself with."

18

The next couple of days at the tribunal echoed the first two. Each time Jonathan Haughton and Edmund Cottam tried to launch a seemingly strong offensive against the clone, their efforts were scuppered by a dose of Tamworth rhetoric, which demonstrated more and more the clone's right to the name, the title, and the family of Haughton. The media was not in the dark about it either and paid close attention to everything being recorded – especially with the outcome of the case having a potential impact on the rights of clones, and the law, throughout the nation.

At the end of the most recent day at the court, Tamworth and his team went back to headquarters to settle in for the evening. There was much to celebrate as they perused the newspapers and the television channels for the latest updates and opinions polls. Aside from the regular postings about the tribunal, another main headline that afternoon was the announcement that the *Forever Together* Clinic was to temporarily cease operations, pending an investigation by the regulatory bodies into their own conduct. This was bad news for many out there who had already parted with money for the development of a replacement clone but good news as far as the anti-clone campaigners, such as Tommy Dale, were concerned. This news was debated by the team at Tamworth's headquarters with mixed opinions. On the one hand, it was good the clinic was being put to task for their involvement in causing the *Haughton Dilemma* (as the case was referred to by the media) in the first place. On the other hand, it was discomforting for John that the world would sooner feel safer shutting the problem down entirely instead of exploring the possibility of extending basic rights to clones. But a deeper debate on the subject was for another time and the discussion was quickly wrapped up for the evening.

They all sat around the table in the lounge, feasting on the buffet of chicken wings and pizza that had been ordered in especially for John. Tamworth poured himself a whisky and relaxed back in his chair. He looked towards Des, who had been examining the polling reports of the case on his laptop – typing with one hand, while he crudely cradled a half-eaten pizza slice with the other.

"What news, Des?" he asked. "Any changes?"

"Well, most of the polls out there still predict a victory for the other guy, Boss, but it's no longer clear cut," Des mumbled with his mouth full. "The margins for many of these have significantly narrowed."

"Well, that's some good news," Tamworth remarked triumphantly. "Any polls out there in our favour?"

"Well, none of the conservative ones have budged much," Des answered, "but there was a poll conducted in California, which asked people for their views on John's disposal should he lose the case...and they have overwhelmingly voted against it, with 95% calling for a revision of the current laws."

"Any polls closer to home?"

"Well, the *Chicago Echo* conducted a poll asking people who they want to win...with 58% backing our John."

"Interesting!" Tamworth commented with thoughtful interest. "There seems to be a clear difference between asking people who *will* win the case, compared to asking them who they *want* to win." He then turned to where John was sitting and noted John's glum and silent indifference on the matter.

"Cheer up, John," he said to him. "The polls are narrowing with each passing day. Very soon we'll be swinging them completely. Not long now!"

"And more and more people out there appear to be on your side," Mina added. "I think we've succeeded in winning round some of the reluctant doubters."

"I agree," said Tamworth. "You're beginning to win the popularity vote, now, if not the sympathy vote; and while it may not win us the case, it may just save your life."

"How so?" Mina asked.

"Well, think about it, Mina," Tamworth chuckled while giving John a playful nudge. "They can't possibly dispose of him now. He's far too popular. A lot of people out there are starting to admire the man, and there will be hell to pay if he comes to any harm – whether it be at the polling stations or even out on the streets themselves. Sure, there will still be opponents out there...but would they risk martyring him?"

"You are a genius, Boss!" Des remarked as he raised his drink in salutation. "This might even mark your big return to mainstream politics."

"Well, I'd be lying if I said the thought hadn't occurred to me," Tamworth replied, cupping his tumbler as he pondered.

John, who remained silent and thoughtfully distant throughout the conversation, finally spoke to get his own views across.

"If it's all the same to you guys," he said as he slowly looked around at the three of them, "I don't give a damn about your party politics or how popular I am. I don't care if people out there like me. I don't even care if people hate me. All I want is to go back home and be with my family...for *me* to be with *my* family and for the world to leave us alone!"

"I understand how you must feel," Tamworth replied solemnly, "but you must admit that while the past few days have no doubt been stressful, they have also been fruitful. There's no harm in celebrating."

Tamworth's reassuring words were of little comfort to John, who sat there, still nervously melancholic and nursing the drink in front of him.

"But I know my counterpart," he said "and we've all seen his legal team in action. There's no way he's going to go quietly into the night without a fight. You may think he's brought out the big guns already but believe me, Arnold, he's far from beaten."

"We never claimed it would be easy, John," Tamworth responded, "but as a soldier...of sorts...even you should understand our optimism when we are beginning to gain ground – ground which I am not prepared to relinquish any time soon. I would have at least thought you'd be more confident about our progress."

Mina was nearby listening in on the conversation and had been staring at John attentively as Tamworth rambled on about their (and his) successes. She could tell that there was more to John's pessimism. He had a longing, distant stare down towards the table. His gaze wasn't necessarily 'at' the table but more through it, and his eyes barely blinked.

"What's really got you down, John?" she finally asked him. "It's not the tribunal, is it? It's something else."

John turned his head towards her and looked up.

"It's Friday!" he finally spoke. He forced a tight smile as he began to explain further. "On Fridays, later on from now, that is, Cassy and I would normally be curled up watching *Friday Night In* on the television."

"Oh, I love that show!" Mina said. "I forgot it was back on the air. Would you like me to switch over to it when it comes on?"

John shook his head and sighed. "You don't understand, Mina. I'm not supposed to be here. I don't *want* to be here. I'm *supposed* to be at home with Cassy."

"You miss her, don't you?" Mina guessed.

"Yes, I miss her. I want to see her again – and Jack, too. I'm bored of being cooped up in here like some prisoner, and on top of that...today is our...well... wedding anniversary."

Mina smiled and placed a comforting hand on John's shoulder.

"Oh, I didn't realise," she remarked in a sympathetic tone.

"I've never forgotten an anniversary," John added, with a shake of his head.

"I'm sure we can swing you by to see her tonight if it means that much to you," Mina declared, still stroking his arm. She then turned her head round towards Tamworth. "What do you think, Boss?"

Tamworth shook his head dismissively at the idea. "Out of the question!" he said. "It's still not safe for him out there on the streets. One hint that he's the clone and he'll be a walking target. No, He's much safer here. If you like I can contact Cassy and have her escorted here?"

"But it's not the same!" John argued in frustration. "At home, we would have alone-time together and cosy up on the sofa. Here would be no better than a conjugal visit!"

"Believe me, I sympathise, Mr Haughton," Tamworth replied more formally, "but the fact remains it's just not safe for you. You can bet your life that the anti-clones out there will be watching us like hawks, hoping to get you on your own."

"You can't have it both ways, Arnold!" John then pointed out.

"How do you mean?"

"I mean you cannot sit around, drinking and patting yourself on the back for a job-well-done...claiming the polls are narrowing and that we are winning the people over but at the same time moaning about how everybody still hates me! As far as I'm concerned those polls Des keeps bringing up mean sod-all if the streets still aren't safe for me!"

"But one step at a time!" Tamworth pleaded. "The case will be for nought if anything were to happen to you."

"And what exactly will happen to me if I did sneak home?" John argued. "It's like you said...would the anti-clones *really* risk martyring me? Are you prepared to test that theory or was that just a load of pretentious trash you just spouted?"

"I imagine that I'm correct in my assumptions, particularly with the organised groups," Tamworth stubbornly replied, "but I cannot speak for the psychotic lone-wolves out there. Besides, with all the attention being generated about this tribunal, the outside of your home will be teaming with hungry paparazzi, eager to get a sneaky scoop at the first opportunity."

Tamworth took a quick gulp to finish his drink and then rose from his feet; a move accompanied by a yawn and a long stretch.

"It's getting late now," he said calmly. "Too late for petty bickering and too early for taking unnecessary risks. I think I'll turn in for the night. We still have a long week ahead of us."

Tamworth collected his files and neatly piled them onto a different table, away from the greasy buffet.

"Des, you'll make sure that the security arrangements are carried out, won't you," he ordered. Des said nothing but raised his hand in a gesture of acknowledgement as he continued to scan the news websites.

"Mina...John," he then added. "I suggest you two get some rest also. I guess we can talk more about visitation rights in the morning, and I'm sure we can come to some reasonable arrangement."

And with that, Tamworth signalled a goodnight to the others with his hands, took his leave for the evening and closed the door behind him. There was a moment's pause before any of the others left in the room spoke.

"Hmph! Visitation rights, indeed!" John hissed, angrily.

"He means well, John," said Mina, "even if he is a little overprotective now and then."

John turned around swiftly to face Mina. "So, who's Billy Reece?" he quickly asked. Mina twitched a little at the sudden and unexpected question.

"That's a bit out of the blue!" she remarked. There was a subtle laugh in her voice to disguise her discomfort.

"Someone mentioned his name today," explained John, "and I noticed that it made Arnold rather uncomfortable. So, who is he?"

Mina and Des looked at one another awkwardly – each trying to decide silently which one of them, if at all, would fill him in.

"Billy Reece was a bit of a low point in Arnold's career," Mina eventually began.

"A *bit* of a low point would be an understatement," Des then commented sarcastically. "But he was also a long time ago and unconnected to anything we are doing now."

"So, who was he, then?" John continued to press.

"Billy Reece was a notorious criminal from about ten years ago who was supposedly killed during a police raid," Mina continued.

"It was later discovered that Billy Reece had arranged for a clone of himself to be created," said Des. "This was of course, back when commercial cloning was still in its infancy and the laws hadn't yet been tightened up."

"The cops located the clone and promptly arrested him," said Mina. "They figured that as the clone possessed much of Billy Reece's memories, he should stand trial instead. It was a controversial move, but the families of those hurt by the original Billy Reece wanted some form of closure and in their eyes, somebody had to pay."

"So where does Arnold Tamworth come into this?" John then asked.

"It was Arnold who took the case on and represented Billy Reece's clone," Des explained. "In doing so, he argued that the sins of the father are not necessarily in the sins of the clone, so to speak, that Billy and his clone were two different people and as such it would be wrong to convict the latter of crimes he did not commit."

"In return, Arnold convinced the clone to compromise and cooperate with the authorities," Mina added. "In one massively detailed recorded confession, Arnold got the clone to spill about Billy Reece's involvements in numerous crimes. He even told them where treasures were stashed and where all the bodies were buried."

"At the time, the clone seemed genuinely remorseful about his predecessors' behaviour and wanted to put things right," Des continued. "Afterwards, Arnold managed to lobby enough sympathy to secure the clone's release from custody and saved him from almost certain death. After which...he disappeared."

"So why does the name haunt him now?" John asked.

Mina took a deep breath through gritted teeth as she began to elaborate further. "It later turned out that the 'clone' Tamworth had been defending...wasn't actually a clone at all but rather the *real* Billy Reece."

"I'm sure you can work out what happened, Mr Haughton," said Des. "Quite simply, Billy Reece had activated and then murdered his own clone, and took his place before the feds arrived. Then, with the help of Mr Tamworth, he openly bragged about his crimes and fled the country before the truth came out. That so-called 'confession' of his became nothing more than a middle finger to the authorities that allowed one of the most wanted criminals at the time to walk away Scott-free."

"Many people got it in the neck," Mina said, "but Arnold got the brunt of it and his reputation was shot to pieces."

"And left him somewhat gun-shy about taking on clone-related cases," added Des.

"But he's taken *me* on, hasn't he?" said John.

"Indeed, he has," replied Des as he began to theorize further. "To put a military slant on it, Mr Haughton, the Billy Reece incident was Arnold's *Vietnam*, so to speak – an absolute disaster he would rather forget. You, on the other hand, are his *Desert Storm* – the chance for him to come back and remind the world what he's still made of."

John's sighed and shook his head as another realisation began to sink in. It was a realisation that he hadn't been completely oblivious to but hadn't been confirmed until now.

"So, what you are saying is...I'm just some pet project of his?" he said accusingly.

"Well, when you say it like that it makes him sound like some contemptible jerk," Des remarked.

"He *is* a jerk!" John replied sternly. "A smart one, I'll give him that, but a jerk all the same. I just knew he was doing this to suit his own interests in some shape or form, but I didn't really know what it was until now!"

"Oh, come on, John," Mina pleaded. "Okay, so he's not perfect, but Arnold is on your side right now when nobody else is. Surely that must count for something."

John hummed a doubtful tone in response. He swigged down the remains of his drink and then slammed the empty bottle onto the table. He then rose from his seat, moved towards the window, and began to stare out into the evening while he pondered. He then spun swiftly to face Mina.

"Tell me, Mina," he began to inquire. "Am I a prisoner here? Or a hostage, maybe?"

"No," she answered, with a look of confusion in her eyes.

"So, if I want to see Cassy tonight..." John began.

"But what about all that stuff Arnold warned you about?" Mina interrupted. "The dangerous men...and the paparazzi outside your wife's home?"

"And as I said," John replied, "he cannot have it both ways – and besides, I feel safer if the press is patrolling the area."

"How do you mean?" Mina asked.

"Well, if there *are* lone wolves out there waiting to get hold of me," John explained, "they're hardly likely to do it on live television, are they?"

"Not entirely sure that's how it works, John," said Des, looking doubtful and shaking his head.

He turned fully to face Mina and Des and made his position clear.

"I'm going to see Cassy and Jack," he insisted, "and I'm going to see them tonight."

And with that, John moved towards where his jacket was hanging and where his outdoor shoes were placed and began to get himself ready to leave.

"But what about Arnold?" Mina pleaded. "He's not going to be happy about this."

"Arnold doesn't need to know, does he? At least not until tomorrow," John replied. "Anyway, sod him! He may be my lawyer and, for the time being at least, my guardian, but I'm not some petulant teenage boy he can just 'ground'. Besides, I'm starting to think he cares more about resurrecting his career than what I personally want from all this."

As John proceeded to tie his shoelaces, he took note of the brief and awkward silence that had now filled the room – the fact that neither Mina nor Des seemed to have anything to say to rebuke his brief rant, and not for the first time either did he have this gut feeling kicking in. Nevertheless, he put his feelings to one side for now. If he was going to leave Tamworth's headquarters, then he was going to need assistance. With his shoes tied and his jacket on, John straightened up and gestured for the others to join him. "Well?" he remarked. "Are you coming along, or what?"

Des and Mina looked at each other briefly. Mina was the first to stand up and with a nod and a smile, she moved towards the coatrack to fetch her own jacket. Des remained seated for the time being, not yet convinced.

"And what about the press?" he inquired. "Even if we snuck you out and got you back before dawn, the boss is surely gonna find out."

"That's why I need you guys!" John said with a smile. "I need you two to help sneak me out of this place, get me over to Cassy's and then, I don't know..."

"Deal with the press?" Mina guessed.

"Precisely!" John replied with a nod and a grin. "Just get me there and create a distraction. Make them think I'm still in the car with you. In the meantime, I'll sneak out and move around them at the first opportunity."

"This an army thing?" Des joked.

"Something like that," said John. "I just need a way in, and you guys are going to give it to me."

As Mina applauded and cooed in excitement at the thought, Des began to rise from his seat.

"I'll get the car ready," he said with a sigh.

19

The plan went off without a hitch. As Des pulled the car up around the side of the building, Mina managed to sneak John out into the back seat, while she got into the passenger seat next to Des. Getting past the guards wasn't too much trouble either, with Des informing them that he had been given the evening off and was taking Mina out to the movies. Lying to the guards in this manner wasn't necessary, as John Haughton wasn't a prisoner and could technically have left whenever he pleased. There certainly didn't appear to have been any orders for the guards to keep him detained. Nevertheless, it was agreed among the three of them that the less the guards knew about this, the better. No point in having them face the wrath of Tamworth too, should he ever find out what had happened.

After a brief but non-eventful drive through the evening, they eventually reached the neighbourhood of John's home (and Cassy's house). Des slowed the car to a crawl and drove carefully up and down the streets to assess the situation. It was dark, late in the evening and although there were news vans stationed nearby, with some reporters even sitting around a makeshift campfire, there wasn't the 'mob' of reporters which John, Mina or Des had expected.

'So much the better,' John thought to himself. *'This'll be easier than I thought.'*

"Stop here, Des," he said. Des obliged and pulled over by a thick area of bushes. As John stealthily climbed out of the car, he instructed Des and Mina to drive further down, closer to the news vans, and set up their 'distraction'. As the car moved off, John waited in the bushes for the signal. He watched as the car came to a halt a little further down. He then saw Mina exit the vehicle and begin to conspicuously creep around. She continued this until some of the reporters began to take note, with a couple starting to walk over to the vehicle, armed with their cameras. As soon as Mina caught sight of them, she casually walked back towards the car and signalled for Des to wind down the back window, and from there, she began to fake a conversation with the now-absent clone.

"It's no good, Mr Haughton," she declared, not too loud, but loud enough for the nearby press to overhear. "We'll have to come back here another time. Too many journalists crawling around." She watched carefully as the journalists crept closer and then she smiled.

"What was that Mr Haughton?" she spoke. "You actually want to? Well, I wouldn't advise answering their questions just now."

Upon hearing those words, the nearby journalists began to quicken their pace towards the car, beguiled by the prospect of an exclusive scoop, like moths to a lamp. Once they were close enough, Mina quickly climbed back into the car and wound up the windows, which, fortunately for her and Des, happened to be made from a secretive one-way glass, which allowed them to keep up the pretence for a few more minutes and buy John precious time to make his move.

John looked out towards the car and sure enough, more and more journalists were surrounding the vehicle. He saw his chance and began to sneak across the street, taking care to stay within the shadows.

Meanwhile, inside the Haughton/Summers residence, Cassy was wide awake. It was fast approaching the time that *Friday Night In* would be on the television and she had done all she could to replicate the evening she would have had with John. A glass of red wine was out on the table, along with a cup of tea, milk, and no sugar, for herself...and a cup of coffee, milk, no sugar, for John. Cassy didn't expect John to be home that evening but understood why. Nevertheless, the need to make the coffee had another purpose, namely, to recreate the familiar aroma that would have filled the room at this time of the evening. It was a bittersweet moment for Cassy as she placed the coffee on the table. The lighting was perfect, the drinks were out, the television reception was...adequate...but it was not lost on her that the most important aspect was missing. John himself. Cassy, however, was getting used to his absence but this brought her little comfort. She thought back to her time with Jonathan and his army days, when he would be deployed for weeks, sometimes months, but he always found a way to come home eventually.

With little Jack now asleep in his cot and only a few minutes to go until Friday Night In would be broadcast, Cassy sat in her dressing-gown, curled up on the sofa and watched the commercials roll by on the television. She became teary-eyed as she tightly cradled a nearby cushion for comfort. Suddenly, she heard a noise outside. She was already aware of the journalists further down the road, but this noise was closer and seemed more intrusive. Cassy heightened her senses and stood up slowly, listening out for any repeats of the mysterious sounds. At first, it sounded like rustling bushes, followed by footsteps and a knock against a wall. Cautiously, she moved to the front door to make sure it was locked and bolted. She quickly glanced out of the porch window before moving steadily to the back door to ensure that it too was locked. Afterwards, she moved back into the living room and stood quietly, listening out for another sound. The clock in the hall chimed the hour of 10 pm; a sound which briefly startled Cassy for a few seconds. She listened to each chime, but on the seventh or eighth chime,

her concentration was interrupted by a clear and distinct second sound – the sound of objects being knocked over and rolling on the ground, and more disturbingly, it from inside the house – the downstairs bathroom, to be precise. This was not her imagination, as she originally assumed. This time she was sure. Cassy moved over to the fireplace and reached down for the poker. Armed and ready, she moved over towards the downstairs bathroom. On the way, she noticed a can of furniture polish on a shelf and grabbed that also, with the intention of blinding the assailant before pummelling him. The bathroom door was slightly ajar, and the light was still off. Cassy readied herself for the attack. She wasn't going to call out the cliché 'who's there?' warning, nor was she going to gently open the door. Upon hearing another sound coming from within the room, which confirmed her fears of an intruder, Cassy moved quickly. She kicked the door open with her foot, charged in, and let loose the furniture polish. At the same time, she elbowed the light switch, which was located on the wall behind her. As the light came on, Cassy watched as the figure fell through the open window and forward rolled onto the floor, coughing and spluttering as the polish spray filled the room. She stood there ready, with the poker raised in the air to strike the man as he sat up.

"Who the hell are you, you creep!" she bellowed, believing the intruder to be one of the paparazzi chancing his luck. "You get the hell out of my house or I swear the only exclusive scoop you'll be getting will be this poker right up your…"

Cassy paused just before finishing as the man gathered himself up and slowly raised his head to reveal himself. As he did so, he kept a defensive arm raised on the off chance that Cassy would carry out her threat. To Cassy's surprise and relief, it was her beloved John. As she looked down at where he was, she could see garden flowers strewn across the bathroom floor, and John himself covered in mud and compost. There was no question of where he got the flowers from so late in the evening. As he stood up and patted himself down, he picked up one of the flowers and showed it to Cassy, his other hand was also out in a welcoming gesture.

"Happy anniversary, love," he sheepishly declared as he struggled to get the words out between relentless coughs from the furniture polish.

Cassy looked at the flower and then back at John. A few seconds were required for her adrenaline levels to drop but afterwards, she smiled, dropped the poker, and ran towards John, where they passionately kissed and embraced each other.

"Oh, John, I've missed you!" she laughed with joy.

"And I've missed you too!" he replied. "I knew I had to come home to you. There was no way I was going to forget about tonight."

"Our anniversary," Cassy said with a smile.

"Well, yes, that too," John replied with a mischievous wink, "but mainly *Friday Night In*. It turns out that Mr Tamworth is not a big fan of it!"

They both laughed together at the joke and made their way to the living room and sank down on the sofa together. No sooner had he finished his humorous remark, than the long-awaited show began to air on the television. As they sat together, Cassy took hold of a fleecy blanked and wrapped them both up in it for warmth. John looked around the living room and immediately noticed the wine, the cup of tea and the coffee, laid out on the table.

"Were you expecting company?" he asked her.

"No," she answered. "I was just...hoping...for you to be here with me."

She lifted the cup of coffee and passed it to John. Fortunately for him, it was still warm. Cassy looked out towards the window.

"Do you think they know you're here?" she asked, referring to the nosey journalists.

"Oh, they know I'm in the area somewhere," said John. "Just not necessarily 'here'. I'll be gone before they know what's happened."

Cassy's smile dropped slightly, but not fully.

"So how long *are* you here for?" she asked him. John gave her a loving look and lifted his free hand to affectionately stroke her face.

"I'm going to be here with you tonight," he answered, "and in the morning I'm still going to be here to play with Jack but cannot stay for too long after that, I'm afraid. I'll need to be back when the tribunal resumes."

Cassy turned and rested herself back against John's body for comfort. John, meanwhile, stroked her hair and kissed her forehead as they both relaxed in front of the television.

"You know, Jack's missed you too," she said. "He's going to be so excited to see you when he wakes up."

"I hope so," John replied, "and I promise that after all this is over, I will never leave you two."

"So, you think there really is a chance for you at the tribunal?" Cassy then asked.

"For *us*," said John. "A chance for *all* of us. And whatever happens...whatever the outcome...I'm not going anywhere."

20

During that same evening, Jonathan Haughton (the original), was also out and about, but unlike John, he had no anniversary to celebrate. To him, the date itself was largely irrelevant and meaningless, so while his own legal team had retired for the evening, Johnathan attempted to find solace at his local bar. The luxuries he had that night were more basic than those of John and Cassy. He opted to gorge on potato chips and salted peanuts, while he unceremoniously washed them down with a range of beers. He sat there at the bar and glanced up at the television. He paid no real attention to the football highlights being shown but became more attentive whenever the news updates were aired – although much of the news that day wasn't good.

Although he remained largely confident of an eventual legal victory, Jonathan was not oblivious to the criticism that had been thrown towards him and his legal team – namely his aggressive and vindictive approach to the tribunal, and also his apparent intolerance of his clone counterpart. Victory or not, his attitude and methods did not appear to sit well with a growing section of the public that had now taken an interest in the case. The only good news came from the polls, which continued to show him ahead in public opinion overall, but at the same time, it wasn't lost on him that this lead had gradually shrunk since the beginning of the tribunal.

Suddenly, Jonathan's attention was drawn towards a full glass of ice-cold beer which had been placed directly in front of him by the bartender – a friendly supportive friend of his by the name of Joey Casey.

"This one's on the house," said Joey with a sympathetic smile. He took away Jonathan's empty glass and gently pushed a fresh drink of beer under Jonathan's nose.

"Thanks, Joey!" Jonathan remarked silently as he picked up the drink and put it to his lips. Joey leaned across the bar and angled himself to see what Jonathan was watching on the television. It was another one of the news updates reminding the public about the clone's latest triumphs in court, courtesy of Alice Beecham's media crew. Joey quickly grabbed the remote and switched the channel back over to the sports channel.

"I wouldn't beat your head over it, Jonny boy," said Joey. "Your clone is just the nation's flavour of the month, that's all. It'll soon blow over and we'll all move on to some other oddity to whine about."

"I guess I underestimated him," Jonathan said mournfully. "I should have known not to do that with my army training. I stumbled at the first hurdle."

"How do you mean?" Joey asked curiously.

"You need to know your enemy before you engage," Jonathan explained, "and I *should* have known him better than anyone."

"Yes, that was a cheap shot from his lawyer," Joey remarked. "That stuff he spouted about your transplants and injuries, that is. Very disrespectful if you ask me."

"So, what do *you* think, Joey?" Jonathan then asked candidly. "As a betting man, that is...what would you say my chances are?"

Joey pondered for a few seconds as he continued to clean the beer glasses that were lined up in front of him.

"As a betting man..." he answered, "not a legal expert, mind you, but a betting man...I think your chances are still pretty solid, my friend. After all, it's not like *your* life is on the line. I mean, the outcome of the trial isn't going to result in *your* disposal, is it?"

"For now, anyway," Jonathan remarked, after which Joey smiled and lightly shook his head in a tutting motion.

"I think you're safe," he said reassuringly. "The ordinary people just wouldn't allow it."

"And the clone?" Jonathan inquired. "What do you think of him?"

"Well, if he really is like you, then I'd say he's an alright kind of guy," Joey answered truthfully. "Don't get me wrong, though, I've nothing against clone replicants, or whatever you want to call them."

"Yeah, and this is the part where you defensively tell me that some of your best friends are clones," Jonathan chuckled, taking another sip of his drink to hide his smirk.

"Nah!" Joey replied. "Never had the pleasure, but I'm sure they're nice enough people. The point being that no matter how nice this guy might be...he isn't you; not really. Whatever bull-crap they stir up over at the courts won't change the fact that *you* are Jonathan Haughton. The same Jonathan Haughton who used to come into my bar and raise the roof. The same guy who took a blade to the kidney when that wannabe gangster tried to shake me down, and still came out on top. I've never seen that clone guy ever come through my doors. Only you."

Jonathan forced a smile and was mildly comforted by the support he still had among his old friends. Joey then leaned over the bar and moved his face closer to Jonathan's. He looked around carefully before speaking again.

"On that note, Jonny-boy," he said quietly, "you never did tell me where you'd been all this time. All I ever got was from what I read in the papers, as well as hearsay. This some official secrets thing?"

"Something like that," said Jonathan. "But beyond the official reports, there's not much more to say. I hardly remember all of the events myself."

Before Joey could press Jonathan for more details, their conversation was suddenly interrupted by a strange and unsavoury character staggering his way towards them from a nearby table.

"Hey, you!" the stranger blurted towards Jonathan as he tried to stay upright. "I know you...you're that Haughton fella!"

"What of it?" Jonathan replied, avoiding immediate eye contact with the man.

"See?" Joey suddenly joked as he prepared to leave them to it. "Even the mindless drunks in here can tell you're the real deal!"

"Yeah, that's right!" the drunk man sluggishly said. "You're the guy! The *real* deal!"

Jonathan tried to take no notice, but the persistent man dragged over a nearby stool and sat right next to him. The unhealthy stench of the man's breath as he spoke was borderline intolerable.

"You know, you make me... hic! ...you make me laugh!" the man continued to slur. "Your doppelganger is out there screwing you over and you're letting him! He's out there screwing your *woman* and you're letting him!"

"Hey, that's enough, pal!" Joey interjected as he returned to the scene in a less jovial mood. Jonathan said nothing in response but instead summoned up as much resilience as he could to contain his increased annoyance with the stranger.

"Hey, hey, we're all friends here!" the drunkard went on. "I hate clones every one of them. If you ask me, hang 'em all up! That's what I'd do to my clone if I had a clone and caught him messing with my woman."

At that moment Jonathan turned around and glared angrily at the inebriated fool.

"Are you trying to be funny?" he barked.

"Me?" the man exclaimed, using both hands to gesture to himself as he swayed loosely on his barstool. "No, not me, sir. I'm on your side. You see, Haughty...I can call you 'Haughty', can't I? No matter. You see Haughty, my woman left me as well. A beautiful sexy bird, she was. Left me for my brother...my own treacherous flesh and blood! You on the other hand...you're lucky...*your* woman left you...for *you*. And if I were in your place, I would tell you...tell me...whatever...to fu...."

"Alright, that's it!" Joey interrupted again as he furiously made his way round to the other side of the bar. "Out! I've had enough of you!". He then grabbed the man forcefully by the collar of his crinkled shirt and dragged him unceremoniously towards the door.

Jonathan looked around at the other guests, who had paused their activities and were now watching the commotion. Once Joey had taken care of the drunkard, they turned and looked back towards Jonathan. Aware of their observation, he downed the rest of his beer and glared at them.

"What the hell are you all looking at?!" he growled. "I'm Jonathan Kenzie Haughton! ME! And I'll have words with anyone who says otherwise!"

Immediately the spectators returned to their own business as Joey re-entered the bar.

"Just ignore him, Jonny-boy," he said as he prepared another drink. "He's an idiot, but your true friends...me, your army-buddies, your poker-mates...we all know who you are. No court case is ever going to change that!"

Joey then placed the drink in front of Jonathan.

"One more for the road?" he offered. This, however, Jonathan declined. He slowly spun out of his stool and steadied himself. He could handle his drink better than most men and although he wasn't as drunk as the other man at the bar had been, he nevertheless started to feel tipsy and fatigued.

"That's me done for the night Joey!" he declared as he reached for his jacket. "I'm the hell outta here!" – and with that, he slowly moved towards the exit and pushed his way out onto the streets. It was clear and largely cloudless, but it was also quite windy. Although the temperature outside was not what one would describe as unpleasantly cold, Jonathan felt the cold, nevertheless. Like many others before him, he had allowed himself to be taken in by the myth of alcohol keeping you warm. With a silent shiver under his breath, he pulled his jacket collars tightly around him and began the long, slow, and tiresome walk back to the apartment in which he was staying.

21

John spent the next few days with Cassy and Jack. For the entire weekend, he focused his attention entirely on his family and divided his time between them, from cooking and baking with Cassy and crawling around the floor with Jack as they engaged each other in the game of 'peek-a-boo!' – much to baby Jack's noticeable delight. John relished every minute of what he had missed for so long – and as he started to think again of the impending tribunal it made him more determined to succeed. Such happiness right now...such contentment. These were 'his' experiences, and he'll be damned if anybody was going to take them away from him.

As is the case with all people enjoying the moment, the long weekend flew by in no time and John needed to get back to Tamworth's headquarters in order for them to plan their next moves. He thought about how he was going to get back – whether he should risk public transport, walk back, or contact Tamworth and get Mina or Des to collect him. Before he could decide, however, his thoughts were interrupted by an urgent-sounding knock at the door. John and Cassy both paused for a few seconds. Cassy signalled for John to move back from the window, while she looked out.

"Who is it?" asked John.

"It's Des, I think," said Cassy, "but he's not alone. There appears to be another man with him, and he looks...armed."

"I'll see to them," said John. "You take Jack upstairs."

"No!" Cassy insisted. "You stay and *I'll* get the door."

"Ms Haughton!" a voice called out from outside. "Do you mind if I come in? It is rather urgent!"

Cassy moved towards the front door, all the time signalling for John to remain out of sight. She approached the door and placed her hand on the handle but paused before opening it.

"Is that you, Des?" she called out.

"Yes, Ms Haughton," replied Des. "May I come in?"

"*You* can," Cassy replied, "but unless my husband is under arrest, I would appreciate it if your friend remained outside."

There was a slight pause before Des responded.

"We are here to escort Mr Haughton back to headquarters," Des explained. "If he's in then let him know that there is a car round the back waiting for him and that Mr Tamworth wants him back within the hour."

Without needing to open the door, Cassy acknowledged Des' instructions, which allowed Des and his guard to walk away. John gathered his belongings and prepared to leave from the back as instructed. He embraced Cassy a final time and kissed Jack goodbye. He cautiously left the house and followed the directions set out by Des. Sure enough, a black vehicle was waiting for him. He immediately noticed it was more secure looking than the vehicle that had previously dropped him off a few days ago. John approached it and climbed into the back. Immediately the car sped off in the direction of the city centre and towards Tamworth's headquarters.

The journey back was uncomfortably quiet, and although John didn't expect to hear much from the armed guard, he got very little from Des – only short statements, which killed any chances of a casual 'conversation', if only to pass the time. John noticed that Des' demeanour was more formal than usual. He guessed that Tamworth must have given him and Mina the third degree for allowing him to go home to Cassy.

When they arrived at the headquarters, they found the outside more active than usual. There were hordes of reporters hoping to get a quick picture of the clone. Des slowly moved the car through the crowd until he was safely through the gates; after which the guards moved out to push the crowd back.

John and Des exited the vehicle and entered the building. Immediately John was aware of the fast-paced activeness of the staff everywhere. He was escorted directly to Tamworth's office, where he saw Mina, who gave him a similar look to the one Des had given him in the car. He clocked sight of Tamworth walking towards him and readied himself for a showdown.

"Ah, the prodigal son returns!" Tamworth announced sarcastically.

"Now look here, Arnold," John began sternly. "Me going out last week was my idea and..."

"What you choose to do during your spare time makes no difference to me, Mr Haughton," Tamworth interrupted. "You've made that perfectly clear. But I would appreciate it more if you were accompanied by some form of armed backup next time. Anything could have happened to you out there and I'm not going to invest my time defending the rights of a corpse."

"There was no danger," John argued. "I saw to that."

"Oh no?" Tamworth replied sternly as he produced one of the tabloid newspapers of the day and tossed it down onto the table for John to read. John stared down at the main headline and then reached down to pick up the newspaper. It read:

'Clone vs Man – Now it's War!!!'

"I've joked about that headline once before," said Tamworth. "I wish I hadn't now."

John read the article carefully. The report was about an attempt on Jonathan's life, which had taken place over the weekend – incidentally the same evening that John had been with Cassy. According to the report, on the way home from a night out in a city bar, Jonathan Haughton, the human plaintiff in the much-reported *'Haughton Dilemma'* was ambushed by a group of unknown assailants who chased him down and assaulted him. Although he was able to fight off a few, causing considerable damage in the process, Jonathan was eventually subdued, shot, and beaten.

"The police are treating it as attempted murder," Mina explained, as John continued to read over the article. "All of the news channels are reporting on this right now."

"And for all we know, it could easily have been *you* that night!" Tamworth added. "So, if you don't mind, you go nowhere from now on without me knowing about it!"

"How did he manage to get away?" John commented under his breath.

"Apparently he was rescued by some good Samaritans," said Tamworth, "and dare I say, some rather conveniently-armed Samaritans at that."

"He's been in hospital for the past few days, under armed guard," said Des. "Only a few news outlets have been allowed to interview him."

"So far many fingers are pointing at you, Mr Haughton," Tamworth said half-accusingly. "Would you mind telling me where you were that night?"

"Are you kidding me?" said John in a defensive tone. "You know very well where I was. Just ask Mina and Des."

"Oh, I know where you were," Tamworth answered. "I know where you were up to the point in which they dropped you off, but I can neither confirm nor deny your whereabouts later."

"Cassy can," said John.

"Cassy *would*," Tamworth replied, "whether you were there or not."

John grew increasingly agitated by Tamworth's accusing tone.

"What exactly are you saying?" he demanded, drawing attention to the newspaper in his hand. "Are you accusing me of having anything to do with this? Why would I do that when I'm winning the case?"

"These aren't my thoughts," Tamworth assured him, "and for the record, I believe you. But nevertheless, our opponents won't see things that way. All they'll see right now is that somebody attempted to murder your counterpart. Had they succeeded then the case would have likely collapsed in your favour. Surely you must see how his death would have been an advantage to you."

"But you said it yourself, Arnold," said John, "that could have been *me* that night. What makes you so sure that those responsible weren't actually after me and got him by mistake?"

"And an easy mistake that would be to make," Tamworth replied. "All the more reason to keep you under close watch for the time being until we get to the bottom of this."

"What have Jonathan's team been saying about it?" asked John.

"Nothing publicly, just yet," said Tamworth. "I've been in contact with Cottam, who has only seen him once in hospital so far. Both of us agree that this situation has just escalated. Neither of us is sure what the motives of the culprits were, and nobody is sure which one of you they were targeting. In any case, there are obviously people out there who wish to rule this by the sword. Logically, the case ends if one of you is dead. 'One person, one identity', remember? If you die, then there is no case to answer – nor would there be any clarification on current laws concerning clone replacements. If *he* was to die, however, you go free. The 'legal' obstacles for your existence would be removed, but you would have no more 'rights' than when you started out."

"So, what's Cottam doing?" Mina inquired. "Is he giving Jonathan a curfew too?"

"You bet your bottom dollar he will," Tamworth answered. "Until this dies down, both Haughtons are going to be placed under tighter protection."

Very soon, their conversation was interrupted by Des, gesturing to them from in front of the television. "Err...Boss," he said. "You might want to come and have a look at this!"

Everyone in the room turned to face the television screen as Des turned up the volume. He had just tuned in to one of the news reports and on the screen was the face of Tommy Dale, being interviewed on his take on the recent events.

"Oh, this was clearly an attempted murder!" Dale began as he talked theatrically into the journalist's microphone. "To think that Mr Haughton, a decorated and wounded war hero, should be treated with such contempt by the courts, such contempt by the politicians, such contempt by the media...should now be forced into hiding simply for fighting for what he believes...and what *I* believe...is right!"

"So, have you spoken to Mr Haughton?" the journalist asked. "Has he said anything to you yet about what happened to him that night?"

"Mr Haughton is in my protective custody right now," Dale replied, "and will not be answering any questions to the media until he is fit and ready. However, witnesses from the area have disclosed what happened, and a detailed report is being pieced together by the police as we speak."

"Mr Dale," spoke another reporter. "What do you think the motives were behind the attempt on Mr Haughton's life?" Tommy Dale grinned slightly before answering.

"Well, naturally I can't really say what the motives were as we have no idea who they were or who they might have been working for," he said with a calculating and manipulative charm in his voice. "I suggest we allow our good detectives to do their jobs and make that full report."

"But what do *you* think?" asked another journalist. "What are your thoughts on the notion that clones may have been involved?" Dale smirked again before answering.

"Well," he said with a sigh, "again, I cannot say either way, but if you were to ask me...and indeed you *have*...I would say that clone involvement, or some form of pro-clone extremists, is certainly something to take into strong consideration. After all, it is no secret that the clone of Jonathan Haughton would have been the main beneficiary had this cowardly act succeeded."

"So, are you suggesting that the clone and his associates hired someone to take out Mr Haughton?" the journalist asked. Dale let out a brief chuckle at the notion.

"Again, it would be wrong of me to put words into people's mouths during an ongoing investigation, but naturally we cannot rule anything out at this time," he began. Afterwards, he turned to face the cameraman and glared down the lens, as if he knew that John, Tamworth, and the others were watching.

"All I can say," he continued, "is that if he *did* have anything to do with the attempt on Mr Haughton's life, then there will be serious ramifications, both legally and politically. That, I am sure of!"

Tamworth and the others watched open-mouthed as the interview with Tommy Dale ended and the news switched back to the television studio, where the presenters began discussing Tommy's points carefully.

"Well, that's just brilliant!" Tamworth growled. "That's all we need right now! Tommy-bloody-Dale getting involved!"

"This is bad, isn't it, Boss?" Des commented.

"It certainly is!" Tamworth remarked. "Right now, we're not sure who the real target of that attack was, or whether it was even connected to the ongoing case. For all we know, it might just have been a random midnight street-mugging."

"Either way, they're going to try and drag our John through the mud!" Mina exclaimed. "It's not fair!"

"It certainly isn't," Tamworth agreed. "If we were to assume that Jonathan was indeed the intended target, and if we were to also assume that the culprits were indeed some kind of pro-clone extremist group...then they've certainly done a lot of damage to our cause right now. Our sympathy vote is going to erode fast, along with our popularity. Whoever they were may just have undone all our good work up to now! And I bet that right now, somewhere out there, Tommy Dale is laughing at us!"

22

On the night he was attacked, Jonathan Haughton didn't lose consciousness instantly. The effects from a mysterious blow to the head, coupled with a gunshot wound across the leg, caused his body to fall limp to the ground. His vision began to darken, but he was still able to hear sounds for a minute or so afterwards. The next thing he heard were shots being fired, but the shots themselves were not directed towards him. He certainly didn't 'feel' as though he had been shot again. Nevertheless, he could hear a range of shots, followed by the sounds of panicked men and what sounded like an ongoing street fight. Jonathan tried to crawl away but was still too limp and continually drifted in and out of consciousness, confused and dazed. Soon the sounds of fighting stopped and the men who had attacked him had gone. Jonathan lay there in the dark, face down on the wet ground, still unable to see. He heard the sounds of people gathered around him. He then felt somebody kneel next to him and place fingers against his neck to check his pulse. Then he heard the faint sounds of the men conversing.

"Is he still with us?" said one of the voices.

"Yep, just about," said another. "I think we can move him."

"Great!" the first voice responded. "Get Frankie to pull up the car and we'll get him in. You grab his arms I'll get his legs. Careful now!"

The last thing Jonathan remembers before fully passing out was the sensation of being roughly handled and carried off the ground. The next time he opened his eyes, Jonathan was no longer on the streets. Instead, he found himself in a featureless room, lying in a single bed and staring up at a blank ceiling. As his vision gradually returned, he immediately recognised that he was in a hospital. The full details of what caused him to be there was still a little cloudy but simply 'being there' meant that he managed to escape. As his memories came flooding back, Jonathan's feelings of relief (that he was now out of a very bad situation) soon made way for the conclusion that somebody must have helped him. Confident that he could move, he sat up quickly and looked across at a nearby mirror to assess the damage. His face was non-worse for wear, albeit a few superficial cuts and bruises but thankfully no signs of permanent scarring. Remembering the bullet which had grazed his leg, he then looked down to see that his leg partially plastered but intact. No bones were broken. He was sore in several places, but not so much as the back of his head, where a mysterious blow from behind had floored him before his attackers began to close in. Jonathan was so preoccupied with checking himself and ascertaining where he was, that he was unaware of the presence of a second individual in the room, who sat quietly and patiently on a chair nearby, watching him. Eventually, the mysterious figure began to speak.

"I must say that you're one tough cookie, my boy," said the man. Jonathan turned his head towards the voice and beheld a middle-aged man in pale casual clothes sitting across from him. He was wearing a large bull-hide and straw

177

cowboy hat and was sat there, leaning forward slightly so that his hands were resting on a wealthy walking stick, which sported a shiny brass handle shaped like the head of a bald eagle. The man lifted his hat slightly to reveal his face – a face that Jonathan recognised instantly.

"You...you're..." Jonathan stammered.

"Thomas Huckabee Dale," the man replied with a smile. He tipped his cap respectfully towards Jonathan as he spoke. "But you probably know me as good old 'Tommy'."

"Tommy Dale," Jonathan replied thoughtfully. He gave a nod of acknowledgement before forcing through a sarcastic smirk. "You're not somebody I would normally associate with the word 'good' if I'm honest."

"Oh?" Dale remarked with raised inquisitive eyebrows.

"Nor are you somebody I would *want* to associate myself with," Jonathan continued.

"I see," Dale said with a patient sigh, which was accompanied by a grin of irony. "I'll just add you to the ever-growing list of people who don't 'fully appreciate' what I'm doing for them...but will no doubt thank me later all the same."

"Thank you?" Jonathan sarcastically replied. "For what?"

"Boy, how do you think you ended up here?" Dale exclaimed. "Do you think that you casually beat your way out with your macho ninja moves, walked over to this hospital and just knocked on the door?"

Jonathan looked around at the room again.

"That said, I *do* admire your valiant efforts," Dale continued with a chuckle. "My associates told me you managed to take out quite a few of your assailants before they finally got the better of you."

"Where am I?" Jonathan asked.

"Isn't it obvious, boy? You're in a room at the city hospital, and I've taken steps to ensure that you are well cared for during your stay."

"How long?"

"You've been here a couple of days so far," Dale started to explain. "I've had armed men stationed outside your room. Nobody has been allowed in here apart from myself, the necessary doctors and nurses and... shall we say...'trusted' members of the press."

"Press?" Jonathan inquired.

"Sure!" Dale replied. "I saw to it that you are treated in a 'public' hospital. None of this 'behind-closed-doors' rubbish just because of this ongoing legal spat you have with your clone. That way, the public can see for themselves how things have started to get out of hand with this tribunal...and what they tried to do to you."

At this point, a nurse entered the room with a tray of food for Jonathan and a cup of coffee for Dale. The two of them paused their conversation briefly until she had left the room again. Jonathan took a sip of his orange juice and looked inquisitively towards Dale again.

"Who's *they*?" he asked him. "Are you referring to the people who attacked me?"

"The people who tried to *kill* you, you mean!" Dale responded emphatically.

"How do you know?" Jonathan replied. "It was dark and rainy at the time. For all we know, it could have been some of those hooligans out there wanting my clone out of the way. They just got the wrong man, that's all."

"Are you sure?" Dale asked. "My associates told me you tried to reason with them at the time. Do you not remember that?"

Jonathan thought for a moment. "No," he eventually answered. The finer details were still a vague blur to him. Dale then leaned forward a little more so that he was closer to Jonathan's bed.

"I agree it would be much easier for your clone to be attacked considering the context of the tribunal and its implications," he said, "and while I would understandably sympathise with the views of those who would be involved, I am not here to officially condone their actions, for obvious reasons."

"And yet you don't condemn them either, I notice," Jonathan replied with another smirk.

"Regardless of what you think, you should thank me all the same," Dale responded in a more formative tone. "Those men were out to kill you that night and would have succeeded had my associates not been in the right place at the right time to watch over you. And when I say you...I mean *you*."

"Again, who's *they*?" Jonathan insisted. "And why would they want *me* dead?"

"Mr Haughton," Dale started to answer. "It is an undeniable fact that all political desires have their extremities, regardless of where they are on the political spectrum. For you, the case you have against your clone may simply be just a small-time quarrel that has...shall we say...gotten out of hand. If you win, you get back everything that you lost following your unintended absence. But that's not what it's become. The outcome of the case, whatever decision is made, will have ramifications across the whole of our nation regarding the status of clone replacements, and it is no secret that I'm rooting for your side to win."

"So, what's that got to do with what happened to me?" Jonathan asked.

"Quite simply," Dale answered, "as much as there are sensible people like me who want to do all they can to see you win your lawsuit, there are also unhinged people out there who seek the same outcome for your clone."

"You mean I was attacked by a gang of pro-clones?" Jonathan exclaimed with a hint of doubt in his voice.

"Is that so hard to believe, Mr Haughton?" Dale argued. "It appears as though society accepts the existence of 'anti-clones' easily enough but the perish thought of it ever being the other way round. Believe it or not, Mr Haughton, there is such a thing as a black racist."

"So, I've been targeted by pro-clones," Jonathan acquiesced.

"Or just 'clones'," Dale suggested. "Or maybe both. In any case, they want you out of the way to make way for your replacement. Think about it for a minute, Mr Haughton. Logically speaking, if your clone disappears it would solve all your problems. Admit it, you must have considered it yourself at some point – and it is his disposal that you are hoping for, is it not?"

Jonathan said nothing but kept his eyes focused on Tommy Dale with curious interest.

"So, by the same logic," Dale continued, "it stands to reason that all of *his* problems would be solved if *you* were out of the way. After all, you've been declared dead before. How would things be any different?"

"So, you're saying that those men tried to kill me...so that my clone can win the tribunal?"

"So that the tribunal would collapse entirely," Dale explained. "While it may appear as though you've been on the back foot in recent times, many out there, myself included, are confident of your eventual victory. The thought that a second-rate laboratory experiment can legally replace natural flesh and blood, such as ourselves, makes my skin crawl! Trust me, Mr Haughton, I want you to win and I wish you all the best. I just fear that your lawyer's 'by the book' approach may be slowing you up a bit."

"He's good at what he does," Jonathan said defensively, "and he knows his stuff."

"I know," said Dale. "I never said that Mr Cottam was 'bad' at his job...just 'limited' somewhat. Not prepared to go that extra mile to get the job done faster."

"What do you mean?" Jonathan asked.

"Well, your image, for a start," Dale explained. "That Tamworth fellow has made your opponent out to be the victim, harassed by the law and by a vindictive squaddie who refuses to compromise. If the *clone* had been attacked that night, instead of you, then you can bet your bottom dollar their propaganda machine would have burned the midnight oil to use it to their advantage."

Jonathan then forced an eager contemplating smile as Dale continued.

"But it was *you* who was nearly killed – and by pro-clone extremists – possibly clones among them…and I intend to see to it that your story gets out. The fact that you are a war hero, who has been through a lot and has lost everything that you hold dear, will certainly rattle people from all sides when they find out what they tried to do to you."

Jonathan thought for a minute before responding.

"Suppose you're right about everything," he said. "Suppose it wasn't mistaken identity and I was indeed targeted that night. I can certainly imagine the press coverage and the interviews that could be conducted from this very room. But to enlist you into my services? You're Tommy Dale. Leader of the extremist *Humans First* group. I'm not so sure that getting into bed with a racist troublemaker will inspire peoples' confidence in me. No offence meant, of course."

Tommy smiled at that comment and let out a short snicker.

"Ah, the old bigot-brush again," Dale sighed again. "A label which my enemies use too quickly without any real substance. Yes, it is no secret that I oppose the creation and use of clone replacements by the rich and naïve. It is abhorrent to the natural order of things. Nor is it a secret that I oppose extending the franchise to them, among other things. After all, would you give the vote to your pet? Would you grant workers' rights to your car? Or your toaster? Of course not! In my view, a view shared by many, if you give these clones such powers, insignificant as they may appear at the beginning, they will use them to 'take' more."

Dale then sat up again in his seat and took a deep breath.

"Yes, Mr Haughton," he continued. "And you *are* Mr Haughton. This is so much bigger than your petty spat with a watered-down copy and when you finally realise that and accept it...you are going to need people like me to get you through."

As soon as he had finished speaking, there was a knock on the door, accompanied by multiple eager-sounding voices a little further down the hall.

"Come in!" Dale called out, before commenting to Jonathan. "Sounds like your fan base has arrived."

The door opened and one of Dale's associates poked his head through the gap.

"Mr Dale, the press is gathered outside for him again," he spoke. "They're wanting to know if he's well enough to talk, yet."

"Well, that's really down to him," Dale declared, looking across to Jonathan. And with that, he stood up and gathered his things. He walked over to Jonathan and offered him one of his business cards. He smiled in satisfaction when Jonathan took it.

"The doctor will no doubt be discharging you later today, Mr Haughton," he said. "What you decide to do when you leave here is entirely up to you. If you wish to call upon my services, then I stand ready to help. If not, then I wish you well all the same. In the meantime, I suggest you use your newfound fame to your advantage. Let them take a few pictures, answer a few questions for them. Trust me, it'll do wonders for your image."

Jonathan said nothing. He simply nodded in acknowledgement, sat back in his bed, and looked carefully at the business card.

"In the meantime, I'll leave you to it," Dale concluded as he made his way to the door. "Mull it over for a while. Think about it. Speak to Cottam if you like...then get back to me when you're all better. It's been lovely to meet you, Mr Haughton."

Tommy Dale left the room and closed the door behind him, leaving Jonathan to consider his offer. He walked off down the corridor, with his associate accompanying him alongside.

"So, did he agree?" the associate asked.

"That man has the opportunity to save our nation once again. This time from itself," Dale replied confidently. "Give him time."

23

At the request of Jonathan Haughton's legal representatives, the ongoing tribunal had been suspended to allow him to fully recover from his ordeal and for the police to continue with their investigation into the incident. The delay bought time for both sides to plan their next moves, but Tamworth was far from happy with this arrangement. He knew that the longer this case was drawn out the more chance there was of public opinion swinging back the other way. He needed to maintain public support for the clone to minimise the risks of 'disposal' should he lose the case. Tamworth's first move was to organise an impromptu press conference for John so that he could directly address the attempted murder of his opponent. With help from Alice Beecham and some well-placed sympathetic journalists, John was once again allowed to go on air to promote his opinions and once again, Tamworth remained off-camera to ensure that John got the attention he needed.

The main aims of the press conference were for John to distance himself from the attack on Jonathan, condemn the attack itself, and shoot down any conspiracy theories that he was in any way involved. At first, he managed this admirably. People did ask him about who might have been involved and whether he thought it was just a random attack, but as the interview progressed, the questions became heavier and more probing. John was asked about his thoughts on the idea of Jonathan's potential death being beneficial to him. He was also asked about his thoughts on rumours of a pro-clone extremist group, which, on the advice of Tamworth's team, John was forced to condemn. It was only when he was thrown a curveball question regarding the *Forever Together* cloning facility that he started to become unstuck and show some signs of confusion or discomfort.

"It's no secret that the *Forever Together* clinic has been ordered to suspend operations due to my, shall we say, premature activation," he said to the journalist, "but that's a separate matter and currently beyond the scope of my own court case."

"But should they be found guilty of negligence," the journalist pressed, "does that not impact your own case?"

"Admittedly," John began slowly, choosing his words carefully, "the clinic is ultimately responsible for my early activation, yes, but at the time, they had it on good faith, from recorded documents, that the client in question, my counterpart, had died. That, however, is an error that extends beyond the clinic and I'm sure that after a full investigation they will no doubt be..."

"But what about the allegations of gross misconduct?" another journalist interrupted. "Allegations of corrupt, unethical and illegal actions that have taken place at the clinic itself - and not just yourself, but other human clones as well?"

John paused for a minute, not quite sure what to say, and when he eventually opened his mouth to say something, he was quickly silenced and whisked away Tamworth's associates, who politely and conveniently ended the press conference.

For the rest of the day, the news headlines focused more on the investigations of the clinic, rather than John Haughton's case. It was a relief to all that the media wasn't trying too hard to connect John to the attack on Jonathan, but John's failure to address questions about the clinic risked further criticism from some outlets.

Back at headquarters, John and the others were discussing their next moves. John turned to Tamworth and asked him, "What do you know about the ongoing investigations at the clinic, Arnold?"

"I don't know too much about it," said Tamworth. "Only what has been officially reported and that they've ceased operations pending investigations."

"Such as?"

"There have been ugly rumours about the clinic and what's been going on at that place," Tamworth began. "Rumours of cloning methods which go beyond the law. Rumours of genetic modifications, eugenic experiments...the kind of stuff you tend to read about in science fiction novels."

"But the kind of things that *could* happen for real?"

"In a manner of speaking, but the laws on commercial clone replacements have always been pretty airtight. Should it be found that the clinic has indeed been bending the rules, there will be hell to pay and deservedly so."

"So why didn't you tell me this before the press conference?" John asked.

"To be honest I didn't think they'd be pressing you so soon on the matter," said Tamworth. "They were meant to be asking you about the incident with Jonathan. Besides, I didn't want you to get drawn too far into that debate.

Condemning the clinic at this stage might work against us but defending them might suggest involvement in anything the authorities might unearth."

Tamworth then sat closer to where John was seated and leaned in closer to him.

"Which brings me to my next point," he said quietly. "Are you aware of any malpractice or wrongdoing taking place at the clinic?"

"I don't know," answered John. "I wasn't really in there for long."

"But did you ever see anything out of the ordinary?" Tamworth pressed. "Did you hear any discussions at all? Surely you'll have memories of all the times your counterpart went in for his memory uploads?"

"Well, there was this talk of a hormone or chemical that they embedded into me," John suggested. "It was some additional coding in my mind that is meant to...sort of...calm me down and help me accept the fact that I am a clone replacement."

"We know about that already," said Tamworth, "but that's a normal and accepted procedure. Not enough for any conviction."

"We?" John asked inquisitively. "Are you the one investigating the clinic, Arnold?"

"I'm...involved," said Tamworth, tilting his head from side to side as he spoke. "I'm not heading it up but any useful information that comes my way, I pass on."

"Isn't that a little contradictory, Arnold?" said John, looking bemused. "You're fighting for my rights but at the same time damning the place that created me?"

"There's no conflict of interest as far as I can see, Mr Haughton," Tamworth explained. "Your right to live and malpractice at the clinic are separate issues deep down – that is, if you're not in any way involved."

"Why would I be?" asked John

"I don't know, Mr Haughton," Tamworth replied, "but the more attention that's focused on the clinic, the more we will need to tread carefully. The other Mr Haughton and his legal team are on the defensive right now and it's only a matter of time before they start to bare their teeth, and they will stop at nothing to find something wrong with you – some flaw in you or your design that they can exploit. This is why I needed to ask you what you knew, or know, about the goings-on at the clinic, so we're not suddenly caught with our pants down out at court."

"Well, as I said, I'm not aware of anything myself," said John, "and my memories of all my visits to the clinic have brought up nothing out of the ordinary. The memory uploads always seemed pretty straightforward."

Tamworth sat back on the sofa and assumed a more relaxed posture, breathing a faint sigh of relief.

"That's what I wanted to hear, Mr Haughton. At the very least we have plausible deniability to fall back on."

"Plausible deniability?"

"What I mean is," explained Tamworth, "should the investigators unearth anything damaging about the clinic you can genuinely deny any knowledge of it and hopefully be disconnected from the case. You have plenty on your plate after all."

Not long afterwards, the group began to hear faint noises coming from the outside. Mina and Des got up from their seats and peeked through the blinds to see what it was.

"It's a group of people gathered outside the headquarter gates, Boss!" said Des.

"Are there many?" Tamworth asked.

"No, Boss!" said Mina. "I'm counting about ten or so people."

"What are they doing?" asked John.

"They look like they're holding a demonstration. Some of them look to be holding placards but I can't make out what they're saying."

"Look at their faces, then," Tamworth suggested. "What do you see?"

"Some of them look rather intimidating, Boss," Mina reported, "and a few of them appear to be sticking their fingers up towards our building."

"These will be protesters no doubt calling for your arrest, Mr Haughton," Tamworth suggested. "This is all Tommy Dale's doing!"

"But he's safe here, isn't he, Boss?" Mina remarked with a slightly panicked tone. "They can't get to John from here, surely?"

"It depends," said Tamworth. "Are they giving the guards a hard time?"

"No," Des answered as he peeked through the blinds again. "The guards are on standby, but the protesters are just dallying around."

"That won't last long though, Boss!" Mina warned. "Do you think we'll need to get John out of here?"

"Not just yet, Mina," Tamworth answered. He then turned to face John again. "But she is right, John. The protection that we afford you while you are in this building is on borrowed time and the clock is ticking. At some point, we may need to consider relocating you to a safer environment before the situation gets worse.

24

As soon as Jonathan Haughton had recovered, a date was set to resume the tribunal. When that day arrived, John, Tamworth and the others arrived at the courthouse and quickly made their way up the stairs, with John flanked on all sides by Tamworth and his team. The armed guards provided by the court struggled to keep the angry crowd at bay and were unable to silence them. It was a much larger crowd than the last time they were there, and most of them appeared to be anti-clone agitators, armed with intimidating placards and handfuls of mud, eggs and paint which they planned to launch. The car that John had arrived in had already been through wars after having to make its way through the smaller group of protesters stationed outside Tamworth's headquarters. Once they were safely inside, the guards lined up along the entrance to block the crowd as started to close in.

Once the people in the courtroom were settled, Judge Taylor-Beckett took a moment to read out the minutes from the previous sessions to bring people up to speed. John looked towards the back of the court where Cassy was sitting. He smiled confidently at her and she smiled back. He then looked back towards the front and to where Jonathan was sitting. He appeared non worse for wear, save for a few cuts and bruises, and the bandages on his leg had been painstakingly hidden from view.

"It's rather strange that he's not made more of an effort to broadcast his injuries," John commented.

"I agree," said Tamworth. "He appears to have gone to great lengths to hide the serious ones. I wonder what he's up to?"

"If I may begin, Your Honour," Cottam announced as he rose from his seat. "My client has requested he be allowed to examine the defendant."

"He?" Taylor-Beckett asked, pointing towards Jonathan. "Not *you*?"

"Not me, Your Honour," Cottam clarified. "My client feels that as it is he who has made the complaint, he should be given an opportunity to speak to John directly during these proceedings."

With a slight shrug, Taylor-Becket nodded and signalled Jonathan to begin his case. Jonathan started by calling John to the witness stand, which John obliged. Tamworth looked towards Cottam, who then gave him an approving nod. Tamworth grinned. *"He wants to try and play my game,"* he thought to himself. *"This should be interesting."*

He then looked on with increasing suspicion but was also interested in how it would play out. After all, John had survived the awkward press conference so he should be able to survive this encounter, so long as he kept his cool.

"During this...examination," Jonathan began, addressing John in the stand, "I want you to consider the following question: Why do you think you are better than me?"

John said nothing but gave a calculating stare back at his rival.

Jonathan then began his attack, where he focused primarily on John's so-called memories. He asked John to publicly recall several events from his past, ranging from times at school to more recent; and every time John answered Jonathan reminded him that he (the clone) was not there for any of those events and therefore those 'memories' of his could not possibly be his.

"Those aren't your experiences," Jonathan would declare with a satisfied smile. "They're mine!"

During this line of questioning, John looked to be on the back foot. Whenever he tried to argue back with examples of more recent (and important) events, such as his 'marriage' to Cassy and the birth of baby Jack, they were quickly shut down and deflected. Jonathan had carefully been coached by his lawyer in preparation for this session. The methods he used were Cottam to the core but with a hint of Tamworth thrown in for good measure.

"My lawyer recently told me a story about a man who once professed to be the world's leading expert on sharks, on account of his extensive research over the years," Jonathan then said. "But that didn't stop a shark from taking one of his legs away when he went swimming with them."

"Get to the point!" John grumbled impatiently.

"My point is that second-hand knowledge pales next to true experience," Jonathan explained. "Granted, you possess all my memories, such as my time at school and my time in the forces...but that's really it. Perhaps you have reflected on them differently, but you have never really lived those memories as I have. You have never fought or suffered or sacrificed as *I* have. You are little more than a spectator. Hell, you probably know as much about karate in your mind as I do, but if we were to settle this dispute man-to-man, your lack of muscle memory would inevitably betray you. That is something that can never be uploaded. It is developed with experience and therefore something I have, which you are lacking."

"Are you asking me to fight you?" John remarked.

"Fortunately for you, no," Jonathan laughed, "because that would be the end of you."

John looked around at the court as he tried to keep his cool. Tamworth glared at him, trying to signal to him to hang on in there as Jonathan continued to try and bait him.

"Unlike you, I have actually lived the life that you can only 'remember'," he went on, "and, had I not disappeared, who is to say that I wouldn't have also lived the life that *you* have had also? Who is to say I wouldn't have been the same husband and same father...and couldn't be in the future? After all, you've managed it okay, and you are a clone of me – a stand-in. I, on the other hand, offer the complete package as the *real* Jonathan Haughton!"

Some of Jonathan's supporters in the crowd began to make encouraging noises of approval, while John was temporarily paralysed with increasing rage. He knew that Jonathan was attempting to bait him and throughout the examination fought back the urge to bite, but with the opinions of the courtroom looking as though they were starting to sway, he could take no more and, to the delight of Jonathan and Cottam, he finally gave in to his emotions.

"I'll tell you why I'm better than you!" he roared, wagging his finger aggressively at his opponent. "It's because you're nothing but a relic of the past, and that's where you belong! You can blurt out all the things in the past that *you* did, rather than me, all you want! You want to show off about all the past events and things you did? Well then, let's play that game! Let's talk about those!"

John then proceeded to list off examples from his memories that shed light on some of Jonathan's faults and regrets from the past; from things he did as a teenager, such as his involvement in the bullying of a classmate at school, to more recent misdemeanours, such as video piracy, shoplifting, traffic offences and minor drug abuse – some of these offences he was never indicted for. Jonathan listened carefully as the more unpleasant and embarrassing parts of his life began to spill out for all to hear, but he remained strong and undeterred.

"But that's all in the past," John concluded, "and we should be talking about n*ow.* I am a husband and a father – two things *you* have *never* been! And even if you were, you're not perfect! There were times in your past when you should have been there for Cassy, occasions when you forgot about dates or failed to notice when she was depressed. Admit it, you weren't the most reliable boyfriend in the world. Both of us know that!"

John paused for a moment to gather his composure. The room filled with the sound of faint mutterings from the crowd. Jonathan however, remained silent but visibly tensed.

"I, on the other hand, have not," John argued as he continued his counteroffensive. "I may have the memories of those unfortunate events, but through your o*wn* claim just a few minutes ago, those were *your* actions, not mine. I have never missed a birthday, nor an anniversary and have strived ever since my activation to be a better and more reliable person than you ever were – the Haughton that Cassy fell in love with! *That* is why I'm better than you!"

Following his powerful counterattack, John sat down and folded his arms, triumphantly awaiting Jonathan's response. He wasn't kept waiting for long.

"Are you kidding me?!" Jonathan exclaimed. "People can change their ways but not necessarily their very being, you moron!"

Suddenly, Judge Taylor-Beckett banged his gavel and signalled for Jonathan to retract his derogatory statement. Jonathan apologised, calmed himself again and continued his rebuttal.

"This case recently became a debate about identity, namely that of 'Jonathan Haughton', an identity which is rightfully mine," he said. "What makes up an identity is not just who a person is today, but also who a person was. Did Ebenezer Scrooge cease to be 'Ebenezer Scrooge' when he turned his life around? No! He changed his behaviour and outlook but also remained that person. People change all the time, for better or for worse."

"But you admit that *you* did all of these things, right?" John arrogantly quipped.

"Yes," Jonathan admitted, looking down to the floor, "I admit to all of them. All those things you mentioned were done by me, not you."

The clone cracked a tight smile as he began to feel his opponent back on the ropes. However, Jonathan wasn't finished and tilted his head back up again.

"I also regret most of those things, as you would attest to," he said, "because that is who Jonathan Kenzie Haughton is. Not perfect but then nobody is – and you think that makes you better than me? What right have you to assume *my* identity if you're not prepared to bear the burden of my past mistakes? I, at least, am prepared to live with them."

"Now hang on a minute," John interrupted, sensing a trap. "It was you who pointed out that I never did those things."

"But it was *you* who argued that by not doing those things you are suddenly better than me!" Jonathan argued back. "Being 'Jonathan Haughton' is about the bad times as well. You can't just cherry-pick your way through *my* life and only take credit for the good things! Yes, I've let Cassy down before and yes, it probably contributed to her affair, but we moved on from that because our love was stronger."

John suddenly gave a puzzled look when he heard that last point.

"Her affair?" he commented.

"And I suppose you're going to pretend *that* didn't happen either!" Jonathan remarked. "It is one thing to ignore the past but another thing entirely to rewrite history!"

John scrunched his face up in confusion.

"Cassy? Affair?" he commented again to himself. He then looked towards where Cassy was seated but she was too embarrassed to glance back at him and instead buried her face into her hand.

"When did that happen?" John said quietly, still looking confused and shaking his head. There were sounds of confused murmurings coming from the audience. His reaction hadn't gone unnoticed by Tamworth or Cottam, who both jumped out of their seats to demand different actions from the judge. While Cottam was insistent on continuing with the examination, wishing to question John himself, Tamworth demanded a recess. As the murmurings grew louder, Taylor-Beckett banged his gavel again and demanded silence. To Tamworth's relief, he was granted a recess. John sat back in his chair, looking pale and scratching his head in confusion. Taylor-Beckett signalled for Tamworth to approach the bench and leaned forward to quietly advise him.

"I've allowed this case to continue this far, Arnold," he spoke quietly. "However, I must also warn you that this recess is on borrowed time. I think we owe him that much, at least. But if what I think has happened, *has* happened...then I may be forced to make a ruling that will not be in your client's favour."

"This isn't over!" Cottam warned Tamworth, before moving away again.

"It is for now!" Tamworth growled back. He then called Mina and Des over to him.

"What's happening, Boss?" Mina asked. "What's going on?"

"What's going on is that you guys are getting him out of here!" said Tamworth, pointing towards John. "Take him back to headquarters and get him rested."

"Is he okay?" Mina asked

"He's just...fatigued," answered Tamworth. He then glared back at where Cassy had been sitting. The seat was empty, but he just managed to catch sight of her as she made her way through the crowd and out of the courtroom.

"You guys look after John," he told the others. "I'll meet you back later."

Afterwards, Tamworth left the courtroom and went after Cassy. He soon caught sight of her again and hurried to cut her off. When he caught up with her, he grabbed her by the shoulders and frog-marched her into a nearby room where they could talk privately. Once they were inside, Tamworth slammed the door shut and glared angrily at Cassy.

"Would you mind telling me what all that was about?" he demanded.

"It... it's in the past!" Cassy answered. "Like Jonathan said, we worked through it."

"Worked through what?" said Tamworth.

There was a brief pause while Cassy tried to find the right words to use.

"Jonathan and I were going through a rough patch in our relationship," Cassy began. "I was used to him being away on army missions, but there were also times when he was AWOL with me."

"AWOL?"

"He'd be home from service but not always be with me. He'd be out at the bar with his comrades, sometimes forgetting birthday gatherings and other important things between us."

"So, what happened?"

"Things started to become unbearable," Cassy continued. "I still loved Jonathan and all but the more he seemed distant from me, and the more he let me down, the more I felt lonely and unappreciated...so I made a mistake."

"Was it a one-night-stand?" Tamworth guessed.

"More like three," Cassy admitted. "I felt guilty afterwards and quickly called it off and confessed to Jonathan during a long heart-to-heart. He was hurt, understandably, and regardless of his faults, I knew it could never justify cheating on him like that. It was a strain on our relationship for a while, but we managed to make it through."

"So, if this was something which happened between you and Jonathan," Tamworth began, "then how come John doesn't know about it?"

"What?" Cassy remarked.

"Don't get innocent with me, Ms Haughton!" Tamworth growled. "I saw your face in the courtroom as well as his. He genuinely knew nothing about this affair of yours, and you didn't seem at all surprised by that; embarrassed, yes...but not surprised. So why *didn't* he know? Surely he possesses those same memories?"

"Because he doesn't!" Cassy blurted out, suddenly.

"What?"

"He hasn't got *all* of it," Cassy said again with a tearful sigh.

Tamworth moved closer to her and stubbornly folded his arms. "Enlighten me!" he ordered.

"When the time came to activate the clone," Cassy began to explain, "I didn't want us to go back to where Jonathan and I had been in our relationship. Even though we worked it through on the surface, it was awkward at times. Jonathan was constantly looking over his shoulder and questioning me whenever I went out alone or was home late – and I began to suspect him sometimes, wondering if he was ever seeing another woman, to get back at me."

It didn't take too long for Tamworth to put the pieces together, and probably the same pieces that Cottam and Judge Taylor-Beckett had picked up on also.

"Oh, bloody Hell!" he exclaimed as he stepped away from her slowly. "You changed him, didn't you! You went and had those memories deleted! That's why he doesn't remember...and that's also why you prefer him to the other Haughton!"

Cassy's said nothing in reply, and her silence confirmed Tamworth's theory.

"For heaven's sake, Ms Haughton!" he exclaimed again. "What the hell were you thinking?! Do you have any idea what you've done?!"

"I wanted to start afresh and have things as they were," Cassy pleaded, "but I swear that I only deleted memories of the affair and its repercussions, nothing more!"

"What you did was violate protocol for your own selfish needs!" Tamworth argued back. "Scars take time to heal and serve as reminders. Living with them and in spite of them...THAT is how you're meant to deal with it!"

He then walked over to the door to leave Cassy to reflect on her actions, but not before throwing out a stern warning to her.

"You tried to modify a designer-boyfriend in John as a quick-fix to your personal problems," he said, "but your reckless attempts to bury the past may very well have signed his death sentence!"

25

Over the next day or so, Tamworth and his team retreated back to headquarters to regroup and reflect on Cassy's recent confession. Although what she said was between her and Tamworth, it wasn't long before news outlets and internet forums were awash with rumour and speculation – damaging enough if nothing concrete.

That evening, Mina entered Tamworth's office and found him sitting back into his chair and pondering his next moves as he cupped and twisted his half-filled tumbler. He eventually caught sight of her and tilted his chair forward slightly.

"Any word from John?" Mina asked him.

"He's still in pieces over Cassy, I believe," replied Tamworth.

"Still not speaking to her, I take it?"

"Nope!"

"I guess he's not taking it too well, is he?" Mina remarked.

"No, I don't suppose he is," said Tamworth in a jaded tone. "All this time he's been fighting a legal battle to keep the life he's had with her, only to find out that she had an affair one time. Would *you* be happy with that?"

"No, I suppose I wouldn't," said Mina. "If anything, I'd be..."

"Confused?" Tamworth began to guess. "And incensed?"

"Well to be honest Boss, I *am* confused," Mina replied. "I mean, why did she do that?"

"Search me," Tamworth replied as he began to take another sip of his drink. "I'm not a marriage councillor."

"No, I mean, why did she have John's memories altered?" Mina then said. "I mean, didn't she and the other Jonathan work it out?"

"Apparently they didn't move on as far as she would have liked," said Tamworth.

Mina looked out into the direction of the room in which John had shut himself.

"So where does this leave them?" she asked.

"Back to square one I would think," said Tamworth, "which is where I am right now."

"What do you mean, Boss?"

"I'm afraid you're going to have to prepare him for some more bad news, Mina," Tamworth declared in a defeated tone. "I cannot fight this case for him anymore."

"You cannot be serious, Boss!" Mina exclaimed. Her eyes widened in astonishment at his sudden admission.

"We'll lose if we continue," Tamworth said. "There's no way we can convince the tribunal that our man has the most right to the identity of 'Jonathan Haughton' when he most certainly isn't; not now he has been altered."

"But what about his other rights?" Mina pleaded. "What about his right to a life?"

"A *different* life for John, with a different identity, *was* my fallback option," Tamworth explained, "but the actions of Ms Haughton have put pay to that. A clone activated before the original has died is one thing but tampering with the memories of a clone has always been a big no-no. This'll open up a can of worms on whether or not the 'design' of John can ever be permitted and whether or not his continued existence would encourage others out there to attempt the same thing."

"Is there nothing at all we can do for him?" Mina pleaded again.

Tamworth sighed for a minute and pondered before answering. His eyes tilted up to the featureless ceiling as he thought about his remaining options.

"I'm afraid there's not much left we *can* do, Mina, my dear," he started. "The only thing would be...but it's a long shot."

"What is?"

"Go back to basics," Tamworth replied. "Rather than fight for his identity, we must go back to fighting for his right to exist, as you suggested a moment ago. If I can convince the tribunal not to dispose of John as a one-off special consideration, and then maybe talk to Cottam again and see if I can get him to agree to allowing John to live with a separate identity. If we are successful, John will live, and afterwards, it will be up to the lawmakers to close the legal loopholes and prevent cases such as this from ever happening again. No doubt Cottam will demand we forfeit our counterclaim, which would be more than reasonable at this point."

"You *know* what John would say about that plan," said Mina. "Where would it leave him and Cassy?"

Tamworth paused for a moment before answering.

"He may have to forfeit her as well," he said. "Assuming he still wants to be with her after all that's happened."

"And what about his son, Jack?" Mina said sternly. "Do you think he'll be so ready to give him up too?"

"He may not have a choice," said Tamworth, shaking his head. "If we fight this and lose, then John may die. If we yield, then there is a slim chance that 'Jack's father' may live. Perhaps one day they could meet up again but..."

"How can you be so cold about this, Arnold?" Mina rebuked. "John's done nothing wrong! Nothing! He's about to have everything taken away from him and you just sit there with your drink and your pathetic arrogant wisecracks while...while he's hurting!"

"Perhaps *you* could comfort him," said Tamworth provocatively, catching Mina off guard. If his intention had been to bait her...it worked.

"Oh? And what's that supposed to mean?" she demanded.

"Well, you obviously care that much for him," Tamworth remarked, "and with Cassy possibly out of the picture..."

Mina's eyes narrowed in annoyance at what Tamworth was insinuating.

"Are you serious?!" she said accusingly. "Or is it the drink talking...*again*!?"

"Mina, are you really blaming my drinking habits for the way you behave around him?" Tamworth responded. "I know you like to provide a sympathetic ear for listening and a comforting shoulder to cry on – but there's a big difference between a 'hug' and a 'cuddle', you know!"

"What?" Mina exclaimed. "Is that what you think has been happening?"

"Is it not?" said Tamworth.

"No!" Mina protested in disgust.

"Well, I suppose we can add that one to my ever-growing list of misfires," Tamworth replied with raised eyebrows, taking yet another sip from his tumbler.

"Unlike you, I actually *care* about what happens to John!" Mina argued back. "To me, he's not just some prop in a pathetic vanity project!"

"Well, I don't pay you to 'care', Mina!" Tamworth said sharply as he began to show a slight annoyance towards her impetuousness. "I pay you to..."

Tamworth didn't have time to finish his point. Within seconds Mina had leaned forward, grabbed hold of the jug of water that was situated by the whisky bottle and threw its contents towards him. She then slammed the empty jug back down onto the table and glared at her soaked and visibly surprised employer.

"You know, Arnold," she barked afterwards. "You can be a right jerk sometimes!"

Although Tamworth was initially startled by Mina's impulsive act, he kept his composure, determined to get the last word in.

"My my...was my humour too dry for you?" he chuckled sarcastically, as he began to pat himself down.

"Got to hell!" Mina barked back; and with that, she turned around and stormed out of the room, leaving him drenched, cold and alone.

***

Elsewhere, John was having a difficult time processing the recent revelation about what Cassy had done. Despite Tamworth's attempts to explain the context to him, he remained confused and upset. He could not understand why Cassy had deleted those memories from him, nor did he have any idea what to feel. After all, the affair itself took place a long time ago and hadn't involved him directly, but now that he had become aware of the affair, there was now a trust issue developing – one that will inevitably eat away at them both, as it had done before with the other Jonathan.

That said, Cassy and the other Jonathan had moved on from it before and so maybe he could as well.

'*If I could just speak to Cassy alone,*' he thought to himself, '*maybe we can talk things through...move on together...but this time I won't make the same mistake as him. I'm better than that – better than him. This time I'll forget.*'

But beyond the inner ponderings, John was also aware of the reality – that in terms of memory, and perhaps thought as well, he was Jonathan Haughton. Simply forgetting and moving on was a task easier said than done. After all, the other Jonathan no doubt believed the same, and look where it had got them.

John sat quietly in the dark and remained silent and confused. The food that was set beside him, his favourite chicken wings, remained untouched and cold. He didn't feel like eating anyway. Instead, he stared in an almost trance-like state at the viewscreen as he flicked through the many television channels. Each channel, one after the other, was the same thing – news updates, coverage of the tribunal and scenes of the gathering crowd outside the Tamworth estate. Eventually, he caught sight of an image on the screen which grabbed his attention. He switched back to it and beheld the face of Tommy Dale. He was being interviewed by the press on the day's events.

"I've said it before and I'll say it again," Dale began. "This cannot be allowed to continue! Clones with engineered memories?! This is something straight out of a horror story! I tell you now that this is a very slippery slope. You allow this one through and you allow more."

"Are you still confident of Jonathan Haughton's victory?" asked the journalist questioning him.

"I've *always* been confident of Mr Haughton's victory," Dale answered. "I just want to see that all is done right by the law."

"And what of the clone?" the journalist then asked. "Are we to assume that you are in favour of his disposal, should the law require it?"

"I believe that the law *does* require it," said Dale. "That at least is my interpretation."

"But what of the opinion of others?" said the journalist. "The numerous polls out there that show many people opposed to the clone's disposal?"

"Ah the old bandwagon fallacy," Dale remarked with a cheeky, confident grin. "There was a time when most people thought the earth was the centre of the universe, but that didn't make it so. If our laws can be so easily swung by ignorant opinion, then we as a nation are truly lost."

"But some people out there are suggesting that you are likening the circumstances of the clone to those of some draconian Dangerous Dog Act," the journalist suggested. "Scheduled for destruction based on breed while not actually committing any offence."

"I think his battered and bruised human counterpart may disagree with you on that one, my friend," Dale suggested.

"So, you *do* believe the clone was responsible for the attempted murder of Jonathan?"

"My beliefs are irrelevant," Dale answered slyly, "which is precisely my point. It is the law that should decide."

"And should they decide to let the clone live?"

"Foolish...and unlikely...but c'est la vie. However, if you ask me, that clone was doomed from the beginning. In a way, I feel sorry for him with the lawyer he's landed himself with."

"You mean Arnold Tamworth?" the journalist asked.

"That washed-up manipulative charlatan doesn't give a fig about him," Dale continued. "He just wants to upset the apple cart. A modern-day King Canute who thinks he can reverse the tide of opinion."

"Yes," the journalist appeared to acknowledge but then slyly pointed out that King Canute actually tried to demonstrate that he *couldn't* alter the tide. Unfazed, Tommy Dale smiled and continued.

"And after that demonstration, he hung up his golden crown and never wore it again," he said, "as Mr Tamworth ought to when this is all over."

"Indeed!" quipped the journalist as he began to turn to face the camera.

"If I may be permitted to add one more thing," Dale then said before the journalist could conclude. "There was a time when Mr Tamworth and I batted for the same team, so to speak."

Upon hearing those words, John's eyes began to widen in curiosity and as he started to pay more attention, he noticed Tommy Dale turn to face the camera, almost as if to speak to him directly.

"Now, I'm all for a fair trial and all," Dale continued, "but if I were in the clone's position...and if you're out there watching this, clone...I'd have probably done my homework first on the man who would be representing me. And don't just take my word for it. Check the records, check the internet and check all the videos...and then ask yourself whether or not your man is doing all of this for you...or really all for him?"

26

While the mood at Tamworth's headquarters remained sombre following the recent revelations and Tommy Dale's television appearance, the same could not be said for Edmund Cottam and *his* team, where the chicken wings ordered in for celebration were almost depleted.

"To the first of many victories!" Jonathan declared triumphantly.

"Agreed," said Cottam with a satisfied smile. He was careful not to express too much excitement. He knew they still had to tread carefully.

"And it's all thanks to you, Edmund!" Jonathan declared. "I couldn't have pulled it off without your coaching and guidance."

"It's really thanks to *you*," Cottam replied. "Not many people have managed to rattle Arnold Tamworth like that in a courtroom. It's about time he was knocked down a few pegs."

"And the clone, of course!"

"Yes, him too," Cottam agreed, "but we mustn't get complacent. We have them on the ropes for now but who knows how long that will last. That thing about Casandra's affair really touched a nerve with him though. Was that...true?"

"Every word of it," said Jonathan. "But the past is the past and Cassy and I got over it long before my disappearance...but the interesting part about it is that 'John' didn't know,"

"Yes, I noticed that too," Cottam nodded. "Something happened there...and we need to work on them to find out what it is."

"I can tell you what happened right now!" said Jonathan. "They messed with his mind back at the clinic. He has no memory of it...because he literally has *no* memory of it. I know the difference between denial and obliviousness and that clone really had no idea."

"If they *have* deleted aspects of his memories...or rather *your* memories, then we have them bang to rights," said Cottam. "Obviously the amount of memories uploaded into a replacement clone is subject to the monetary cost, but deliberate cherry-picking has always been illegal. Alas, all we have, for the time being, is speculation rather than proof."

"So how do we get it?" Jonathan suggested. "Do we bring him in and interrogate him?"

"You'd be interrogating the wrong person," Cottam replied, shaking his head at the thought. "It is unlikely that the clone would consciously be aware of such alterations. Nevertheless, we'll see what comes out. My advice is to take what we have right now."

"And what *do* we have, right now?" Jonathan asked.

"I received word from Mr Tamworth not long ago," Cottam revealed. "He's offering to...negotiate."

"Negotiate?" Jonathan remarked. He sat up quickly as the news piqued his interest.

"Tamworth is offering to retract his client's counterclaim to your identity," Cottam explained. "If the terms are agreed upon then you win. You get back what you lost before your disappearance, and possibly more if you decide to pursue the clinic through the courts for their part in this sorry mess."

"And what are *his* terms?" Jonathan asked. "I suppose he'll want me to leave his clone man alone!"

"That's more or less it," Cottam nodded. "If there is scope for preventing John's disposal then he is prepared to back down and possibly secure a new name for the clone by court order. Furthermore, Mr Tamworth is even prepared to back a further motion to prevent situations like this from ever happening again."

Jonathan paused momentarily and began to think about the offer.

"Of course, I will only accept the offer with your approval," Cottam then added.

"And what of Cassy?" Jonathan asked. "Do I get her back? And my home?"

"That's not really for me to decide," said Cottam. "Or the courts for that matter."

"Then we may have reached an impasse," Jonathan grumbled. "No matter what he calls himself he'll still be a thorn in my side as long as he's still around!"

"May I ask you something, Mr Haughton?" said Cottam as he poured himself a cup of tea. "Do you hate clones?"

Jonathan didn't immediately answer. He simply sat there and stared into nothingness – almost as if he were in a trance. At first, Cottam didn't think he had heard him, so he slowly moved closer to where Jonathan was sitting and spoke a little louder.

"What?" Jonathan remarked, turning quickly, and looking slightly surprised.

"Do you hate clones?" Cottam repeated, before adding, "Throughout this tribunal, you appear to have a certain...aversion to them."

"No, I don't hate clones, Edmund," said Jonathan, shaking his head slowly. "If I did then I wouldn't have invested in this replacement scheme in the first place. Although now I wish I hadn't."

"So, it's just him then?" Cottam guessed. "Just one clone?"

"Just him," Jonathan nodded again. "He's not meant to be here. Not yet. Can you imagine what it's like...coming home to discover a doppelganger in your place. He's taken your home, your woman..."

"I get the picture, Mr Haughton," Cottam interrupted calmingly, "but do you think Cassy will take you back if you have your clone disposed of? Think about it. I suggest that you win one battle at a time. Win the case first...and win Cassy later."

Jonathan fell silent and, for a brief moment, began to contemplate Cottam's advice. Cottam was still a little concerned by Jonathan's recent blankness. It wasn't the first time that he had mysteriously tranced like this, coupled with the fact that Jonathan had shown signs of agitation throughout the tribunal.

'*Was this fatigue?*' he asked himself.

A few moments later, Cottam's thoughts were interrupted by a knock on the door. When he answered, he saw that it was one of his clerical assistants.

"Sorry to interrupt, Mr Cottam," she said, "but there is a Mr Dale at reception. He says he has no appointment, but he seems very insistent to see you both."

"Tommy Dale? Here?" Cottam remarked. "You'll have to tell him to come back with an appointment, Cheryl. I've no time for..."

"He's here because *I* invited him!" Jonathan interjected. Cottam turned and looked at Jonathan with bewilderment. "You?" he commented.

"I want to hear what he has to say," said Jonathan. "It is the least I could do for the man who saved my life."

"Mr Haughton," said Cottam nervously. "I feel I must advise you against his involvement. His reputation alone might scupper..."

"Nevertheless, I want to hear him out," Jonathan insisted, again growing more agitated. "Bring him in!"

Cottam turned back to Cheryl, his secretary, and quietly nodded. A few minutes later Tommy Dale was escorted up to Cottam's office. He sat down and rested himself against his walking stick. He said nothing initially but instead offered a cheeky smug smile towards the other two.

"Well," he finally spoke, "here we all are and with endgame approaching."

"We're not out of the woods yet," Cottam warned. "We've only rattled them. Nothing more."

"Yes, I must congratulate you both on your efforts to date!" Dale chuckled. "And my compliments to you, Mr Cottam, for helping our young man here get one over on the illustrious Arnold Tamworth. I must say, that alone made my day. But while I don't doubt your capabilities and legal expertise, Mr Cottam, I am not entirely convinced that you have what is needed for that final push to the finish line."

"Push?" Cottam remarked, slightly insulted. "How so?"

"With all due respect, Mr Cottam," Dale explained, "you and I handle things, shall we say, rather differently, wouldn't you agree?"

"I handle things fairly and *legally*," replied Cottam defensively.

"As do I," said Dale, with a slight smirk. "But I learned many years ago that there's a *Greek* way of doing things and a *Roman* way of doing things."

"What do you mean?" asked Jonathan.

"What I mean is," Dale explained, "your lawyer here, while very good at his job, likes to handle things as the ancient Greeks would. In medicine, the Greeks would analyse the symptoms, diagnose, and then provide the necessary remedy for the problem to go away. They also applied this line of thinking politically – whenever they encountered a threat, they would analyse the enemy, work out their weaknesses and defeat them accordingly – and be ready for that threat should it ever return."

"And the Roman way?" Jonathan asked.

"The Roman way was far more pragmatic, my boy," said Dale. "While the Greeks focused on the 'cure', the Romans focused on 'prevention'. They drained swamps and passed laws on public health. They took steps to ensure that people didn't get a disease in the first place. Politically if you attacked Rome, you either ended them or they ended you. They didn't sit back and wait to be attacked again. They followed their enemies back, hunted them down and utterly destroyed them...making sure that they were never a threat to them again – perhaps even salt the soil of their lands for good measure."

"So, you're the Roman?" Jonathan guessed.

"I am a conqueror!" Dale replied as he gave Jonathan a serious and determined stare. "You have them on the ropes, so I say go after them and take them out. You may never get another opportunity! He's a goddam clone for heaven's sake! A freak of nature – no... not even that!"

"Put them on dying ground and they shall live," Cottam then quoted out loud.

"Huh?" Dale remarked dismissively. "What are you harping on about?"

"Sun-Tzu's *The Art of War*," Cottam replied. "A cornered animal will likely bare its teeth. If we give them no way out, they *will* come out fighting."

"So, let them!" Dale chuckled. "As good old Abe said, *'A house divided against itself cannot stand'* – and from what I've gathered, all's not well on the Tamworth front."

"How do you mean?"

"What I mean is, my boy," Dale said to Jonathan, "they're divided right now and weakened. We should therefore weaken them further...and then strike! After all, you want your woman back, don't you?"

"Yes!"

"And you won't if *he's* alive. That I guarantee!"

John thought for a minute as Cottam attempted in vain to persuade him away from Dale's suggestions.

"So how do we weaken him?" he asked. "When do we strike?"

Tommy Dale's smile widened triumphantly at Jonathan's response.

"Well, my boy, the fightback has already begun!" he declared. "My media machine has been burning the midnight oil since the tribunal recessed to break the clone's popularity."

"You mean lie?" said Cottam.

"Lie?" Dale remarked with another quick chuckle. "Oh no! No! The truth will do just fine for now. I've seen to it that there have been enough leaks concerning the clinic investigations that can be tied to the clone – and while we don't have anything concrete, I'm confident it'll be enough to put pressure on the authorities to act. Soon, they will be unable to renew his diplomatic immunities...and THAT is when we will strike."

"But what of Tamworth?" said Jonathan. "He will no doubt still protect him."

"That's if he wants it," Dale remarked.

"How so?"

"As I've already said, Mr Haughton," Dale explained. "My media machine has been quite busy. My private investigators and agent provocateurs have been working around the clock long before you took me in. Working for *you*. As we speak, I have arranged for some of their findings to be smuggled over to John for his eyes only – and I believe that when he gets a hold of them and reads them...he'll probably ask for another lawyer."

Tommy Dale then poured out a drink from one of the decanters on Cottam's cabinet. He raised a glass towards Jonathan and smiled.

"Divide and conquer!" he said. Jonathan smiled back and nodded.

"And the proof, Mr Dale?" Cottam inquired uncomfortably. "Will it be there at the clinic? And if so, how do we go about getting it?"

"I'll get it," answered Jonathan with renewed confidence and determination in his voice. "One way or another...I'm going to get it!"

27

Just as Tommy Dale had planned, a large envelope of 'evidence' was successfully smuggled into Tamworth's headquarters. It was addressed to John, with further instructions that the 'urgent' documents contained be for his eyes only. There was a cover letter accompanying them, from the desk of T.H. Dale, which outlined the overall contents of the documents and his (Tommy Dale's) reasons for sending them. The wording of the letter came across as obnoxious as it was diplomatic. It made it clear that whilst Tommy Dale did not pretend to be looking out for the clone's best interest, he was, nevertheless, a stickler for a 'fair trial' and believed that John at least deserved to know more about the man defending him.

John sat expressionless as he poured through the documents, although he need not have bothered. Most of the information contained in them was no different to the websites that Tommy Dale had mentioned during his previous television appearance, which accused Tamworth of fraud and hypocrisy. There were further details that cast doubt on Tamworth's credibility, including the so-called 'Billy Reece incident'. Up to now, John had dismissed many of these accusations as hearsay or 'fake news', but the documents in his hand confirmed many of the anonymous and formerly baseless accusations about his lawyer – ones he hoped had been false and risked scuppering his own position if they were true. Angry, John clenched his fist tightly, mercilessly crunching the sheets of paper he was holding and, with a quick shake to the head, he stood up and briskly made his way to Tamworth's office. When he got there, he found the door slightly ajar and could hear Tamworth in his office, conversing with Alice Beecham about the publicity of the case and ways of diffusing the explosive revelations concerning the recent disclosures. John stood there and listened in.

"And what of John?" Alice then asked. "And the clones who work here? Will they still be protected?"

"I believe John is still safe enough here for the time being," Tamworth said, "but of course, once they start smashing our windows, I'll rethink my strategy."

"Well, I think this is starting to get out of hand, Arnie," Alice then replied. "According to recent reports, violent attacks against clones across the city have increased substantially since the case began and will probably get worse once the finer details of this become public."

"It's probably out there already, to be fair," Tamworth said solemnly. "I've been swamped all day by phone calls from victimized clones seeking my protection and wanting to use my office as some kind of sanctuary. I've had to advise them away of course, on account of the mob outside."

"You're enjoying this, aren't you," Alice commented lightly, "all this attention you're getting?"

"Admittedly, my involvement in the Haughton case has elevated me somewhat among the clone community,"

Tamworth replied with an arrogant smile, "I think they see me as some kind of saviour."

Unwilling to hear any more, John nudged open the door and stood there in the doorway. He still had the incriminating sheets clenched in his hand. Tamworth and Alice quickly took notice and ceased their conversation.

"Is everything okay with you, Mr Haughton?" Tamworth asked, immediately noting the expression of annoyance on John's face.

"You slimy son of a bitch!" John remarked with an accusatory growl.

"I beg your pardon?" Tamworth exclaimed with raised eyebrows.

"You don't care about me, at all," John said accusingly. "All this is just to feed your ego. You couldn't give a damn about me...or Mina...or any other clone for that matter!"

There was a brief pause between the two as they locked gazes and began to size each other up. Alice, meanwhile, sat there silently – unsure of what to say, or whether it was appropriate to say anything at all.

"I think we'll wrap this up, for now, Alice," Tamworth then said, still looking towards where John stood. He then dismissed Alice in order to leave him and John alone. Alice quickly packed away her things and slipped out, shutting the door behind her. The two men continued to stare at one another until Tamworth broke the silence.

"What are you playing at?" he inquired insistently.

"What are *you* playing at?" John responded angrily. "This isn't a game! My life is on the line and from what I've gathered, you couldn't care if I even existed!"

"Who have you been talking to?" Tamworth asked. "It's Cottam, isn't it? What's he been saying?"

"No-one's been talking to me," John replied. "But he was right about you, wasn't he? And Tommy Dale, too."

"Oh, Tommy Dale!" Tamworth scoffed as he threw himself back in his chair in frustration. "So now you're getting words of wisdom from that bigoted buffoon?"

"Bigot or not, he's right about you, isn't he?" said John as he forcefully flicked the sheets of paper across Tamworth's desk. Tamworth stared down at them with indifference.

"What the hell are these?" John demanded.

"My political voting records by the looks of it," Tamworth replied, "although you knew that already. So, what of it?"

"According to these, you voted against more clone-based recommendations during your tenure as a politician than you had ever voted in favour," John said accusingly. "And these documents over here record the numerous times you actively tried to put the clinic out of business! If you had had your way, then me, Mina, and many other clones out there wouldn't be alive today. So why are you even bothering with me?"

Tamworth poured himself a small glass of whisky from the bottle that was on his desk and relaxed back in his chair. He looked patiently at the visibly angry John before answering.

"In 1972," he began, "President Nixon, an outspoken critic of communism, paid a friendly visit to communist China – a meeting which led to a softening of relations between the two powers."

"Oh, spare me the pretentious history teacher crap and get to the point!" John barked.

"The point is, if Nixon, of *all* people, thought that such a meeting would be a good idea then it surely had to be,"

Tamworth explained. "Nobody else could have pulled that off without jeopardising their own reputation. And likewise, if I of *all* people am fighting for the rights of a clone then it surely adds more credibility to your cause, don't you think?"

"You are full of it, you know," said John. "And if I remember correctly, Nixon's reputation wasn't exactly one to aspire to."

"Well, not for *that* reason, anyway," Tamworth chuckled.

"And this stuff with the clinic?" said John. "No doubt back-up legislation to appease the tougher voters. How long will it be after my case is over before you decide to jump ship? You don't care if you win this case or not. You just want to upset the applecart. You're a political anarchist. How can I trust you, now, when you don't really care about clones?"

"Are you finished?" Tamworth said angrily. His facial expression suddenly switched to a more serious look. He then pointed to a nearby chair and gestured for John to sit down. John initially refused but after a more forceful tone of insistence from Tamworth, he eventually obliged; after which Tamworth continued to explain his position.

"Okay, Mr Haughton, cards on the table," he started. "Firstly, I did not deceive you about my intentions. My voting record is in the public domain for all to see and I stand by them, but believe me, I still have your best interests at heart."

"How?"

"You are right in the sense that if I had had my way, you would not exist at all, as you have so crudely put it," Tamworth began. "If I'm honest, I've never believed in the concept of human cloning. When we have a planetary population of over eight billion people consuming our limited resources, we certainly don't *need* to replace people. I also don't believe in the current reasons for human cloning. The whole 'replacement' thing sickens me. It's just a bunch of self-serving wealthy toffs who would rather live in denial and avoid the agonizing pain of bereavement. It's as pathetic as swapping out a dead hamster and praying that the kids don't find out. As Shakespeare put it: '*it is better to have loved and lost than never to have loved at all*'. If you ask me, the whole concept of creating a replacement human is a con – an exploitation of the rich and vulnerable."

"So why *are* you helping me if you don't think I should be here?" John asked.

"I am helping you," Tamworth answered, "because you *are* here."

John gave a puzzled look as Tamworth continued to speak:

"When scientists of the time produced the first successfully cloned animal back in the 1990s, a sheep they affectionately called 'Dolly', it was, to all extent and purposes, still a sheep. If you sliced it, cooked it, and served it on a plate with mint sauce and vegetables it would have still tasted like regular mutton. At the end of the day, regardless of *how* you came about, you are still a human being, Mr Haughton, which in my view entitles you to basic human rights. In short, while I may not agree with *how* you were created, I still recognise you for what you are – a living human being – and I will defend to the death you're right to live as such. But that doesn't mean I have to like you."

"And the Tamworth Manifesto?" said John. "Just more pretentious crap from a self-serving opportunistic hypocrite?"

"Don't confuse that legislation with something that promotes replacement cloning," Tamworth warned. "It isn't.

It's merely there to protect existing clones such as yourself from persecution. I'm not a monster, after all."

"Are you sure that's it?" said John. "Nothing to do with your career ambitions?"

"I would like to think that a genuine desire for equality in our society would be enough," Tamworth replied. "It has taken our civilisation long enough to move away from the petty racial distinctions that once divided us, and I for one resent the idea of a two-tier system where some are more equal than others. *That* is what I am fighting to prevent, Mr Haughton."

John relaxed more as he began to make sense of Tamworth's logic. In one way, he had a point, but at the same time John couldn't escape from the fact that he was still being used as a political pawn – and he resented being used. Tamworth continued to read John's disapproved expressions.

"You know you could be a lot more appreciative considering the circumstances," he said. "Trust me, nobody else out there would have been able to carry you this far. If it wasn't for me, you'd probably be dead by now – disposed of – either by the state or by your irrational counterpart; and that outcome looks more likely now thanks to your wife's selfish tampering!"

"Got to Hell!" John retorted. "When this is all over, I don't want to ever see you again! You stay away from me and my family!"

"Suits me, Mr Haughton," Tamworth replied with a shrug. "But let's see if we can make it to that stage first, shall we?"

The two of them didn't have time to fully defuse their spat. No sooner had they finished speaking when they heard an almighty smash coming from the nearby window.

Tamworth tensed up in his seat while John dived to the floor. Both of them quickly got up and crept over to the now-broken window. They saw the jagged rock on the floor nearby that had been hurled from the crowd outside, which had now grown into an uncontrollable baying mob. The two of them observed the people below shouting and hurling abuse. The guards managed to keep the gates firmly closed but were beginning to struggle against increasing numbers trying to force their way in. The fact the guards were armed was no longer a deterrent.

"I think our time here might be over," said Tamworth. "We may need to start packing very soon."

"Yeah, you're right," said John in feigned agreement. "I guess my time here is done!"

"Oh, you think you can just leave?" Tamworth remarked, staring at John, and reading his intentions. "Good luck with that. That mob out there will probably tear you to pieces!"

"That mob out there started because all of this got out of hand," John retorted, "but at least they're honest about how they feel about me."

"Look John, I know you're hurting right now, I get it," pleaded Tamworth. "The tribunal, this whole Cassy thing...I appreciate that it's driving you insane right now, but I implore you to lay low and not do anything rash. Like I said before, I'm not in the business of defending a corpse."

"You might have more success if you did!" John barked back; and with that, he stormed out of the room and left Tamworth alone once again.

28

Following his spat with Tamworth, John retreated to his room and sulked in the dark. He was an angry man and angry at everyone. He was angry at Jonathan for the torment he's caused, angry at Cassy for her part in his mind-alterations and especially angry at Tamworth for what he saw as two-faced duplicity. John Haughton was fast running out of people to trust.

It was later when Mina entered the room – herself annoyed by Tamworth's insensitivity earlier but calmer and more composed than John seemed to be. She gently pushed open the door and knocked on it twice to alert him of her presence.

"Mind if I come in?" she asked quietly. John didn't answer.

"I'll take your silence as a 'yes', then," Mina concluded as she walked in. The only light in the room was provided by the glare of the telly, which was still showing unfavourable news reports of the case. Mina could see that John was trying to keep it together. Mina came in quietly, sat down beside him and said nothing until he spoke.

"You knew what he really thought about clones didn't you?" he said, avoiding eye contact with Mina as he spoke.

"John, I..." Mina began.

"I saw it in your face when we first met," said John, "when I made that quip about him genuinely caring for clones. I should have listened to my instincts back then."

"But he *does* care about clones, John," said Mina.

"Pfft! He cares about his career more."

"He's a politician, John," said Mina pleadingly. "That's what politicians are like, but that doesn't mean he doesn't care about *you*. He's trying his hardest to ensure that you live through this, victory or no victory."

John turned and looked at Mina.

"I don't like being used," he grumbled, "and nor should you!"

"Oh? How do you mean?" asked Mina inquisitively.

"He has other clones working for him," said John, "and yet he chose *you* to look after me. Now, why was that?"

"Because I'm the best," said Mina, "...and I wanted to."

"And because he thought your 'Collette' backstory might rub off on me somehow," John theorized, "and possibly butter me up towards accepting the option of having an alternative identity. It certainly would have made things easier for him."

"He means well, John," said Mina. "Admittedly when he's had a few drinks, he can be rather...direct...but believe me, he's out for your best interests in the long term."

"Well, I'm not sure he can help me now, Mina," John sighed. "Once my secret becomes public, that's it. I'm done for!"

"Arnold's gotten you this far," said Mina, "and while things are down just now, he's come back from worse. I'm sure that even if we lose the case, Arnold's gonna sort something out for you to protect you from disposal."

"Can he protect me from *him*?" said John, referring to Jonathan's determination. Mina knew immediately whom he was talking about.

"He'll try," Mina answered.

"Not good enough, Mina!" said John, shaking his head dismissively. "I know him more than anyone, remember? He won't accept any deal preventing my death and even if he did, he won't rest until I'm out of the way. There's only one thing for it...I need to leave."

"Leave?" Mina exclaimed in surprise. "You mean run away?"

"Call it what you want, Mina, but I've had enough," said John. "The only thing left for me is to leave the country now, while I still can...take Cassy and Jack with me..."

"No, John!" Mina pleaded. "You said yourself that Jonathan wouldn't stop hunting you. If you left now, without Arnold's protection you're going to make things so much worse for yourself!"

"Worse for myself?" John huffed. "How can things possibly be worse? I'm not going to stay here and wait for the all-clear to end me. They'll need to catch us first and I'm going to get a head start."

"But John, Arnold can still protect you." Mina pleaded again. "You're safe as long as you are here with us."

"But for how long?" John asked. He then drew attention to the distant sounds of the angry mob being kept at bay outside the headquarters. "I don't think even he can keep them out for long!"

"So, what would *you* want to do?" Mina asked, almost putting John on the spot. John thought for a moment and then suddenly had a brainwave of his own.

"Wait a second, Mina," he said as he began to spill his plans to her. "This whole situation came about because my memories had been tampered with before my activation, right? When certain memories had been deleted."

"So?" Mina nodded.

"So, what if we simply put those memories back into me?" John suggested. "Would they not have the original memories on file back at the clinic? If they do then we could simply restore them and upload them into me!"

For a moment, Mina seemed doubtful about the plan.

"So, what do you think?" John asked her.

"I don't know, John," she replied. "It's never been done before. We can't be sure it's even gonna work."

"That's because it's never *needed* to be done before," said John. "But if it *does* work then problem solved."

"Or it might create *new* problems, John," Mina warned. "Have you thought about that?"

"In what way?" asked John.

"Think about it for a minute," Mina began to explain. "Everything about you since your activation has set you apart from Jonathan. You said it yourself, that he's not been the same since he came back. He's quick to anger, easily confused and erratic. He's nothing like you. Maybe the absence of those missing memories helped to shape the person you are today. Maybe *that* is the person Cassy fell for. Do you really want to risk losing it all?"

"I can't see how that could happen, Mina," said John confidently. "It makes no difference now I know about the affair. Maybe this way I can better understand why she did it...with the bonus of having the complete package."

Mina sat there and said nothing. She continued to feel sceptical about the plan, which was made worse by the sounds of the roaring protestors outside. After all, how on earth were they going to make it past that lot?

"One thing is certain," said John, almost reading Mina's concerns, "I'll need some help getting out of here."

He then looked at Mina and took her by the hand.

"So how about it?" he then asked. "Are you with me on this?"

29

The next morning Tamworth stood behind his desk with his back to the door. He was just finishing up a tense-sounding phone call and when he hung up, he turned slowly and noticed Des standing there, holding his tray of breakfast, which, aside from the full-English platter, included an extra-large black coffee and a cold glass of water with some aspirins on the side. Tamworth looked ad Des slightly puzzled.

"Where's Mina?" he asked him.

"Dunno, Boss," Des answered. "I haven't seen her all morning. She must have gone out for some errands."

"Maybe so," Tamworth muttered, shaking his head slightly. "She's probably still in a huff from yesterday."

"Say what now, Boss?" Des inquired

"Oh, Nothing Des," Tamworth replied as he signalled for him to place the tray onto the desk. Immediately he saw the newspapers that were on the tray also and scanned their headlines. They didn't make for pleasant reading.

"Something up, Boss?" Des asked – although he need not have had to. He could read Tamworth's morbid expression to see that things weren't going so well.

"That was the court secretary speaking from the office of Judge Taylor-Beckett," said Tamworth with a frustrated sigh. "He was just informing me that John's diplomatic immunity from detainment will not be considered for renewal."

"But why?" Des asked. He picked up Tamworth's coffee and handed it to him. Tamworth took a quick swig and shook his head from side to side rapidly in a bid to wake himself up properly.

"They told me they were unhappy about recent revelations concerning John's alterations at the clinic," Tamworth explained. "They feel that extending his immunity at this time would be...how did he put it...'inappropriate'."

"Well, that sucks!" Des exclaimed. "And it doesn't leave us much time either."

"It expires *today*," Tamworth revealed. "After today they can file for his arrest, bring him in and there will be nothing I can do about it. Either we get things sorted with the case soon or we may lose John altogether – and it would be unwise to separate him from our protection even if he was under police custody. It's bad news whichever way you look at it."

Tamworth then signalled for the glass of water and aspirin and as he did so, he noticed that Des had something wedged under his arm. It appeared to be a folio.

"What's that you've got there?" he asked him. Des took out the file and placed it on the desk.

"Just something I came by which I think might be useful to you, Boss," he answered with a smile.

Tamworth didn't read the file immediately. He simply stared down at it, and then looked at Des' grin again.

"Enlighten me," He demanded.

"I was doing some light reading of the leaked documents gathered so far regarding the clinic investigations," Des began to explain. "These ones here, relate directly to Jonathan Haughton."

"You mean *John* Haughton?" Tamworth corrected him.

"No, Boss," Des insisted. "I mean *Jonathan*."

"Well, you have my interest for now," Tamworth remarked. "So, what's in it?"

"I've not looked at the whole thing myself, Boss," Des began, "but these particular files refer to Jonathan's disappearance during the mission and why the vehicle he was in had crashed."

"It was shot at, wasn't it?" said Tamworth. "At least that's what the official report suggested."

"And as far as the official report was concerned it certainly *looked* that way," Des continued. "But more, let's say, 'unofficial' reports, point out that the location of the wreckage was nowhere near their intended target, and what's more...Jonathan was the one driving."

"So, what of it?" Tamworth asked.

"Jonathan Haughton remembered nothing of the crash itself," Des pointed out. "All he remembered was a sudden dizziness taking hold en-route to their objective, followed by an overpowering migraine. Then he woke up alone among the wreckage. There was no indication of enemy interference."

"Are you suggesting that Jonathan crashed the vehicle himself?" Tamworth asked.

"Not intentionally, if this report is anything to go by," Des suggested.

"Des," Tamworth insisted, trying to hurry him to the point. "What *exactly* does the report say?"

"Well, Boss," Des began, trying to speak more plainly, "the report appears to have found some link between what went on at the clinic and the crash that wiped out Jonathan's team. Financial records show that Jonathan had been a regular visitor to the clinic – something Jonathan himself admits to. He opted for regular memory uploads in case he was ever killed in action, and as a result, the authorities have started looking into the possibility that such regular contact with the machine might have messed with him in the head somewhat."

"In what way?"

"They think it might have caused some subtle damage to his brain, which caused him to black-out completely during his mission. They believe it was some sort of neural shock. That's why he had no memory of who he was when he woke up. It was as if his brain had temporarily reverted back to its factory settings."

Upon hearing Des' theory, Tamworth's face lit up in delight.

"Des, you genius!" he said gleefully. "Your words have sobered me up more than this coffee ever could. Tell me more!"

"Certainly, Boss," Des obliged. "Further investigations have uncovered other cases of adverse mental effects on clients who used the upload machine regularly, ranging from epilepsy to amnesia. I guess Jonathan's symptoms were more distinct because he was there so often. Whatever the machine does to retrieve and copy people's memories, Boss...it's doing something else as well...and it's not pretty. Research also seems to suggest that discontinued use would do little to reverse the damage caused already."

"Well, I must say even I'm astonished, Des," Tamworth commented. "And I can also see why they might have tried to hide it. That's one hell of a smoking gun you've brought me."

"Thank you, Boss."

"So, all of this really *is* the fault of the clinic," said Tamworth. "Gross negligence at best! It'll also explain Jonathan's apparent erratic behaviour as well. Both John and Cassy have commented before that he hasn't been the same man since he came back – and all this time we thought it was PTSD from the mission."

"I suppose the question now is how you plan to use this, Boss," said Des.

"Oh, I plan to use this, alright!" Tamworth declared. "Just humour me for a minute, Des, and hear me out."

"Alright Boss! Shoot!"

"Let's just say that the upload machines at the clinic have indeed messed with Jonathan Haughton's mind in the long-term. It might be safe to say that the damage had been happening for a while but hadn't yet been detected, right?"

"Right, I guess so."

"So, what if Jonathan's mind was already damaged enough by the time of his final upload. Wouldn't those problems theoretically manifest in the clone also?"

"I don't know, Boss," Des remarked, looking slightly confused as he tried to keep up.

"Either way I might be able to see a way around this mess," Tamworth explained carefully. "If my theory is correct, then by that logic, not only has the clinic messed with the clone's memories...it is also responsible for messing with Jonathan's also."

"Go on?"

"Jonathan's mind hasn't been all there anyway. There have been times he's shown confusion, forgetfulness and even aggression, apparently...and all the fault of the clinic. So, who cares if aspects of John's memories have been deleted now? There's every chance that Jonathan will lose those same memories eventually at this rate. Besides, who's to say that any mental problems being downloaded into the clone wouldn't have erased those memories anyway in the long term?"

"I kind of get it now, Boss," Des smiled.

"Damn right!" Tamworth cried out jubilantly. "I think this revelation of our own just might do the job of saving our John's skin. We just need to convince the jury out there that John's absent memories would have been inevitable even without the alterations. It won't win us the case, but it might just save his neck!"

Des and Tamworth rejoiced at the plan and began to put things into action.

"Go get Mina and John in here, now!" Tamworth ordered. "They're going to want to see these files also."

Des began to move towards the door but before could leave, one of the telephones on Tamworth's desk rang out and Tamworth stopped Des in his tracks.

Tamworth picked up the phone and spoke to the other end. Des looked on as Tamworth's face dropped slightly, trying desperately, but failing miserably, to conceal the inconvenient news being given to him.

"Yes," he said down the phone. "Yes...Righto. I see. Ok, thanks for the update."

He then put the phone down and bit his lip in an awkward panic.

"Something up, Boss?" Des inquired.

"You could say that," Tamworth replied. "That was one of my operatives at the police station. It looks like we're going to be having some company very soon!"

"Soon? How soon?" Des asked.

"Very soon apparently," Tamworth replied. "Evidently our opponents are wasting no time in taking advantage.

Word's out that they're preparing to send a squad round to pick him up and take him in for questioning."

"What for?" Des remarked. "What are they gonna charge him with?"

"I don't think that really matters to them right now," said Tamworth. "It might be to do with the recent investigations at the clinic. Then again it could be to do with that previous attempt on Jonathan's life."

"But he wasn't anywhere near him that night!" Des insisted. "Believe me, I know."

"All I know is they're on their way and we're running out of time," said Tamworth. "They might even want to talk to us as well."

"So, what do we do now?"

"I want you to find Mina and tell her to stay with John," Tamworth instructed. "Then get the guards ready. Nobody gets through those gates unless they are genuine police officers!"

"And if they are?" Des inquired.

"If they *are* then there won't be much that we can do to stop them," said Tamworth. "In the meantime, I'll get Miss Beecham on the line to initiate damage control."

Des nodded and left the office. With precious little time remaining, the staff set about making rapid preparations for the impending arrival of the police. With Des on the lookout for John and Mina, Tamworth remained in his office and began dialling frantically. While he waited on hold, he thought about his limited options, and whether he would hand John over to them or try and sneak him away while he still had time. His thoughts were quickly interrupted by a sound on the other end of the line.

"Alice, you there?" said Tamworth down the receiver.

"I'm here, Arnold," Alice replied. "Is everything okay?"

"For now," said Tamworth, "but it might get a bit busier soon."

"How so?" Alice asked.

"I don't have much time to explain, right now," said Tamworth, "but I've just got a tip-off from one of my contacts at the Chicago Police Department. They're sending a squad round to bring in the clone."

"My goodness, that's big news, Arnold!" Alice said in surprise. "Can I get in on this?"

"That's why I'm contacting you, Alice," Tamworth confirmed. "No doubt our visitors may bring their own media with them and I can't say that I trust their impartiality. I need us to strike first and give me time to figure things out for John. At least if his arrest is made public, they can't risk damaging him."

"Well, you can count on our network for impartiality, Arnold," said Alice. "What do you want me to do?"

"Just the usual for now Alice," Tamworth instructed. "Activate the mic and cameras at your end, watch and record...and thank you. Tamworth out!"

As soon as Tamworth ended the call, he activated the cameras. He then sat back in his chair and watched the CCTV images of the outside of the building as the minutes counted down. So far, no signs of any police cars but he knew they were on their way. All he could see were the intolerant anti-clone protesters calling for John's blood and attempting to force their way past the guards.

'*How on earth are we going to sneak him through that lot?*' he thought to himself.

Just then, Des entered the room. Tamworth noticed he was all by himself and looking as white as a sheet.

"Where's John?" he asked.

"Gone!" Des answered. "And Mina too. I can't find them anywhere!"

"Gone?" Tamworth remarked. "Gone where?"

"I dunno, Boss," said Des. "I've looked everywhere."

"Well, where the devil are they?"

Just then, Des pointed towards the view-screen and drew Tamworth's attention to a couple of police cars and police vans pulling up outside the building. He looked at them carefully, for they had almost been fooled before.

"What do you want us to do about them, Boss?" asked Des.

"Their vehicles seem legit," said Tamworth. "We'll have to let them in. Once they've produced their credentials bring them up to my office."

Tamworth continued to watch the screen as officers poured out of the vans. They were heavily armed, but as with the vehicles, their weapons also appeared standard for police officers. Tamworth however, continued to remain cautious and double-checked the microphones for Alice.

Several of the police officers entered the premises, while the rest remained outside and helped the security guards hold the mob at bay. As instructed, Des escorted the main officers to Tamworth's office. They knocked and then entered. Before Tamworth had the chance to throw them off with his brash wit, the leading officer cut him off and started to speak.

"Mr Arnold Tamworth," said the lead officer, producing his papers. "We have a warrant to bring in the clone identified as 'John Haughton' and a second warrant to search these premises."

Tamworth took the warrant and perused it carefully. It looked genuine enough.

"Bring in?" said Tamworth. "You mean arrest?"

"We mean, bring him in for questioning," said the officer. "Think of it also as protective custody."

The officer then took out his identification card and handed it to Tamworth.

I am Captain Elliot Jones and my associate here is Sergeant Smith," the officer confirmed. "And we would appreciate your full cooperation in this matter, sir."

Tamworth looked at the officers' ID badges. Again, they appeared genuine, but that didn't stop him from raising his eyebrows in surprise when he saw what their names were.

"Smith...and Jones..." he commented as he scrunched his face in amazement, fully aware of the irony being played out.

"Really?" he then groaned.

30

Neither Tamworth nor Des knew exactly when John and Mina made their daring escape, but it wasn't long before the police had arrived. John's tactical thinking, embedded into his memories since he was activated, assessed the situation, and figured, wisely, that the best place to hide from the enemy was sometimes to be right under their noses. As the angry mob continued to shout, push, and throw objects towards the guards and the building, John and Mina snuck out when it was evening and, wearing dark hooded attire, they immersed themselves within the crowd, doing their best not to draw too much attention to themselves. When the police vans arrived, the crowds were forced to disperse to let them by, giving John and Mina the perfect opportunity to sneak away.

Through the evening, they stealthily made their way to the clinic, taking multiple means of transport and walking some of the way. Throughout the journey, they continued to keep their heads down to avoid arousing suspicion. Once they arrived at the Forever Together clinic, they found the place largely locked down, with most of the lights off and guards patrolling the grounds, albeit at large distances from each other. This gave John and Mina an opportunity to sneak through. Using the night to their advantage, the two of them snuck around and past the guards until they found their way in – a window that seemed to have been left open. They both climb in and looked around, using a small torch that Mina had nabbed from headquarters. The room in which they found themselves was nothing special, just a hospital room, so they carefully opened the door and scanned the darkened corridor. As they moved out, they noticed how locked down the place really was, for there was no automatic lighting responding to their movements and the nearby camera appeared to be deactivated - 'appeared' being the operative word, however, and taking no chances, they continued to slink carefully through the shadows.

They looked around carefully, trying to find their bearings, and as they did so, little snippets of memories started to return to them.

"I remember this place," said John in a low voice. "Not as dark, but I remember being around here."

"Me too," Mina whispered. "It doesn't seem as vivid as my official memories, but I *am* beginning to remember."

"Any idea where we are?" asked John. Mina shook her head.

"I don't quite know how to describe it, John," she said. "It's there but..."

"But what?" John asked. Mina paused briefly to rephrase.

"It's like waking up after having a vivid dream," she started to explain. "Much of it has gone out of your head already, and you quickly realise that it's a dream...but you still remember little things in great detail. You know, those parts of a dream that stay in your head and don't go away."

"I'm starting to feel that way too," said John. "I also have some memories of this place, but I've always looked back upon it as...a dream."

"One thing is for sure," Mina remarked, crossing her arms across her shoulders for warmth, "it's quite chilly in here...and kind of creepy."

"I know how you feel," agreed John. "I don't like this place at all."

"Well let's not stay here longer than we need to," Mina then suggested. "Where do you think they'd keep your old memories?"

"I'm not sure," replied John. "There's probably an archive room somewhere. I think they would have been digitally stored somehow. We just need to find the place."

They continued to look around, searching the rooms and the different levels. The more they searched the clinic, the more familiar the place became, and it wasn't pleasant. The more they remembered, the creepier it became. Each darkened corridor they approached with caution, and each mysterious clang or bang caused them to flinch and freeze like terrified rodents. Soon they arrived at a room that was all too familiar to them. It was a large chamber, containing rows and rows of tube-like containers – each large enough to fit a fully-grown human inside. However, this was different from what they remembered. Aside from the darkness and the eerie silence, it was also cold and empty. Not one of the tubes contained anything. John approached the nearest one and brushed his hand down the sides as more memories of the place came flooding back.

"I remember this," he shuddered. "This is where we are made, grown and kept...right before we are activated."

"Me too," Mina replied, also shuddering slightly. Her breath began to become heavier as she spoke. "I think..."

"What?" asked John.

"I think I might remember waking up in here," Mina said. "I remember looking out and banging on the glass, screaming for help, and men...men in white...they..."

"They what?"

"I... I don't know," said Mina. "I've not thought about it in a long, long time. I always used to think it was just a bad dream."

"That's not all!" John then remarked as a sudden realisation sent a chill down the back of him. "I remember others being here, in the other tubes. Some of them looked less developed than me. So, where are they?"

"Maybe they were activated?" Mina thought.

"So soon? And all of them?" said John. "I doubt that. Something's happened to them. Tamworth told me that with the clinic under investigation they've had to cease operations. So that might mean they..."

"Oh my!" Mina remarked as she too began to think the same as John. "They've been disposed of!"

"They might not have had any choice," said John. "Just dispose of them and refund the money. Ask no questions and move on! It's sick!"

"And I've got another bad thought, John," Mina then said. "How exactly *do* they dispose of a clone? We all know it basically means 'death', but I've never really thought about it."

"It's probably not something one needs to think about after making it through the activation stage," said John.

"But how?" asked Mina.

"I don't know," John answered. "Probably do something similar to an abortion for those in the early stages, and for those closer to activation...I dread not to think."

"John, we need to get out of here!" Mina exclaimed. "I'm getting scared!"

"They've...killed...all the remaining clones," John growled through gritted teeth, "like they were nothing...like we were just playthings to be tossed away!"

"Come on John," said Mina. She then took him by the arm and led him out of the chamber. Both had to pause for a deep breath to recover from the haunting memories rushing back to them. It was as if their very presence there had started to unlock secret stories embedded far down in their subconscious. They were frightened and angry.

"Murderers!" John exclaimed, still through gritted teeth and with fists clenched tightly.

The two of them proceeded to make their way down the next corridor. Eventually, they came to a useful map of the area that was fastened to the wall. They looked carefully and managed to locate the 'Archive Room' but there were several.

"We could split up here and go to each one," John suggested. "Are you okay with that?"

"I think I can manage that," Mina said unsurely.

"Ok, I'll look in Rooms A and B, while you take this passage and look in rooms C and D."

"What am I looking for, exactly?" Mina asked.

"I'm not entirely sure what it is physically," said John, "but anything to do with our saved memories. Check the computers if you can get into them. Also, check the filing cabinets for any paperwork and see if you can locate one of those upload machines. I cannot remember where it was but we're gonna need it if our theory works."

In the darkness, the two of them went their separate ways – each taking a different corridor towards their respective archive rooms.

Mina came to the first archive room. It was dark and the computers were all powered down. She tried to switch one of them on, but it did not respond. As she stepped across, she could feel her feet kicking piles of paper across the floor, and she could hear the bushing sounds as they moved. She shone her torch down towards the floor and beheld a mess of shredded pieces of paper strewn everywhere. Either the place had been searched recently or there had been a clandestine attempt to destroy any incriminating evidence connected to the clinic. Mina moved on to the next room and was greeted by a similar sight. Undeterred, she knelt down and started to pour through the remaining documents that hadn't been shredded.

Unfortunately, she didn't find anything connected directly to where John's original memories might be stored, or anyone else's for that matter, but what she *did* come across certainly made for interesting reading. It was a record of serious health risks to people uploading their memories into the banks. There were cases of adverse effects on the clients' mental well-being, ranging from slight memory losses, more common migraines and, in a more serious case, albeit rare, signs of an onset of dementia. There was no concrete explanation at present, but there seemed to be a direct correlation between the frequency of a person's memory uploads and the severity of their symptoms.

'This might explain why Jonathan Haughton has been acting so erratic,' she thought to herself. *'I've got to tell John...and let Arnold know, too.'*

As Mina continued to consider her next steps, her thoughts were suddenly interrupted by sounds of a commotion coming from down the hall. She could hear voices and what sounded like something, or someone, being thrown around. As she made her way to the area, she came across two figures struggling around one of the medical labs; with a dark-hooded man getting the better of another, who appeared to be one of the clinic's scientists. As the hooded man threw the other man around, he knocked over tables and chemicals and broke some of the glass containers. As Mina looked and listened, her eyes widened in horror. In the dark she couldn't immediately recognise the clothes...but she certainly recognised the voice.

"What did you do to me?!" shouted the man repeatedly, as he grabbed the trembling scientist by the collar and rammed him forcefully against the metal walls.

"Please, Mr Haughton, I can explain!" the scientist moaned. "Just...let me go!"

"You went and messed up my head!" shouted the other man, "and you're going to put it right! Get me into one of your fancy machines and put my memories back. *All* of them!"

"I can't!" the scientist pleaded.

"What?"

"It's not as simple as that, Mr Haughton. It only works one way. What you're suggesting has never been done before. It's not...legal."

"Not legal?" the hooded man cried. He then raised his arm up to strike the scientist hard, but at that moment, Mina ran into the room and grabbed his arm.

"John! No!" she cried out. "Stop it!"

John turned to face Mina. He looked at her slightly perplexed – almost taken aback by her presence. As he began to calm slightly, Mina continued to speak gently. She then showed John the papers she had found.

"I wouldn't use the upload machine, John," she cautioned him. "Here, look what I've found."

She handed John the sheets and continued to speak as he scanned them by torchlight.

"I think there might be something wrong with Jonathan," said Mina. "He used the machine so much that it might have caused some damage to his brain – perhaps some irreversible damage."

She then looked at the scientist for confirmation and asked him, "Isn't that right?"

The trembling scientist nodded frantically, still recovering from John's assault.

"This is a dark place John," Mina continued, "with dark men doing dark deeds. It's got to Jonathan and it'll get to you if you try to upload any deleted files."

"Files?" the scientist remarked. "What files?"

"The memories," said John. "The ones that I... I mean...*he* uploaded."

"There are none," the scientist replied. "Not anymore."

"How so?" asked Mina

"Once a clone has been activated, the account is emptied," The scientist explained. "It's the law. It helps to prevent multiple replicates from being created. Once uploaded we keep them stored until the next upload, if any, and then we wait until a physical clone has been successfully developed. Once the clone is prepared, we then upload the memories into it. We then keep a copy of the memories stored until activation and release. As soon as the release forms are signed and processed...the files are purged."

"So, there is no way you can return John's deleted memories?" Mina asked. "None at all?"

"Are you sure you have no copies?" John asked. "In case anything goes wrong?"

The scientist shook his head anxiously as an angry John looked on. However, John wasn't convinced. He could see the sweat running down the scientist's face and the fact that his eyes kept glancing out towards the corridor. John looked out in that direction also.

"You're lying," he then said accusingly.

"Please, Mr Haughton," the scientist begged. "There's no guarantee that we still have it stored and even if we did..."

"Then what?" Mina asked.

"If we did then it would wipe away all your new memories in the process," the scientist answered. "In theory, at least."

"What do you mean?" asked Mina in confusion.

"It's like...like reformatting a computer," the scientist began to explain. "To make room for the new update, the current files need to be removed. It would be like starting over."

John and Mina looked at one another briefly as they began to take in what the scientist had said. John slowly moved towards Mina to say something to her, turning his back on the scientist in the process, but as he did so he quickly spun back around and walloped the scientist roughly, sending him crashing to the floor and out cold. Mina was surprised by John's sudden, violent and disproportionate outburst.

"What the hell did you do that for?" she hissed. She knelt down to check the man over. Thankfully he was still alive.

"They've screwed me!" he growled. "I should never have let them."

"Let them what?" Mina asked, catching John's words but not quite understanding.

"Doesn't matter," said John, shaking his hooded head. "My memory files are still here, somewhere – that much, I know. We just need to find it and..."

"Are you mad?" Mina remarked, realising the fatal flaw in John's suggestion. "John, do you even realise what you're saying?"

"What? Why? What's wrong?" asked John.

"Well think about it, John," Mina began to explain. "If the process works as he claimed it did, then the only memories they would have in storage would be everything up to the last upload before Jonathan's disappearance."

"So?" replied John, still failing to realise the problem.

"But nothing else after that," Mina pointed out. "You would lose every memory of everything you've done following your activation – your relationship with Cassy...and baby Jack...you wouldn't have any memories of him either! Everything that sets you apart from Jonathan...everything which makes you unique...you would lose!"

John's eyes widened in fascination as Mina's theory began to sink in. He tilted his head upwards as he pondered and breathed deeply.

"I'm sorry it's not going to work this way, John," said Mina. "Besides, according to those files I found, using the machine might make things worse. After all, if it's messed up Jonathan then it might mess you up as well."

After listening to Mina's warning, John placed the papers down and forced a sly, pondering smile.

"Well, I found something even more unnerving back out there," he then said, as he pointed out towards the corridor. "Back that way."

"What is it?" Mina asked.

"Come, I'll show you," said John. He then guided Mina out of the room and down the darkened corridor. As they walked, he ensured that Mina was ahead of him.

"Where are we going?" she asked

"I... I'm not quite sure," said John, looking around the place, as if to find his bearings. "I *think* it was this way. Do you remember where I was heading when we split up?"

"I think it was Archive Room A," Mina replied, "and also Room B."

"Ah, that's right!" John remarked. "Do you think I'll still be there?"

Mina was instantly confused by John's strange wording, but before she could say anything, she felt strong arms clamping around her, with one hand covering her mouth. She struggled violently to break free but to no avail, and as John, or at least the person she *thought* was John continued to hold her tight, she realised that the hand across her mouth was also holding a damp rag with a strong chemical smell.

'*Chloroform*' she instantly thought. She wasn't sure if it was chloroform or something stronger, but whatever it was, was overpowering, to say the least. As Mina continued to struggle the noxious chemical began to take effect, weakening her by the second. As Mina began to lose consciousness, Jonathan (as it turned out to be) carefully lowered her to the floor and kept her there until she stopped moving. He then stood up and dropped the rag. He looked down at the unconscious Mina and grinned maniacally.

"Thank you, whoever you are," he smirked. He then looked up at the map on the wall and scanned for the Archive Rooms, A and B; and once he had found it, he made his way through the dark and now-silent corridors.

The clone, meanwhile, was still in Archive Room B, having searched Room A and found nothing. He was greeted by a similar view that Mina had found – shredded and burned papers strewn across the floor. Like Mina he also began to read through the papers, unaware of the similarly dressed figure stalking him from the shadows. Eventually, however, John came across a separate filing cabinet that appeared to hold details on the storage of human memory files and where the digital formats were stored.

"Bingo!" he muttered in delight. He then heard approaching footsteps coming from outside, and, assuming it to be Mina, he turned around and called out to her, only to be greeted by the lurching Jonathan standing at the doorway and brandishing a jagged steel pipe.

"Mina!" said Jonathan with a menacing smile. "So that's what she's called!"

"What have you done to her?" John demanded angrily. He stood up slowly and glanced down at the weapon that Jonathan was holding. Jonathan noticed where John's eyes were looking.

"What? Oh no, I haven't killed her, if that's what you think," he laughed. "I'm not a monster after all. *You* are, but I'm not."

"What the hell do you want?" said John.

"The same thing as you, apparently," Jonathan answered, slapping himself repeatedly across the back of his head. "I want to get my head fixed, but those pesky scientists have scuppered that one now, haven't they?"

Jonathan then prepared his weapon and raised it slowly into the air, causing John to assume a familiar fighting stance in preparation, his fists ready for action. Jonathan looked at him and smiled again. He lowered his weapon and threw it away.

"Nah!" he said mockingly. "That would be too easy."

He then adopted a similar fighting stance, which almost mirrored that of his counterpart.

"This is much more fun, don't you think?" he said.

"You tell me!" growled John.

"Okay," Jonathan smirked and nodded. "Let's settle this right now. Man-to-Man! Let's see how your sparring skills hold up to mine."

"Suites me," John replied, at which point the two men circled each other menacingly. As Jonathan continued to mock, John launched the first strike – a forward kick to Jonathan's ribs. Jonathan blocked it...but only just.

"Very good," he commented in a patronising tone. "You've got some fire in you after all. The clinic really did do a good job, didn't they?"

Soon afterwards, John attempted another move – a low punch towards Jonathan, but Jonathan countered and returned, tripping John in the process and sending him to the floor. John got up and wiped the blood from his cut lip.

"First blood," Jonathan chuckled. "Try again!"

John tried again and was countered for a second time. Jonathan laughed and continued to mock as if he was just playing with John.

"Remember what I told you?" he said to John. "Muscle memory. That's something you can never have!"

Despite John's efforts to scoff at the idea, there was no getting around the fact that in this instance, Jonathan was right, and it was folly to assume that the two were evenly matched for this encounter. As they continued to spar and tussle, a confusing conflict began to develop within John, between his mind and his body. In his head, he knew all the right moves to make, but his body behaved like a rookie on his first day at the gym. John wasn't used to this, but it was his first time putting those inherited memories of combat into practice; and against his more-experienced counterpart, it showed.

They continued their fight, with John giving as good as he could get with an occasional opening, the odd opportunities that Jonathan hadn't considered, which set them apart in terms of thinking – but inevitably it was Jonathan who was victorious.

Jonathan watched as the injured and exhausted John crawled about the floor.

"What were you going to do anyway?" said Jonathan. "Run away? Take my Cassy with you? Take my Jack?"

"She's MY Cassy!" John shouted back as he spat out a glob of blood to the floor. "And he's MY Jack!"

"Is that so?" Jonathan growled in a calculating tone. He then went over to the discarded pipe and picked it up again.

"This ends tonight," he declared as he raised the pipe above his head. "This ends now!" And with that, he brought the pipe down forcefully across John's face and knocked him to the floor. As John lay there unconscious, Jonathan knelt beside him and checked him over. He was still breathing. Jonathan paused briefly to consider his options. He raised his weapon again and prepared to bring it down onto the helpless John...and again if necessary.

'It would be so easy you freak! You laboratory freak!' he thought to himself, but as he raised the pipe as high as he could, a sudden realisation began to set in. As much as he wanted it...as much as it would potentially solve his problem, Jonathan knew that killing his clone there and then wouldn't help his cause in the long run. Jonathan may have been many things in life...but he had no intention of adding 'cold-blooded murderer' to his list if he could help it – nor would his actions inspire Cassy to take him back into her life. As he dropped his weapon to the floor he stepped over the unconscious clone and moved towards the filing cabinet that had caught John's attention.

"Nah, I ain't going to kill you," he said to him. "Like I said before...*I'm* not the monster!"

He then began to search through the same documents that John had found until he had found the relevant one – the location of his former memories.

"Bingo!" he commented with a grin.

Wasting no time, Jonathan activated one of the nearby computers and began to 'hack' into the system. Following the instructions as best he could, he managed to locate the collection of old memory files of the former *Forever Together* clients, including his own. They were in a folder earmarked for deletion and Jonathan sighed in relief to have found it in time. He then grabbed a nearby memory stick and placed it into the computer. He attempted to copy and paste his file onto the stick but was forbidden by the computer's secure server. It appeared that 'copying' files was impossible but as Jonathan quickly discovered, 'moving' them was not – so he dragged the whole file over and waited.

'They won't know,' he thought to himself. *'They're purging it anyway'*.

Once he had finished, Jonathan removed the memory stick, took the still-unconscious John by the leg, and proceeded to drag him out of the archive room and down the dark corridor. He shuffled slowly past each room until he eventually found the one containing the memory upload machine. Jonathan recognised it immediately, even with the dimly lit setting. It was a machine that he had used many times before, although he himself had never personally worked the controls. He quickly examined the machine and then hoisted John into the restraints. He then lowered the metallic headpiece of the machinery over John's head. John was still unconscious at this point but showed signs that he was starting to come round.

'*It matters not,*' Jonathan thought to himself as he began to flick some of the switches. '*By the time we're finished, he won't remember this day.*'

"You know, it didn't have to be this way," he then said tauntingly to John. "I offered to let you live. I offered you the chance to leave and live out your own little life – but as long as there was Cassy and the little one in your life, I should have known what your reply would have been."

Jonathan then began to power up the rest of the machine as he continued to speak.

"Throughout this trial, I kept asking myself, '*If I were the clone instead of you...would I back down?*'" he asked rhetorically. "Then I thought '*not a chance!*' – So how can I expect anything different from the man who was designed to think as I do? ... and at that point, I realised that as long as Cassy and Jack were around, you weren't going anywhere – but there can only be *one* Jonathan Haughton!"

At that point, John groaned a little more as he began to waken. When he regained consciousness, he found himself restrained and unable to move.

"Naturally, I cannot kill Cassy or Jack," said Jonathan, "as that would defeat the point of *my* existence in this world...and then the answer came to me – tonight even."

"Jonathan, what are you doing?" said John as he became more aware of where he was and what he was hooked up to.

"Let's just say I'm giving you a clean start," said Jonathan. "It's funny how neither of us had thought about it before, and I have your friend to thank for that. Mina, wasn't it? No matter...you won't know her at all once this is all over."

John began to struggle more against the restraints as the upload machine began to buzz into action, shouting threatening expletives towards Jonathan as he did so.

"I'll kill you!" he growled. "I'll rip you apart and see that you stay dead this time, you son of a bitch!"

"No, you won't!" Jonathan replied with a victorious grin. "Once I reload these files into you, you won't remember any of this...or anything at all from the last two years. No marriage, no Jack..."

"I'll still remember Cassy," John argued, "and like it or not, she'll still remember me!"

"That's true," Jonathan conceded as he placed his hands onto the final activation switch, "but I figure that if you so desperately want to be me...then I'll be *you*. Does that sound fair?"

John let off another tirade of expletives and threats as he continued to writhe against the restraints.

"I thought so," said Jonathan with a smile. "But don't worry, I'll take good care of them from now on. I'm gonna take them to Florida and see the sights. We've always wanted to go there."

Jonathan flicked the switch and the machine kicked into action. John felt a tingling in his head which began to increase in intensity. It was nothing he hadn't experienced before, compared to all the times Jonathan had uploaded his memories, but it was unpleasant, nevertheless. The knowledge that he was about to have everything deleted was unbearable. He was about to lose everything that made him unique, which set him apart from Jonathan – his very own identity.

Jonathan stood triumphantly as he watched the machine kick into action. Just then, his attention was drawn to the sounds of approaching guards coming from down the corridor. Jonathan knew that he had to get out of there but not before leaning in towards John to give him one final gloat and a warning.

"I'm afraid I have to go now," he whispered hauntingly into John's ear. "When you wake up, this will all seem like a bad dream...that's if you remember anything all."

As the machine continued to work, John remained still, breathing rapidly, and thinking hard about Cassy and Jack. John tried to clear his mind enough so that only those thoughts remained. He hoped that if he thought about them hard enough, they would still be there afterwards, but then again it might make them the first memories to go. Nevertheless, John continued to think only of his wife and baby...whatever was to happen, if they should even be the last things left in his mind...that would be enough.

When the patrolling guards finally arrived, they found John unconscious once again, and still strapped to the machine, but, like a phantom, Jonathan was gone.

31

The following day, Tamworth and Des were released from the police station after being brought in for questioning regarding the whereabouts of the now-fugitive clone. Initially, the police attempted to charge them with obstruction of justice and harbouring a fugitive. Tamworth, however, was able to use his legal intellect to rip apart those charges; namely that John had not been made a fugitive until after his disappearance, and that there was no evidence of obstruction because neither he, nor Des, nor any of the guards or staff back at headquarters, had resisted the police inquiries in any way. Upon leaving the station, the two of them stood outside the entrance and discussed their next moves.

"Well, that was a piece of nothing!" said Des sarcastically.

"They had nothing on us," Tamworth agreed. "Just a publicity stunt to try and discredit us before the next phase of the tribunal. They must think we have something on Jonathan."

"But we do, don't we, Boss?" Des commented.

"Yep, and they must surely know it," said Tamworth. "Hence this charade."

"So, what now, Boss?" asked Des.

"What now?" Tamworth repeated, before answering. "Now we try and find John before the authorities get their hands on him!"

"And Mina too, I'm guessing," said Des. "Where do you think they've gone?"

"You make it sound as if they've eloped," Tamworth said sarcastically, before adding, "No, I know where he'll be. He probably doesn't know about Jonathan's deteriorating condition. Right now, he thinks his back is up against the wall. He's a desperate man. I think he's going to run."

"Run?" Des remarked. "You mean flee the country?"

"If necessary," said Tamworth, "but he won't be alone. I bet he's round at Casandra's right now, packing up and preparing to leave. Oh yes...he's gonna run...but we need to get to him first before he does something *really* stupid."

Using public transport, Tamworth and Des made their way back to headquarters and found it a mess following the police's extensive and rigorous search. They then got into their car and drove to Cassy's address. When they arrived, Tamworth instructed Des to stop the car further down the road, where they then sat and waited. Eventually, they spied Cassy exiting the house with some bags, and loading them into her car. As Tamworth looked closer, he noticed her turning round to face the house and signalling to someone else. Although the large hedge obscured his view of who she appeared to have been talking to, Tamworth guessed that it could only be John. Tamworth then saw Cassy get into her car and drive away. He then saw his moment. He instructed Des to wait in the vehicle while he got out and crept briskly towards the house. When he got to the front door, he found it open ajar, so he carefully pushed it open and quietly moved in. He looked around the rooms on ground level and saw nobody, but Tamworth was convinced that John was around somewhere. He then heard faint sounds coming from upstairs, so he went up and had a look, but not before cheekily swiping a half-filled bottle of whisky, which he had noticed on the counter in the kitchen. Soon he spied what he assumed to be John, in the main bedroom, rummaging through drawers. He also took note of the open and partially filled suitcase resting on the bed.

"Going somewhere, John?" he asked him, catching John by surprise. John jerked round in a startled manner and when he caught sight of Tamworth, he breathed a sigh of relief. For a few seconds, he scanned Tamworth analytically and then continued to pack.

"You really need to lock your front door," Tamworth then said. "Especially in the current circumstances."

"Don't try to stop me, Mr Tamworth," said John. "We've made up our minds. We're leaving while we still have the chance. Me, Cassy...and Jack."

"You don't need to be so formal, John," Tamworth remarked. "Arnold is still fine, you know."

Tamworth then looked down at the bottle of whisky he had swiped earlier. "May I?" he then asked him.

"Do what you want," said John. "I don't care right now!"

Tamworth took a quick swig from the bottle and placed it onto a nearby table. He continued to look on as John prepared the bags.

"By the way, have you seen Mina at all?" he then asked.

"What?" answered John sharply. "Err...No!"

"Really?" Tamworth remarked. "We were kind of under the impression that she absconded with you."

"Well, I've not seen her," replied John.

"Well, she's missing then," said Tamworth. "That's not usual for Mina. She's usually quite reliable. It's a bit worrying, really."

Tamworth noted that John hadn't responded beyond an indifferent shrug.

"Does that not seem strange to you, John?" he went on.

"I am listening, Arnold," John sighed, shoving a pile of clothes into Tamworth's hands, "but as you can see, I've got other things on my mind right now, so make yourself useful and help me pack."

Tamworth placed the pile down, and as he slowly began to fold the clothes, the two men continued their conversation, facing away from one another.

"You don't have to do this, you know," said Tamworth.

"I'm afraid I don't have a choice," John replied. "There's no way the courts will let me live after what was done to me."

"A minor setback, John," Tamworth said, "but I assure you, the fight isn't over."

"How do you mean?"

"I think there's something wrong with Jonathan."

John paused suddenly when he heard that last comment from Tamworth.

"What do you mean?" he asked curiously.

Tamworth then told him about the clinic and the adverse effect the upload machines have had on Jonathan's mind. As he explained the facts, it wasn't lost on Tamworth that John's reaction to it was one of peculiar indifference. His confusion began to develop into suspicion.

"So, we could still be in with a chance, John," he then concluded cautiously. "Running away like this isn't the answer. There is a warrant out for you now and you can guarantee that all the airports will be monitored."

"At least we'll have a head start if we set off now," John insisted.

"You know, are you *sure* you haven't seen Mina about?" Tamworth then pressed. "I'm kind of surprised you're not that concerned."

"No," John said sharply. "When I left your place, I came back here to pack. Now, if you don't mind, I'm a bit pushed for time. I want to get out of here before the police arrive."

Tamworth didn't turn around to face John and instead kept folding the clothes on the pile as he spoke, but he was more cautious in his approach as his suspicions grew.

"None of this adds up, you know," he then commented. He got no response from John, so he continued to mutter, but loud enough for John to hear.

"Mina is missing, you seem more stand-offish and defensive...and the fact it's now been two days since the arrest warrant for you was issued. I'm rather surprised the police haven't staked this place out already...unless, for some reason, they know *not* to look here."

Tamworth did not get the opportunity to interrogate John further, or the man he initially assumed was John; nor did he have the chance to turn to face him directly. The next thing he knew, there was a sharp and painful crack across the back of his head, which caused him to fall to the floor and black out. Jonathan, as it turned out to be, had taken the opportunity to strike while Tamworth's back was still turned. He stood over the unconscious Tamworth and looked down at him with a menacing smile. The poetic irony of the whisky bottle being his weapon of choice was not lost on him either. However, he didn't have time to gloat because he suddenly heard Cassy pulling up in the car outside. Thinking quickly, Jonathan lifted Tamworth's limp body and slowly dragged and rolled it towards the nearby wardrobe. He opened its doors, made room at the bottom, and unceremoniously shoved him inside. He forced the door shut and wedged it closed with a nearby chair. He then picked up the broken glass fragments that he could see and covered the wet patches from the bottle that had soaked into the carpet. By the time Cassy was in the house, she was none the wiser to what had just happened. Jonathan, still posing as the clone, sealed the suitcase and made his way downstairs to greet Cassy; and once the car was packed, they took baby Jack with them and left.

32

The fact that Jonathan and Cassy had left the house had not gone unnoticed by Des, who was still waiting in the car. He had been briefly distracted by a phone call and when he noticed their car drive away, with no sign of Tamworth leaving the house, he ended his call and got out to investigate. After searching around the house, he came to the main bedroom and immediately picked up the familiar odour of whisky that had filled the room. He also noted the damp patch on the carpet and caught sight of some of the broken bottle. Within a few seconds, his attention was drawn to a chair that had been wedged against the wardrobe door to keep it shut. Des removed the chair and immediately the door sprung open, causing the semi-conscious Tamworth to limply roll out onto the floor. Des moved him so that he was upright and began lightly slapping his face in a bid to wake him up. Eventually, Tamworth opened his eyes and let out a dull groaning sound. The first sensation after regaining consciousness, aside from dizziness was a pounding headache. He delicately felt around where Jonathan had struck him and soon came across a tender and painful lump.

"You okay, Boss?" said Des.

"Eh? What?" Tamworth remarked, still dazed from the assault. "Oh, that son of a bitch hit me with something..." He then looked around the room and eventually cast his eyes over to the fragments of glass. He picked up the largest piece and examined it closer, as well as smelling it. "Oh, he's gonna be for it now, the son of a bitch!"

"Boss, I have something to tell you," Des began. "I don't think that was John that Cassy left with."

"Oh, you think?!" Tamworth barked sarcastically.

"No, I *don't* think," Des replied. "I've just got off the phone to Alice Beecham. She told me that the police have arrested John and Mina and are planning to hold them for questioning."

"What? John *and* Mina?" Tamworth remarked. "Why Mina?"

"Apparently they were picked up by security at the cloning clinic. They're being charged with breaking an entry, but they're at the hospital just now and under heavy guard."

Tamworth shot upright and attempted to stand himself up but collapsed back down, still dizzy. Des then stood up and gently lifted Tamworth to his feet and helped to hold him up straight.

"They're not going to leave it there," he grumbled. "They're going to hold him for a lot longer...and then there's Cassy and Jack to consider also."

"So, what now, Boss?" asked Des.

"Give me your phone, Des," said Tamworth. "I'm going to put a stop to this nonsense right now!"

He then took the phone and started dialling.

"If those sons of bitches think they can get the better of *me* then they've got another thing coming!" he grumbled. "Now I get the big guns! I'm gonna get him on assault, kidnap, fraud...and alcohol abuse."

"Say what now, Boss?" Des remarked.

"Oh, nothing," said Tamworth dismissively. "Just get the car ready!"

Des guided Tamworth to the car and helped him into it. As the car sped off, Tamworth continued to make his calls.

"You know where Jonathan and Cassy have gone?" asked Des.

"No idea," said Tamworth, "but we can deal with them later. Remember that we have to deal with John and Mina too, but at least we know exactly where they are. I'm gonna make a few more phone calls and have checkpoints at every airport and transport station. Might slow him down enough."

When they eventually arrived at the hospital, they quickly found the ward in which John and Mina were situated heavily guarded and, wasting no time, (but still needing help from Des) Tamworth headed in and began to work his magic. Through his phone calls he had pulled in all the remaining legal favours he could muster and already the police had been inundated with heavy calls from influential figures who still had some pull. Very quickly, Tamworth was able to browbeat the Commander to release Mina and John on bail (which Tamworth duly paid) on the agreement that both would return for questioning at an approved time and a further agreement that Tamworth himself be present for both interviews (especially John's).

Immediately Mina was handed over to Tamworth's care. John, meanwhile, was still recovering from his ordeal and remained in his room. When Mina saw Tamworth, she smiled and ran over to him. He appeared less thrilled and looked back at her scornfully.

"Arnold!" Mina exclaimed in delight. "I am so glad you are here!"

"I bet you are!" said Tamworth. "What in heaven's name were you doing at that place anyway?"

"We were trying to find a way to put John's lost memories back into him," said Mina.

"What?" exclaimed Tamworth. "You didn't use one of those wretched machines, did you?"

"No, Arnold. We just..."

"Then don't," said Tamworth insistently. "I have reason to believe those things are dangerous. Where's John anyway?"

"That's what I was trying to tell you, Arnold. Jonathan did something to him. He hooked him up to one!"

"He what?"

"I don't know how long he was in it for," Mina explained, "but by the time I woke up the guards had already removed him."

"So, what happened to John?" Des the asked.

Mina hesitated before answering. She then told them about what John had managed to tell her – about Jonathan's plan to re-install the original memory files, effectively returning John to his 'factory settings'.

"Such a procedure would mean he's lost everything since his initial activation," Des commented solemnly, shaking his head in disbelief. "If that's the case then he is truly lost."

"Woah! Wait a minute," Tamworth suddenly realised. "*He* said all of that to *you*?"

Mina looked back at him and nodded.

"So, he still knows you, then," Tamworth pointed out. "So, evidently he still remembers the incident...which means his memories are fine."

"The guards must have pulled him out of the machine before it had finished," said Des, smiling in relief.

"Safe for a few cuts and bruises, I suspect that our friend is just fine," Tamworth chuckled.

"How do you know?" Mina asked.

"Because I, unlike Jonathan, happen to know a bit about how the cloning process works," Tamworth explained. "The machine is used only for 'uploading' memories from paying clients, whereas inserting the memories into a clone is a far more delicate and time-consuming procedure. I doubt any of John's memories have been wiped. All it's probably done is create a digital copy of them, as it is meant to – but that doesn't change Jonathan's intentions, which are unforgivable."

Mina and Des both breathed a sigh of relief, while Tamworth requested that he be taken to John. When they arrived, they saw him in his room, sitting upright on the bed. The three of them entered the room and began to speak to him. Mina entered first and threw her arms around him in delight while assuring him that he was going to be okay.

"Arnold," John then spoke. "We discovered some things at the clinic that we think people need to know. We think it's done something to Jonathan. He attacked us when we were there and..."

"And me too," said Tamworth, "which brings me onto more pressing issues."

Tamworth called the police chief over as John and Mina looked on slightly confused.

"What's he on about?" John asked quietly. Des then leaned over and quietly filled them in about what had happened to Tamworth.

"He's done what?" Mina exclaimed.

"We think Cassy doesn't know," Des explained. "Arnold has already put the word out to the state's main exit points. We now just need to find out where he's taking them. Any ideas?"

Meanwhile, Tamworth was still bringing the police chief up to speed, in his usual confrontational manner.

"It's not that simple, sir!" the officer replied. "We've got a few cars to spare and I can maybe get some roadblocks along the state lines but for now we..."

"Spare me your logistical crap!" Tamworth barked. "We've got a fugitive on the run by the name of Jonathan Haughton. He has two hostages, a woman and a child, and should be deemed dangerous and possibly armed."

"He won't harm them," said John suddenly. "Believe me, I know him well, but he will still be dangerous. Right now, he is pretending to be me and trying to steal my wife and child away from me."

"Your wife?" the officer remarked, looking perplexed. "But aren't you a... I mean aren't you..."

"Oh, for the love of..." Tamworth exclaimed in frustration. "Just get us some damn squad cars!"

"And go where?" the officer insisted, but as he spoke his rebuke was interrupted by a quick suggestion from John.

"Florida!" said John as he suddenly remembered the last thing Jonathan had said to him. "He said he was taking them to Florida."

"Florida?" the officer remarked. "That's a big place. Anywhere specific he might have taken them?"

"Oh, I don't know," said John. "There's certainly plenty down there to keep a family entertained. The list of options is endless!"

"If he leaves Illinois it'll get messy," warned Des. "The more state lines he crosses the harder it'll be to grab him. Different laws down that way will probably be more sympathetic to him."

"The law is the law," The officer replied reassuringly. "If we want him, we will have him."

"And we'll need a couple of helicopters as well!" Tamworth added in a demanding tone. He overheard the conversation about Florida and factored it into his phone call.

The officer looked unimpressed and started to narrow his eyes in annoyance.

"With *no* due respect, Mr Tamworth," he began with a sense of growing impatience, "*I* will be the one directing this search and as such *I* will decide what we use and how. Is that clear?"

Tamworth, attempting to dominate proceedings opened his mouth to answer back but was quickly cut off by now-confident John, who immediately interjected.

"Just..." he began delicately as he placed himself between Tamworth and the officer. "Just find them please, officer, and quickly. The other Jonathan Haughton is pretending to be me, right now, and he has my wife and child with him. I know you might not see her as such, but to me, Cassy is my wife."

The officer quickly composed himself and gave John an approving nod.

"We will do our best within the confines of the law, Mr Haughton," he reassured him; and with that, he quickly left them to make the necessary arrangements.

"You didn't have to be so uptight about it, Arnold!" Mina then commented.

"You know, you're probably right, Mina," Tamworth conceded with a slow shake of his head. "However, I've not had the best experience with the police in recent times, and I'm still a bit irked about it."

"We all are," said John, "but right now I don't want us to waste any more time getting my wife and child back!"

"And find them, we will," Tamworth reassured him, "and then we can put an end to this charade once and for all. Des! Get the car ready!"

33

The car that Jonathan was driving was eventually been picked up by a police helicopter and, unknown to Jonathan, his location had now been relayed to all nearby precincts, with police cars converging from numerous directions.

Jonathan, meanwhile, was becoming increasingly agitated by the sounds of baby Jack coming from the back of the car.

"I can't believe he cries so much," said Jonathan to Cassy. "Surely it's not feeding time again!"

"He hates long journeys, John," Cassy replied. "You know that."

"Can't you shut him up or something? It's doing my head in. I'm trying to think."

Cassy stared impatiently at Jonathan as he drove. He seemed more erratic than usual but for the time being, she put it all down to the stress of their escape. Still, she was surprised and rather upset that he would be so irritated by baby Jack.

"You think this is easy for any of us, John?" she said, with an annoyed expression. "We're all on the run – all of us, not just you. We're leaving everything behind. Nothing is going to be the same again."

"I'm sorry," sighed Jonathan. "And you're right. I shouldn't be taking it out on you two. I'm just a little excitable that's all, but what matters is that we're all together again. How it should be...how it should always have been,"

Jonathan said the last part so quietly that Cassy didn't pick up on the last few words, but before she could get him to repeat what he said, her attention was suddenly drawn to the sight of several police vehicles approaching their position from up ahead.

"John, do you see that?" she remarked.

"Yes, I see them," Jonathan replied. "Hang on!"

He then caught sight of several more vehicles in his rear-view mirror that were approaching from the other side.

"Over there, John!" said Cassy suddenly, pointing outwards. "Take that left there."

Without slowing, the car suddenly skidded onto the next turning and began to accelerate further. Baby Jack continued to wail in the back as Cassy turned around and tried desperately to settle him. As she turned, she looked out of the rear window and saw the police cars turn onto their road and continue their pursuit.

"They're following us, John!" she panicked. "They've found us!"

"Just sit tight," said Jonathan. "They've not got us yet."

As they drove, Jonathan also caught sight of the helicopter above them and realised that he needed to revise his strategy. There was no way he could evade their relentless pursuit and he couldn't stay on the road forever.

"John, what are we going to do, now?" cried Cassy.

"I'm thinking!" Jonathan grumbled. "Just let me think for a minute!"

"They're gaining on us…and there are more coming from over there."

"I'm THINKING!" Jonathan barked impatiently. Cassy sat back in worry as she watched him shaking his head and tugging at his hair with one hand.

"We're not going to get out of this John," Cassy pleaded. "Maybe we should give ourselves up. Maybe Tamworth can protect you like he said he..."

"Screw Tamworth!" said Jonathan with a sly grin. "He won't be able to help us right now."

"John!" Cassy pleaded again, still trying to comfort baby Jack at the same time. "You're scaring me. We can't outrun them like this!"

Jonathan thought for a minute before beginning to slow the car.

"I've got it!" he said suddenly as he pondered more.

"Got what?"

"Well, they're obviously after the clone, right," said Jonathan.

"What?" Cassy remarked, confused over Jonathan's choice of words.

"I mean...they're after *me*," Jonathan continued, "but they're not after *Jonathan* though. Cassy, would you mind joining me in some subterfuge?"

"What do you mean?" Cassy asked.

"I'm going to try and convince the cops that I'm *him*," Jonathan suggested.

"That's not going to work, John," said Cassy. "They're probably going to check you over. Besides, how can you be sure that Jonathan isn't with them already?"

"Oh, I'm sure," said Jonathan after remembering where he had left John. He was also naturally confident of his chances of proving his own identity to the police.

As the pursuing cars began to close in, several other cars up ahead swerved into their path, causing Jonathan to slam on the brakes. After a brief pause, he instructed Cassy to wait in the car while he went over to speak to the officers. The police exited their own vehicles and stood pointing their guns towards Jonathan. As Jonathan raised his hands and approached, another car, not police, swerved into view and stopped suddenly.

"Jonathan Haughton?" shouted the lead officer. Jonathan nodded in response but was a little confused at their choice of name. He looked out towards the mystery car and to his surprise, out stepped Arnold Tamworth.

"Get that man away from them!" he ordered, pointing out towards Cassy and Jack. As Jonathan and Tamworth locked dagger-eyes at each other, the other door of the car opened and out stepped the *real* John, who began to signal across to Cassy in her car. Jonathan's expression was one of intense surprise.

"You!" he hissed.

"The game's up Jonathan!" Tamworth shouted again as two police officers began to close in. Jonathan looked back at his car and saw Cassy shaking her head in shock. As the police began to place the cuffs onto Jonathan he looked back at Cassy with an angry smile – anger that his plan had failed but satisfied that he had proven an important point – that Cassy had failed to tell the difference between him and the clone. In his mind, therefore, there was still a chance for them if John was out of the picture.

Suddenly, another mystery vehicle sped into view and stopped abruptly, skidding to a halt several meters away from Jonathan. The doors opened and two mysterious men with guns got out and began firing at the police and their cars, causing them to duck down for safety but with some officers managing to shoot back. During all the commotion, Jonathan saw his chance to escape and with the flanking officers briefly distracted, he turned swiftly and grabbed one of them by the arm and snapped it at the elbow. As he did so he kicked back at the other, catching him squarely in the solar plexus and causing him to collapse to the ground in agony. He then took one of their handguns and shot a few rounds out towards the police. He had hoped to hit John but was denied the opportunity.

The mystery masked men beckoned Jonathan towards their vehicle and provided cover as he ran over to them and dived in. The car then sped off, leaving the police cars in a damaged state, with many of their tires blown out. As Tamworth, Des and the police emerged from their safe positions, John ran over to Cassy's car. She got out and hurried towards him and as soon as they reached each other they embraced and passionately kissed.

"Oh, John I'm so sorry!" Cassy sobbed. "He told me he was you. I mean...I should have..."

"And so, should I," Tamworth remarked, overhearing what Cassy was saying. "He was clever and manipulative. Took us all for fools."

"What matters is that you're both safe now," said John. "Both you and baby Jack."

"Safe for now," Tamworth warned. "Jonathan is becoming more erratic by the hour. I reckon it's only a matter of time before he does something stupid."

"But Jonathan wouldn't really hurt us, would he?" said Cassy; but as she pondered her own question doubts began to set in.

"You're right, in one sense," John agreed. "It's me he wants out of the way, not you. He thinks that doing all of this will get you back."

"But it won't," said Cassy. "He's not the Jonathan I knew. He's not been so for a long time. *You* are the one I love."

"I know."

"And no doubt *he* knows that too," Tamworth warned again, "and that makes him dangerous. His mind is so unhinged right now who knows what he might do next. You ever seen *Thelma and Louise?*"

"What's important is we are all together again," said Cassy.

"Agreed!" Tamworth noted with a reassuring smile. "But while we're bringing the other guy in, I must insist that you all accompany me back for your protection. Alice's media machine will be working overtime to broadcast these events to the nation. By the time the day is out, I guarantee that public opinion will be firmly back in our favour – and even if the tribunal does deny your right to the identity of Jonathan Haughton, they're not going to dispose of you. That, I can promise, not with the evidence we've mustered over the past couple of days. Besides, after all that has happened, do you still *want* his identity? No, John...you are your own person and always have been. If I were you, I'd stick to being plain old 'John' – a clone with honour, pride, guts and glory."

"I agree with Arnold, John," said Cassy. "If we have to stay in hiding for a little longer then I would rather we be together."

"Alas, hiding it will have to be, for the time being, Ms Haughton," Tamworth remarked. "At least until Jonathan is in custody. Unfortunately, that's easier said than done. We're not in any position to pursue and he's not exactly alone anymore."

Tamworth left John and Cassy to see to baby Jack and went back to liaise with the chief officer and assess the damages. As Cassy lifted Jack from the car, she placed him into John's waiting arms. There was no crying from Jack this time, not like it had been with Jonathan. He nuzzled peacefully against John's warm and comforting chest. Cassy looked on tearfully and smiled.

"Jack knew," she said with a smile. "I might have been blinded for a while, but he knows who his father is."

"I guess kids sometimes know better," laughed John. He looked down at Jack lovingly, but as he began to consider what Tamworth had spoken about earlier, his smile sank into a more serious and sober look. He gently passed Jack back into Cassy's awaiting arms and kissed them both. He instructed Cassy to head over to Tamworth's car while he took care of their bags, but as Cassy turned and approached Tamworth, she heard the engine of the car rev up again. The sound also caught the attention of Tamworth and the police officers, but before they knew what was going on, John sped off in one of the police cars and in the direction of Jonathan's vehicle. Some of the police scrambled to their own vehicles but there was little they could do on account of the damage to them.

"What the devil does he think he's doing?" Tamworth exclaimed.

"He's going after Jonathan!" Cassy guessed.

"The fool!" Tamworth cried out in frustration. "The stupid fool!"

34

As the car continued to power down the highway, Jonathan sat in the back and faced the masked men who had rescued him.

"Thank you, whoever you are," he told them. None of the men replied. They just sat there and stared back at him for a while, still wearing their balaclavas. Jonathan looked back at them and eventually broke the awkward silence once again.

"So, who are you guys?" he asked. "And where are we going?"

"That depends on whether we've got the right guy or not," said one of the men.

"What do you mean?" Jonathan asked. The man then pointed his weapon at Jonathan's head. Jonathan froze tensely.

"That tattoo," the man said. "Show me your hand."

"Afraid that I'm the clone?" Jonathan remarked with a forced smile.

"If we were sure then we wouldn't be having this conversation right now," the man replied. "Now, your hand please."

Jonathan slowly lifted his hand and pulled back his sleeve and reveal to them what appeared to be the clinic's signature barcode on the back of his hand. Unsure of whose side they were on, Jonathan waited patiently to gauge their reactions. As soon as he heard the familiar click of a cocked pistol, Jonathan licked the palm of his other hand and gently rubbed it against the logo, which caused it to smudge away and exposing the fact it was fraudulent (obviously to fool Tamworth and Cassy). Immediately, and to Jonathan's relief, the men lowered their weapons but kept their balaclavas on.

"Looks like we got you out of there in time, Mr Haughton," said the main henchman.

"Who's we?" asked Jonathan curiously.

"We are friends," said one of the others. "We're here to help you end this."

"Mr Dale sends his regards," announced the first man, "and to tell you it's now or never."

"Now or never?" Jonathan remarked.

"The clone must go," answered the main henchman. "You know this. If you go to prison for all of this then he wins and takes your life away. We cannot allow that to happen."

"I agree," Jonathan conceded. "Cassy and Jack should be mine."

"He's a clone," the man pointed out. "A freak of science and an affront to what is proper and natural."

"And it's gone too far!" added another man. "If we kill it now then the trial will collapse."

"No doubt you'll be questioned for your part," spoke the first man again, "but Mr Dale assures you that your reputation will be protected."

"How?" asked Jonathan.

"We're going make it look like self-defence," the man revealed. "If that clone freak is anything like you in his thinking, he'll no doubt be after you just now. We're going to make it look as though he tried to kill you and you fought back, as is your right as an American."

"A true and normal American!" added another.

"You see, Mr Haughton," the first man continued, "clones are an insult to our humanity. When we play God like this we spit in His face and dare him to act."

"And he *will* act," said another man, "with all the fires of Hell."

"Do you really believe that?" Jonathan asked. "I'm not really religious myself, no disrespect."

"This ain't necessarily a religious crusade," the man replied, "but a crusade, nevertheless. Our chance now to put a stop to the needless and sickening replacement cloning industry. Don't get me wrong, I know you don't think the same as we do; after all, you got yourself into this mess by buying into their lies, to begin with, but I would like to think that you can see it now – your mistake."

"It was a mistake," Jonathan nodded. "Yes, I see that now."

"And if we don't put a stop to this madness right now then the same thing can happen to others," the man warned. "Designer humans replacing their natural counterparts – and one by one they'll take over the world."

"That's a little far-fetched," Jonathan laughed. "My clone is just one."

"Is it?" the man argued. "Our most dominant and widespread organised religions started with one. Mark my words, Mr Haughton, this will spread unless we stop it now. Take back your identity before you lose it forever...before you lose it to a fraud!"

Jonathan nodded in reluctant agreement. Deep down he didn't have any bigoted attitudes towards clones. After all, as was revealed in the tribunal, he himself was not exactly born the natural way either. However, his burning disdain for John, combined with the damage to his mind already, has irreparably clouded his judgment. All he could think about was ending John for good – not necessarily for the good of humanity, as the men in the car with him had described it, but certainly for himself and the life he once had.

"I am Jonathan Kenzie Haughton," he declared as he prepared his own pistol for action, "and I will have strong words with anyone who says otherwise!"

Just then, the driver signalled to the others that he had managed to pick up the police radio signal and that word was out about a stolen vehicle, with the clone as the driver.

"That'll be him now," the main henchman smiled, looking towards Jonathan. "Any ideas?"

Jonathan looked out of the car window and thought for a few seconds before answering, "Yes. I have one."

Jonathan instructed the men to pull over, get out of the car and wait, including the driver, and as they did so, he climbed into the driver's seat and sped off further down the road. The men waited along the road as instructed.

Meanwhile, the pursuing John continued to power down the highway, driving the cop car erratically and without sounding its sirens. Eventually, he caught sight of Tommy Dale's men up ahead, who were still standing by the roadside where Jonathan had left them, and still brandishing their firearms. John narrowed his eyes and in a vengeful rage prepared to turn his vehicle towards them, but right at the last moment, he felt an almighty shunt, accompanied by a horrible crashing and cracking sound. Before he could react, Jonathan's car, hidden from view by the trees, had shot out from the side and smashed mercilessly into John's, sending his car careening off the road and down into the wooded area below. John was thrown about helplessly as the car rolled and twisted all the way down to the bottom until it finally stopped.

Still conscious, and miraculously still alive, John wrestled his way out of his seat belt and began to crawl himself away from the wreckage. He didn't get far before Jonathan, whose car had stopped further on, found him. He ran up to John and forcefully kicked him flat to the ground.

"Now you can *really* understand what I've been through!" he ranted. "You want to be me so badly, you worthless freak...well now you've got it!"

Jonathan grabbed the bleeding John, hoisted him to his feet and then punched him back to the ground. He did this several times and as the two of them battled it out, Jonathan had the upper hand throughout much of the struggle.

"Get up!" he mocked. "Get up and fight me!"

John tried desperately to crawl away but was followed by Jonathan, who continued to stand over him. This time he was brandishing a heavy branch.

"You'll never be me!" Jonathan growled.

"I'm *not* you, you pathetic scumbag!" John moaned as he spat out a mouthful of blood. He then turned around to face up towards his nemesis and declared, in no uncertain terms, "I'm *me*!" – and with that, John clasped a nearby rock and launched it straight up at Jonathan, catching him squarely in his face. As Jonathan fell back, temporarily stunned, John struggled to his feet and limped briskly, and painfully, towards the thick bushes up ahead.

Jonathan recovered and staggered to his feet, but when he looked around, John was nowhere to be seen. He scanned the area carefully and patiently.

"You're not going anywhere, Jonny-boy!" he thought to himself. *"I know you all too well."*

"You think you can hide from me, clone?" he bellowed towards the trees. "You wanna play soldier? You wanna play *me?*"

John ducked down in his hiding spot and watched as Jonathan paced around the area, looking for him, but while Jonathan seemed to be 'hunting' like an amateur, John was 'stalking' and biding his time. As Jonathan continued to scan the area, he was soon joined by Tommy Dale's associates, who had made their way down to the bottom. Jonathan smiled at them while sporting the horrible injury across his eye that had been left by John's rock.

"You need proof that I'm still me?" he joked.

"No need," replied the main henchman. "We can tell by your clothes."

Jonathan nodded and smiled.

"Well, he's in here somewhere," he then said. "He can't have gotten too far. We find him and we kill him! This injury here will help with my defence."

"No, Mr Haughton," the henchman suddenly replied. "If we do that, it all goes away."

"Isn't that the idea?" Jonathan remarked.

"Not this way," the man replied. "My boss believes it necessary for the clone to be captured alive and stand trial for the heinous crime he has committed."

"Oh?" Jonathan remarked in slight confusion at the apparent change of plan. "What crime? What's he done?"

"Committed murder," replied the henchman. "Cold, unprovoked and brutal murder."

Jonathan was taken aback by this sudden revelation and received the news with very mixed emotions. On the one hand, a conviction for John for the crime of 'murder' (leading to a possible execution), could play right into his hands – but at the same time...John was a clone...of *him* – and this sudden spike in violence was out of sync, even by his own standards. Immediately, Jonathan's military intuition kicked in as he began to sense something wrong. He stealthy readied his weapon as he continued to speak but kept a watchful eye on the other men in the area.

"Murder?" he remarked in a feigned sense of disbelief. "When did that happen? Who did he kill?"

The henchman stared blankly at Jonathan, before giving him a very clear and obvious answer.

35

When the police eventually arrived at the scene, they were met with what could only be described as carnage. As they moved in, armed to the teeth they could see lifeless bodies of several men strewn around the place. The police searched the area carefully and cordoned off the nearby road. Tamworth, Des and the police chief were not far behind and arrived soon after. They exited their vehicle and began to make their way down, apprehensive about what to expect. Tamworth scanned the area carefully.

'There's no way he would have gotten out of this,' he thought to himself.

Eventually, the chief was called over by the officers nearby and he signalled for Tamworth to follow. They had found a live one. It was one of the Haughtons, but with the officers crowding him, and looking at the extent of his injuries, Tamworth was unable to ascertain whether it was Jonathan the man, or John the clone. Whoever he was, he was battered, bloodied and bruised. Tamworth tried to look at the man's hand, for signs of John's logo, but it was too damaged. The officers carefully moved the man to safety and signalled for an ambulance to take him to the hospital. Tamworth and the chief tried to get the man to say something coherent, but he appeared dazed and confused. As they lifted him into the ambulance, Tamworth made a final attempt to get some answers before he was removed.

"John, can you speak?" Tamworth insisted. "If that's you in there then say something. Nod! Anything!"

"I..." the man struggled under his oxygen mask. "I need my lawyer. I need to speak to my lawyer!"

"I'm here," Tamworth replied, "and don't you worry. We're gonna get you the aid you need."

"No!" the man sputtered aggressively. "I need *my* lawyer! *My* lawyer!"

Tamworth was taken aback by the man's outburst until he managed to force out more from under his mask. He said a name – Cottam! He asked for Cottam.

When Tamworth heard that name, he immediately understood which of the two Haughtons they had found, but John the clone was yet to be identified among the corpses. Before he could get anything further from the semi-conscious Jonathan, Tamworth was escorted back out of the ambulance before it was shut, secured and driven speedily away back in the direction of the city. Tamworth watched as the ambulance moved further and further away until he felt a light tap on his shoulder. It was one of the accompanying officers informing him of the worst news – they had found the 'other guy'.

"Are you positive?" Tamworth asked him.

"We believe so, sir," the officer replied. "Fits the description, at least."

Tamworth's expression was a mix of sorrow and disappointment – for, without the clone, the trial was as good as dead, along with (he assumed) any chance of extending further human rights to other clones in the long run. He looked again in the direction of the ambulance as it finally disappeared from view and began to tighten his fists in increasing anger. In a frustrated rage, he stamped and kicked at the ground, sending pockets of dirt up into the air around him. Afterwards, he calmed down and composed himself once more in front of the startled police officers. The main officer approached him carefully.

"So, do you ever think he'll spill about what happened here?" the officer commented lightly.

"Oh, he'll say *something*," Tamworth remarked. "Whatever comes out will be spun in his favour, I'm sure. In the meantime, officer, I want that man taken in when he is ready – for kidnap, assault...and murder!"

"I'm not sure if we can get him on *that* charge, sir," the officer replied. "Surely you must know that."

"Times are changing," replied Tamworth. "We'll see."

36

For the next few days, Jonathan Haughton would see nobody apart from his lawyer, Edmund Cottam. No Arnold Tamworth, no Tommy Dale, no curious members of the associated press...and no Cassandra. The latter was the only person who Jonathan *wanted* to see – but despite the pleas relayed to her from Cottam, Cassy wanted none of it. As time passed, the only news of what had happened to John was revealed to Cottam by Jonathan – that he had died in the violent conflict at the crash site, but it was not by his hand. Cassy wasn't sure whether Jonathan was deceiving them or if he was speaking the truth, but in the case of the latter, she saw him as the man responsible for killing her husband and Jack's true father – and for that, she could never forgive him. Whatever existed between her and Jonathan...died with John.

After a few days had passed, Arnold Tamworth entered the hospital with the intention of speaking with Jonathan directly. He was greeted by Cottam coming out of the heavily guarded room and stopped in his tracks.

"My client doesn't wish to see anyone right now, Mr Tamworth," said Cottam.

"How is he?" asked Tamworth curiously.

"He's still in a bad way," Cottam explained. "He's recovering well, but still weak for now."

"Is he well enough to talk?" Tamworth asked. "Is he going to spill about what *really* happened to John?"

Cottam looked around carefully before answering and led Tamworth to one side so they could speak more privately.

"I appreciate that you're a little excitable, right now Mr Tamworth," he began, "but the finer details cannot change the fact that your client is dead."

"Did *he* kill him?" Tamworth suddenly asked. "I suppose he wouldn't confess to it if he had."

"According to my client, no," said Cottam. "However there have been some, shall we say, interesting developments since."

"Like what?"

"Like what's really been going on in the background."

"Such as?"

"Such as, who it was who had attacked Jonathan that night."

At that moment, the attention of both the men was drawn to a familiar voice coming from the corridor. It was that of Tommy Dale, who was heading their way and towards the room in which Jonathan was resting. Tamworth and Cottam watched as he conversed with the guards and tried to persuade them to let him through, but to no success.

"Goddamn it, man," Dale demanded, "as his political representative I say it is imperative that I speak to the man right now!"

The guards stood there expressionless and ignored the ramblings of Tommy. Getting nowhere, Tommy Dale gathered himself up again and looked around the area before suddenly catching sight of Tamworth and Cottam. He smirked slightly and waddled his way over to where they stood. He then moved closer to speak to Tamworth directly.

"Well, well, my friend," he said gleefully. "Might I say that you've certainly backed the wrong horse this time."

"Come again?" Tamworth remarked.

"Your clone is in big trouble now," Dale explained, seemingly unaware of what had happened to John. "That's twice now he's tried to murder his original and steal his name. I knew this would happen one day. I knew that a time would come when clones would start taking over, and this is just the beginning. Had that second-rate freak succeeded in his outrageous plot, that poor man in there would have become a martyr to our cause."

"My client is dead!" Tamworth said angrily. Dale looked at him for a few seconds and then smiled.

"Then let *him* be a martyr to *your* cause, Mr Tamworth," he gloated, "but enjoy it while it lasts. Mr Cottam here, and myself, will see to it that our Mr Haughton...the *only* Mr Haughton...comes out of this a true American hero."

As he gloated, Dale placed a hand on Cottam's shoulder in a show of solidarity and asked him to help convince the guards to let him through but was briefly taken aback when Cottam instead swatted his hand away as if it were an insect.

"My client will see nobody right now, Mr Dale," Cottam responded. "Not even you...*especially* not you."

"What the devil are you on about?" Dale exclaimed, unaware, until the last moment, of the policemen flanking him and closing in. "Is this your idea?"

"Yes, it's my doing...and for your own good," Cottam confirmed. "If I allow you into that room my client would probably want to break your neck."

Cottam then gave a swift nod to the policemen, who took hold of Tommy Dale and began to make their arrest.

As they read out his rights, Tommy Dale ranted and struggled throughout and continued to shout threats and expletives as the guards manhandled him away from the area. Tamworth, in the meantime, stood surprised by what had just happened. His eyebrows raised with interest as Cottam turned back to him and began to explain to him recent revelations.

"According to my client," he began, "he and some other men, who claimed to work for Tommy Dale, planned to kill John and make it look like self-defence."

"So, it *was* murder!" Tamworth commented.

"At first," Cottam continued, "but that's not how it panned out. Instead of firing on the clone, Dale's men suddenly turned their guns on Jonathan instead."

Tamworth was surprised by this revelation. It didn't make sense as far as he could see.

"Why?" he then asked.

"Apparently, my client's mental breakdowns and irrational behaviour had caused him to become a liability to Tommy Dale's so-called anti-clone cause."

"They attacked him?" Tamworth exclaimed, twisting his face in bewilderment. "I still don't get it."

"And I didn't either, at least at first," Cottam continued, "but from what I've gathered from all of this, Tommy Dale's long-term plan was to arrange for Jonathan to be murdered and plant enough evidence around to frame the clone."

"But that would..."

"I know," said Cottam. "It would lead to rioting in the streets. Indeed, the paranoia generated of clones murdering their counterparts and stealing their lives is the stuff of horror movies. Governments would be pressured into restricting rights for clones rather than extending them. If anything, it would shut down the *Forever Together* clinic and kill the industry for good."

"I can't say I exactly sympathise for the clinic, though," Tamworth huffed.

"But you would have sympathised with your clone," Cottam pointed out. "For had he survived in Jonathan's place, he surely would have been disposed of – no, instead tried for murder and probably 'executed'."

"So, what *did* happen to John?" asked Tamworth.

"I'm glad you asked," Cottam said with a smile and a nod. "Jonathan claims that upon discovering the plot against Jonathan's life, and probably knowing the repercussions had it succeeded, the clone defended him and opened fire on the attackers. He was killed in the process, but it bought Jonathan ample time to take out the remainder of Dale's men. It wasn't long after when the police arrived at the scene and Jonathan passed out from his own injuries.

"What, just like that?" Tamworth remarked, looking surprised and unconvinced.

"Just like that," Cottam commented back.

"And you believe him, eh?" Tamworth asked doubtfully.

"Of course, I do," Cottam answered. "It seems to make perfect sense to me."

"Oh? How so?"

"Well, for a start it doesn't make sense for him to have killed his mysterious associates if they *hadn't* turned on him – and I also doubt he could have single-handedly dispatched them without help from somebody else – not with the injuries he sustained during the encounter."

Tamworth sank down into a nearby chair to process the terrible news. He looked down to the ground as he pondered and spoke. He sounded like a defeated man – not like Arnold Tamworth at all.

"You would think that John's self-sacrifice would be of some comfort to me," he said with a sigh, "but it's not. This is one case that's gonna have me licked."

"Is that really all you care about?" Cottam asked. "The case?"

"No," Tamworth replied. "Those words are just the ramblings of a single-minded idiot who bit of more than he could chew. I should have just stuck to the basics."

"Well, if it's of any comfort, this case won't, as you put it, 'have you licked'," Cottam then said. "Jonathan has decided to drop his claim entirely. There is no case to answer anymore, save for Tommy Dale's upcoming trial."

"I can't imagine that will win any brownie points with Cassandra though," said Tamworth.

"No, not really," Cottam agreed. "He's been trying to contact her but she's not having any of it. She still holds him responsible for what happened to John."

"So, she should," said Tamworth. "While he may not have pulled the trigger himself, he was still very much involved, right from the beginning. He should shoulder some responsibility as much as Tommy Dale."

"As should *you*, Arnold," said Cottam sternly. "Your reckless strategy shone far too much light onto the clone and made his case bigger than it should have been. It ended him and may likely end you. It's like you said, you should have stuck to the basics!"

"So, what happens now?" Tamworth asked thoughtfully.

"We'll reconvene the tribunal when my client is able and ready," Cottam replied. "What we decide from there will be for his benefit and not the crusade you instigated; but for now, watch this space, Mr Tamworth...We'll be in touch."

And with that, Edmund Cottam donned his cap, gathered his things, and walked away, leaving Arnold Tamworth in the corridor and alone with his thoughts.

37

It was the final day of the tribunal and the conclusion to what many had described as the trial of the century. Whether it be known as the case of *Haughton vs Haughton*, *Man vs Clone* or even *The Haughton Dilemma* (a favourite of the media) – whatever people called it, all agreed that the case had both gripped and divided the nation.

The courtroom was filled with the sounds of mutterings and creative guesses from the bystanders on what the outcome might be and what the Judge would conclude. All were present, Jonathan Haughton and his lawyer, obviously, along with Arnold Tamworth, who now sat alone and was, for the first time in a long time, lost for words. All angles of the press were there, from sympathisers to critics, including Alice Beecham who had been granted a front-row view and, after a prior agreement with Cottam, an opportunity for an exclusive interview with Jonathan once the tribunal had concluded. Mina and Des were also there among the bystanders, as was Cassandra Haughton, her eyes bloodshot from sleepless nights, grief and anger. She remained further back, only just catching a view of Jonathan. He smiled at her through the crowds, but she ignored him and glanced away.

Eventually, Judge Avery Taylor-Beckett entered the courtroom and as he took his seat, Jonathan leaned into Cottam for a final discussion with him. Tamworth sat alone on the other side of the courtroom, with his arms folded. He had a defeated and fed-up look in his eyes. No more opportunities for theatrics, and no chance to have the last word as he used to. He just wanted the day to end quickly so he could retreat to headquarters and pick up the pieces. Everyone sat quietly as Taylor-Beckett scanned over the documents in front of him. He then took off his glasses briefly and looked towards Jonathan.

"Jonathan Kenzie Haughton," he spoke, and as he did so, Jonathan rose from his seat. "I understand that you have come to the decision to request a dismissal of your claim against your late clone counterpart?"

"I have, Your Honour," answered Jonathan. "I see that there is no longer a case to answer, now that the defendant is gone."

"And you, Mr Tamworth," asked Taylor-Beckett, turning to face Arnold. "I imagine that you are happy with this arrangement also?"

"I am happy to a point, Your Honour," Tamworth answered. "But then again I have very little choice in the matter. My client's counterclaim obviously died with my client."

"The court will be noting this in the official records," Taylor-Beckett announced. "However, from my own standpoint, the court is also unhappy with this outcome. We feel that with the money and resources poured into this case already, on top of the immense publicity it has generated, it is for public interests that this tribunal at least tries to come to some satisfactory conclusion."

Taylor-Beckett then looked back towards Jonathan.

"I understand you have a few closing words, Mr Haughton?" he said to him.

"I do, Your Honour," Jonathan responded, "and a confession."

The sounds of silent gasps could be heard around the room as people were curious as to what he was about to say. Tamworth pricked up his own ears and Cassy stared blankly. The courtroom listened as Jonathan confessed his increased bigotry during the tribunal – the fact that he had allowed his personal feelings and increased hatred to cloud his judgment. He admitted to the court that until recently, he had still been pushing for the clone's disposal, blindly seeing himself as the real deal being usurped by an insignificant and cheap copy. Yet, in contradiction, he also saw the clone as a powerful threat who also had a powerful case to exist. During his speech, Jonathan expressed regret that the clone's humanity bore fruit only when he sacrificed himself to save him. This was a notion that some in the courtroom, including Tamworth, Mina and Des found particularly insulting to John's memory – but perhaps none more so than Cassandra, who appeared less than impressed.

"I have no ill will against other replacement clones," Jonathan concluded, "and as such, I call for the dismissal of my claim not only because my clone has died, but also because of the potential negativity that could be triggered for other innocent clones out there. On reflection, I do not wish this private grudge to be responsible for any further suffering. John, my clone, turned out to be a good man, like myself. I see that now, but at the same time, he was not me, either. He was, in many ways, his own person...with his own different identity."

Taylor-Beckett paused briefly to prepare his own closing statement.

"Throughout my career as a judge in this court," he began, "I have dealt with some very complicated cases but none so complicated as this one, where two people, with the exact same DNA, and baring the same memories up to a point, fighting tooth and claw over who has the right to a single and specific identity. It is unfortunate that the extreme administrative error on the part of the clinic and the authorities, which they may in due course answer for, led to this extraordinary set of circumstances."

Taylor-Beckett paused again to allow the records to be updated and took a breath before continuing his statement.

"But..." he went on, "what began as a complaint against the defendant spiralled into a bigger question of identity. If anything, this case has raised, but not necessarily addressed, deep questions about what identity entails. Philosophers through the ages have argued it to be a sense of being – a uniqueness attributed to an individual, a group, or a thing. However, it is not as simple as that. The allegory about Theseus' Ship that was presented by Arnold Tamworth, though compelling, is no basis to define the identity of either man involved in this tribunal. Jonathan Kenzie Haughton, the man standing before us today, did not cease to be so simply because he was reported dead – for that is not how the world works; nor was it ever that way. I put it to you, Arnold Tamworth, that your client's counterclaim, to retain Jonathan's very identity, was as flawed and as futile as the plaintiff's motives."

Taylor-Beckett then looked directly at Jonathan and asked him, "Mr Haughton, were it not for Ms Haughton's desire to remain with the clone, would you have still pursued him through the courts in this manner?"

Jonathan thought for a minute and shook his head slowly.

"No," he answered. "I suppose, had he agreed to leave and start a new life elsewhere...I may have..."

"Precisely!" Taylor-Beckett remarked. "I must be clear to you Mr Haughton, that had recent events not transpired, had this tribunal been allowed to run its natural course, then my ruling would have likely been in your favour...up to a point. Had you only demanded the reversal of the *Identity Redistribution Act*, and for everything associated with you prior to your disappearance to be returned to you, I would have granted it; for it is yours. But no court in the land, dare I say in the world, could ever *force* Ms Cassandra Haughton back into a relationship with you if it is not what she wants. That, I'm afraid, was *never* your decision to make."

Jonathan nodded in agreement. He looked towards Cottam and gave him a quick nod before adding to his closing statements.

"I agree with what would have been the court's findings," he began. "All I wanted was my life back and the life I am convinced I would have had were it not for my disappearance – but I now understand that I have changed."

Jonathan then turned to face Cassy before continuing. By this time Cottam had made his way to the back of the courts to hand her a folded piece of paper. As she slowly opened it, Jonathan continued his plea:

"I am not the man Cassy once knew...and I know that she may never forgive me for the hurt I have caused her. All I ask of her is just one thing...just one chance only to talk to her privately so I can...so that *we* can at least have closure before we move on. For our sake and for that of baby Jack."

Jonathan then called out to Cassy in the audience. By this point, she had read the note and her expression had started to change. It was a slow and subtle change from despair and anger to that of hope. Jonathan locked eyes with her, and she locked eyes with him.

"So how about it, Cassy," he asked, "for old time's sake?"

Cassy said nothing. She looked down at the note once more, and then looked back up again. Then, she slowly nodded in acknowledgement – no smile or frown expressed to betray how she was truly feeling, but there was something about her that had suddenly changed – enough for her to maybe let Jonathan back in, if only for a moment. This hadn't gone unnoticed by Tamworth, who was flabbergasted by her fickle response and was now curious about the note.

'She's lost her mind!' he thought to himself as he gave Cassy a disapproving look. *'She must be mad, to entertain this man after everything he's put her through. Surely, she won't take him back. Surely not!'*

"Well, that settles things, at least for now," Taylor-Beckett declared as he banged his gavel. "The case of Jonathan Haughton vs the man formerly known as 'John Haughton' is dismissed, along with the defendant's counterclaim, but I am sure that as far as the human rights of clones may be concerned, this episode in our legal history will surely mark the beginning rather than an end to the matter."

Taylor-Beckett banged his gavel again and retired from the room. Immediately the crowd began to comment loudly on the result and the media went wild with flashing cameras and noisy reporters. As people began filtering out of the courtroom, Tamworth attempted to chase Cassy once again but was pushed back by the dense crowd which blocked his way. He then turned back and towards Cottam, who was clearing away his papers and took hold of his arm.

"What did it say?" he demanded. "That piece of paper you gave to Ms Haughton. What was it?"

"I cannot say," Cottam answered.

"Cannot," Tamworth insisted accusingly, "or *will* not?"

"I never saw what was written," Cottam replied, "but even if I did...I could not say."

Determined, Tamworth turned back to where Cassy had left, and once the crowd began to thin out, he moved swiftly towards the exit. As he stepped out of the courtroom, he looked around the hallway frantically, but Cassy was nowhere to be seen. He then took himself back into the emptying courtroom and sat down where Cassy had been seated. He looked down and suddenly caught sight of something on the ground. Upon closer inspection, it was a piece of paper – most likely the same piece of paper that Cottam had passed to her. He picked it up from the floor and examined it. It still had the fold lines down the middle but no other marks to show it had been intentionally scrunched up and abandoned, and from that, Tamworth concluded it had been left behind by mistake. Curiously he opened it up and read it; and as he did so, he remained no more enlightened than before. It read, possible cryptically, for all he knew:

'You were right all along. We men are all the same.'

38

Several weeks had passed since the great *Haughton Dilemma* had ended; during which, the media frenzy covering the case, and the subject of clone-rights associated with it, gradually settled back down to the level of indifferent low-key campaigns from isolated groups.

Tamworth sat alone in his office, repeatedly filling his tumbler, and feeling sorry for himself – and all this despite the positives for him that had come out of the affair. Since the tribunal had ended, the media had turned their attention back towards him. Tamworth was back in business, and to all extent and purpose, he should have felt more energised at his new promotion. He had recently been appointed to head up the investigations into the ethical activities at the *Forever Together* clinic, particularly to ensure, as agreed with Cottam, that such cases like John Haughton never happen again. Then there was the issue of further civil rights for clones – a side topic which Tamworth would continue to promote from the sidelines.

Much had happened since the dismissal of the case. Tommy Dale and his associates had been arrested, pending a trial of their own and facing imprisonment if found guilty. Mina had now left the employment of Tamworth's services to take up a position in freelance journalism under the watchful eye of Alice Beecham. It was a mutual and amicable end to a good partnership, but Tamworth knew deep down that her presence would be missed. He still had Des in his services, however, but he was more of a hands-on kind of guy and admin was never his strong point. Mina, on the other hand, was the best secretary Tamworth had ever employed and it would not be easy to replace her...at least without illegally cloning her. Still, he wished her well, bitter as he felt.

Jonathan Haughton, surprisingly as it sounded (and possibly to clear his conscious) offered to testify and occasionally speak out on behalf of the rights for replacement clones, while not campaigning actively. Apparently, he did not want his role in the tribunal to be mistaken for an anti-clone platform – politics had never been his thing. What was even more surprising, however, was how quickly Jonathan and Cassy seemed to rekindle their romance. As promised, Cassy allowed Jonathan that 'one more opportunity' to talk in private, and whatever it was...whatever Jonathan said to her...it must have worked a charm.

'Perhaps Cassy did this for baby Jack,' Tamworth thought to himself. *'Maybe to bring about some kind of normality that I can't see; but if so, it makes this whole episode a waste of time'.*

At that point, there was a knock at the door, after which Des entered the room.

"Des!" Tamworth said warmly. "Come in and sit down. You fancy a drink?"

"Err, no thank you, Boss," Des replied.

"Well, do you mind if *I* have a drink, then?"

"I think you're a few steps on that path already, if you ask me, Boss."

Tamworth pushed himself back into his chair and sank down, still cupping his tumbler and staring across at Des.

"Well," he remarked, taking another sip, "continue as I mean to go on!"

Des stared back at the pensive and sombre-looking Tamworth and read his mood clearly.

"Cheer up, Boss," he said with an indifferent shrug. "After all, you got a lot further than people thought you would."

Tamworth reflected on Des' remark and slowly drew out a smile.

"Yes, I did come close, didn't I?" he concurred. "So very close. Can you imagine the ruckus it would have caused if we had actually won? In any case, I imagine people will now be more mindful of their identity and uniqueness from now on, and not take it for granted."

"Your fans are waiting outside for you, by the way," Des then said. "The press that is, not that baying mob from before."

"Yes...whatever happened to that baying mob from before anyway?" Tamworth replied.

"Dunno, Boss," said Des with a shrug. "Does it matter?"

"A bit," said Tamworth. "It's eerily quiet now, without them. I kind of miss 'em now. Everyone's left me, Des. Mina's left me...John's left me...Alice, well she's a bit busy right now but she's as good as left me. Next thing I imagine *you're* gonna leave me. "

"Not likely Boss," said Des with an indifferent sniff. "You pay me well enough."

"A little too well, I figure," Tamworth grumbled. "I'm glad you stayed, Des. I hate goodbyes, but I also think they're important. Nothing like some closure to reinvigorate the soul."

"So, have you said all of your goodbyes, Boss?" Des asked. "Are you all ready for your journey back to the top?"

"Not quite," Tamworth answered. He took out the mysterious note he had found on the courtroom floor and looked at it again, as mystified weeks later as he had been when he first read it. He handed it over to Des.

"Does this mean anything to you?" he then asked him. "It's a note which Cassy received on that final day at court."

"We men are all the same," said Des, quoting the last part of the note before handing it back to Tamworth. "That's kind of a broad statement if you ask me, Boss. Was it something she said before?"

"I'm not sure," said Tamworth. He then placed his tumbler down onto his desk, stood up, straightened his tie, and picked up his jacket.

"Get the car ready, Des," he then said. "I've got some air to clear."

39

There was a knock at the front door. Jonathan answered it and there stood Arnold Tamworth, alone and strangely more sober-looking than usual. Jonathan stood there and leaned himself against the edge of the doorway.

"What the hell do you want?" he said to Tamworth, with gritted teeth.

"Mr Haughton," answered Tamworth in a mutual tone, before asking, "Is Ms Haughton around?"

"Who is it?" Cassy suddenly shouted from upstairs, and loud enough for Tamworth to hear.

"I'll take that as a yes, then," said Tamworth humorously as he glanced over Jonathan's shoulder and looked towards the stairway.

"It's that Tamworth guy wanting to see you," Jonathan shouted back.

Cassy came down quickly to greet Tamworth. She invited him inside and the three of them moved into the living room to talk more. Tamworth looked around and noted the open suitcases and half-filled cardboard boxes scattered about the place, and was immediately struck with a dizzy sense of déjà vu.

"Going somewhere?" he inquired curiously.

"We're thinking of moving away for a while," said Cassy. "We think a well-deserved holiday will give us a chance to get away from everything that's happened."

"A fresh start," Jonathan added as he tenderly placed his arm around Cassy, "and a chance to be the family we've always wanted to be."

Tamworth looked at them both with slight bemusement.

"That must have been some talk the two of you had," he remarked as he turned to face Cassy directly. "When I first took up this case for you, you were adamant that the clone was the only man for you. I guess it didn't take too long for you to change your mind again. How fickle of you!"

"Now wait a minute..." Jonathan suddenly interjected. He attempted to square up to Tamworth but was held back at the last minute by Cassy's embrace.

"No, darling, no," she said. "We've talked about this." Jonathan took a few deep breaths to calm himself down, while Cassy glanced back towards Tamworth.

"It's true that I loved John, but he's gone now," she explained. "Jonathan and I have talked and... well, we've decided to give ourselves a second chance."

"So, so fickle!" Tamworth quipped again, with a disappointed shake of the head.

"It still took us some time," said Jonathan, "and we're still trying to get things back to normal around here, for all of our sakes, especially for Jack."

"So, you're going to pretend that all of this just...didn't happen?" said Tamworth to Cassy. "Trying to rewrite history like you tried to do with your clone?"

"I made a mistake when I deleted those memories from John," Cassy admitted. "But this is different. We're not trying to hide from what's happened but rather move on from it."

"As we had done before," Jonathan added, "like many other couples have managed when they want it enough."

"I'm not here to argue," Tamworth then said as he forced a reluctant smile towards Jonathan. "I'm just here to congratulate you. After all, you won."

Jonathan moved over to the nearby cot, lifted baby jack out of it and began to playfully bounce him in his arms, much to baby Jacks' delight.

"I dropped the case, remember?" Jonathan insisted. "There was nothing left to win and nothing more to gain by dragging it out."

Cassy took baby Jack from Jonathan and headed upstairs to change him, leaving the two men alone to continue their discussion. There was a brief and awkward pause before either of them said anything.

"Drink?" Jonathan offered.

"Don't mind if I do!" said Tamworth with a more voluntary smile. Jonathan retrieved two tumblers from the cupboard and presented to Tamworth an unopened bottle of whisky. Tamworth looked at the label and smiled again.

"Ah! My favourite as well!" he remarked. "Nothing but the best in this place!"

"It's for you," Jonathan revealed. "She told me about how you like to drink this stuff."

"Aw, you shouldn't have," Tamworth quipped.

"Believe me I didn't want to," Jonathan answered back. "It was Cassy's idea. She wanted to thank you for all the work you did for her and suggested this as some kind of peace offering. Personally, I wanted to punch you in the face. No offence, of course."

"None taken," said Tamworth, "and I'll be satisfied if you don't clobber me over the head with it this time."

Jonathan let out a sly chuckle as he opened the bottle and poured out the drinks. He then passed one of the glasses to Tamworth. They looked at each other silently as they both took a quick sip.

"I see Jack has finally taken to you," Tamworth then commented.

"It took some time, but yes," nodded Jonathan.

"It's funny when you think about it though," continued Tamworth. "Technically, you've become the first example of an original replacing a clone, as opposed to the other way around. After all, all of this was *his* life originally."

"It was *supposed* to be mine," Jonathan retorted, "and besides, it's not like you lost out on anything. You're back up there again with the rest of the political big shots."

"I admit it has been a boost to my career somewhat – albeit a shot to my ego," said Tamworth. "I've been tasked with tightening up the rights of existing clones, whilst also heading up the inquiry into the questionable practises of the *Forever Together* clinic."

"The best of both worlds, then," Jonathan remarked.

"And I suppose I'll need to thank you for your upcoming contributions to the cause," Tamworth went on. "Your unexpected declaration of support for extending the rights of clones is commendable...although I cannot see it happening anytime soon if you're planning on disappearing for the foreseeable future. Were you being genuine, Jonathan...or was that part of your ploy to butter up Cassy?

"Maybe one day, when this has all died down," said Jonathan, "but just to be clear, Mr Tamworth, I'm not like that fool Tommy Dale, or his cronies, and never was. If I was, I wouldn't have invested in a replacement clone in the first place."

"I understand," said Tamworth. "It was just one particular clone you hated."

"We're all still humans, regardless of how we came about," Jonathan replied. "Just like Dolly."

"Dolly?" Tamworth inquired, holding his tumbler to his lips but not quite taking a sip.

"It's something you mentioned one time about that cloned sheep," Jonathan explained, "and the fact that at the end of the day she would have tasted just like any other sheep."

Tamworth's eyebrows raised slightly with both fascination and suspicion as began to recollect.

"Yes, come to think of it I *do* remember having that conversation," he then commented, "...just not with *you*."

Everything suddenly went quiet in the room and as Tamworth's memories of the conversation came back in full, a cold realisation gradually began to set in, the thought of which sent a chill down his spine. He placed his tumbler down onto a nearby table but continued to keep a grip on it. He then stared cautiously at Jonathan.

"Tell me, Mr Haughton," he asked slowly. "Who *really* died that day? The man or the clone?"

Jonathan looked at Tamworth and returned a sly grin.

"Does it matter?" he answered; and with that, Tamworth's suspicions were confirmed. His eyes began to widen in astonishment as he looked over the man more carefully.

"John!" he gasped. "It *is* you, isn't it!"

"Not that it matters," replied Jonathan...or rather, *John,* with a shrug and a sly wink. "And the name is 'Jonathan' by the way."

"I don't believe it! You son of a bitch!" Tamworth exclaimed. "So that's why Jack seems so happy to see you!"

"Precisely."

"And Cassy? Does she know?"

"Oh, she knows," John revealed with a triumphant smile. "That's what we really talked about that day. I told her the truth and she agreed to go along with the subterfuge."

"But why?" Tamworth demanded. "With the other Jonathan dead, you could have returned to how things were anyway. You would have been a legal and legitimate replacement and doing what you were made for."

"Exactly!" replied John. "Complete with all the legal restrictions that come with it...but this way, I get to live a life free from such restrictions – the kind of life the other Jonathan used to have. Would that not be a better way to honour his memories? Besides, people out there would think I murdered him anyway, so I'll never be safe! We reckoned it would be better this way if everyone believes that I *am* him."

"You can't do that, John!" Tamworth warned sternly. "It's stupid and dangerous!"

"Why so angry, Arnold?" John began to argue. "You got what you wanted from this. You wanted the clone to win...and I've won. You wanted an outcome where I wouldn't be disposed of...and I wasn't. You wanted the *Forever Together* clinic to be shut down and investigated and that's happening also. You wanted me to have more rights...and although that's not happened as a clone, I now have the chance to enjoy what our normal naturally-born civilians are entitled to.

"But it's not as simple as that, John!" Tamworth pleaded. "You've already given yourself away to me by accident. If you slip up out there, you're dead...and the repercussions could impact every other living clone out there!"

"Don't pretend you genuinely care for clones, Arnold!" John argued back. "Your little campaigns and speeches for our equality have always been nothing but smoke and mirrors to make the best of a bad situation – to accommodate for the fact that, against your own personal desires, we exist!"

Tamworth opened his mouth again to argue back but stopped short of making a sound. For the first time in a long time, he found himself speechless and immobilised. Perhaps not checkmated...but 'checked' nevertheless.

"I wouldn't complain too much, Arnold," John continued with another accomplished grin. "We all got what we wanted at the end of the day. I've got my freedom and you've got your career back. You're just upset because you don't like being used!"

Tamworth continued to glare at him in disbelief. His fingers tightened around his tumbler as he attempted to subdue his anger. He then released his grip after other thoughts regarding recent events entered his mind.

"Well, you've managed to lie this far," he said. "So, tell me...what *really* happened that day? What really happened to the other Jonathan?"

After a brief pause, John began to reflect and recall:

"As you know, I took the cop car and gave chase. After I was rammed off the road, I crawled from the wreckage to hide. Jonathan found me and we fought. Then some of Tommy Dale's men showed up."

"Planning to kill you?" Tamworth guessed.

"No, as it turned out," John went on. "What I told people about Tommy Dale's plan...to murder Jonathan and try to pin it on me...that part was true. I wasn't sure whether they would have killed me there and then or have me on the run to be hunted down by the law."

"So, then what happened?" Tamworth asked again. "Did you kill them?"

"I didn't have to," replied John. "Jonathan did. Both of us recognised the main guy but for different reasons. I remembered him as one of the fake policemen who tried to take me away that day when we first met."

"Ah, I remember that day," Tamworth commented thoughtfully. "I never did get his name. It was either 'Smith' or 'Jones', I think."

"Well, it turned out that he was also one of the men who 'rescued' Jonathan that night he was attacked," John then revealed. "You said yourself how conveniently placed those 'good Samaritans' had been."

"So, what happened next?" Tamworth asked again.

"After they shot Jonathan, they turned their attention towards me and started to walk over. I had a weapon ready for a final stand-off and at the time I thought I was done for. The next thing I knew, my counterpart had grabbed his gun again and emptied the shells into them while their backs were turned. When I went over to him, he..."

"He what?" Tamworth asked. "What did he do next? Did he say anything to you? Did he still want to..."

"No," said John abruptly. "No, he...succumbed to his own wounds and died right there. I figured that with all the damage inflicted on us both, the police would find it difficult to distinguish clone from man, so I seized the opportunity. I swapped our clothing about, sliced the clinic's barcode from my hand and the rest is history."

Tamworth was taken aback by this revelation. Astounded as he was by the clone's ingenuity, he was also aware of the dangers and the potential implications. As for whether Jonathan died in the way John claimed, Tamworth couldn't help but remain sceptical. What John had described did seem to make sense...but he also sounded as if he was choosing his words very carefully – almost as if he was still hiding something.

"And you are sure there is nothing else you want to add?" Tamworth demanded. John did not give a definite answer. He simply shook his head and looked away.

Tamworth grew increasingly uncomfortable with the position he found himself in. The similarities to Billy Reece were obvious to him. It was Billy Reece all over again but in reverse, and possibly worse, as this time the clone was the problem.

"You'll never get away with this, you know," Tamworth warned. "I cannot allow you to jeopardise the pro-clone cause with your recklessness!"

"Would you really turn us in, Arnold?" said John confidently as he called Tamworth's bluff. "Because surely *that* would undermine the pro-clone cause. And are you also prepared to risk my disposal again? Not to mention your own reputation."

"Oh aye!" Tamworth challenged. "If not me, then somebody else out there will eventually connect the dots and put two and two together. Even if I do keep my mouth shut about this, it would eventually get back to me – the fact that I let you two go!"

"I knew it!" said John triumphantly as he began to move closer to where Tamworth stood. "Nothing but your precious reputation to think about! If only we could somehow disconnect you from our 'reckless actions'. You know...plausible deniability and all."

Tamworth moved slowly towards John in a confrontational manner but immediately backed away again when John stood firm. At that point, their conversation was interrupted when Cassy entered the room again.

"Listen to us, Arnold," she pleaded. "This is the only way forward now."

Tamworth turned to face her and stared her down.

"So, you're definitely okay with this?" he asked her before adding, "I'll wager that this was the plan all along wasn't it?"

"No!" Cassy pleaded. "It's not like that at all!"

"You know you won't get away with this!" Tamworth scoffed. "They *will* find out eventually! I can't let you do this!"

No sooner had Tamworth finished speaking than he felt a painful, and all too familiar, crack across the back of his head before quickly losing control and collapsing to the ground. As his vision began to fade, he saw John standing there with the offending weapon, the whisky bottle, still in his hand. Immediately Tamworth was overcome by feelings of seething pain, humiliation, and disbelief that he had let his guard down like this for a second time.

'Et-tu my friend?' he thought to himself as he fixed his eyes on the treacherous bottle – the symbolic and literal accessory to his downfall – and not for the first time either.

Not long after, Tamworth couldn't see anything at all, but as his consciousness began to fade, he could still make out the sounds of recognisable voices around him.

"Oh, John, what did you do that for?" said the voice of Cassy, who by now had rushed over and was kneeling beside the semiconscious Tamworth. "I didn't want us to do anything like *that* to him. Not after all the help he had given us."

"*I* did!" replied John with a smirk. "It's the least I could do – and a little payback from when we first met."

316

He then cupped the bottle sideways and bowled it across the floor so that it rolled and stopped where Tamworth lay.

"Will he be okay?" Cassy asked.

"No doubt, I'm sure," John answered. "He's just out cold, but if it'll make you feel better, we can easily call for an ambulance on the way out."

Cassy frantically nodded at the suggestion.

"Yes, do it!" she replied.

"By the time he wakes up we'll be long gone," John continued. "And with a bit of luck, he won't remember anything at all of what was said today. Like I said, plausible deniability."

"Remember what from today?" Cassy asked.

"Nothing important, my love," said John; and with that, they gathered their things together, got baby Jack ready in the car, and departed for their big adventure.

THE END